Author Photo: David Royal

SETH INSUA is an Anglo-Spanish writer and artist. He was born in Kent in 1989. He graduated from the University of Oxford with a First in English Language and Literature. He has been shortlisted for the Bridport Prize and *The London Magazine*'s Short Story Competition and was a semi-finalist in the BlueCat Screenplay Competition. He lives with his husband, David, between Newcastle upon Tyne and Madrid. *Human, Animal* is his first novel.

vervebooks.co.uk/seth-insua
sethinsua.com
@sethinsua

HUMAN, ANIMAL

SETH INSUA

VERVE BOOKS

First published in the UK in 2025 by VERVE Books Ltd.,
Harpenden, UK

vervebooks.co.uk
@VERVE_Books

A CIP catalogue record for this book is available from the British Library.

ISBN
978-0-85730-889-4 (Paperback)
978-0-85730-890-0 (eBook)

2 4 6 8 10 9 7 5 3 1

Typeset in 10.75 on 13.35pt Minion Pro
by Avocet Typeset, Bideford, Devon, EX39 2BP
Printed and bound in Great Britain by
CPI Group (UK) Ltd, Croydon CR0 4YY

For my family,
with love & thanks

Under the trees several pheasants lay about, their rich plumage dabbled with blood; some were dead, some feebly twitching a wing, some staring up at the sky, some pulsating quickly, some contorted, some stretched out – all of them writhing in agony except the fortunate ones whose tortures had ended during the night by the inability of nature to bear more. With the impulse of a soul who could feel for kindred sufferers as much as for herself, Tess's first thought was to put the still living birds out of their torture, and to this end with her own hands she broke the necks of as many as she could find, leaving them to lie where she had found them till the gamekeepers should come – as they probably would come – to look for them a second time. 'Poor darlings – to suppose myself the most miserable being on earth in the sight o' such misery as yours!' she exclaimed, her tears running down as she killed the birds tenderly.

– Thomas Hardy,
Tess of the d'Urbervilles, Chapter XLI

Part I
Father's Son

Father

THE COW RUNNING LOOSE IN the orchard is my mother. A blur in the moonlit garden. I watch her from the bedroom window as the nightmare loosens its grip. The animal cry that woke me came from her throat. That streak of hide is her cotton gown. My skin is crawling, but the cows are safe. Locked up, where they belong. And Ma is an easier being to handle.

It's just gone two. I leave my wife in bed and feel my way downstairs. Hunched over, gripping the bannister. My chest is tight. I let out a shuddering breath and ache for sleep. What is Ma playing at? What could have possessed her, out there in the middle of the night? At the back door, I slip on my shoes without untying the laces, grab the heavy duffle coat. Then out onto the frozen path. Cold cuts through my pyjamas, ice crackling underfoot like bubble wrap. I prick up my ears, find the laurel with my fingertips. Let it lead me through the darkness.

Worry is a farmer's right. Live with cows for long enough, their lowing crowds your waking thoughts. Spills into your dreams.

And tonight my brother Mike had come home. Fifteen years my junior, six years dead. I saw him surrounded by the herd, greeting the animals he once called friends. His laughter lines, just the way he was when he was alive. I wanted to hand him the reins and run for the hills. Instead, I wisecracked about his scarecrow hat, lying trampled in the mud when I found him. He made a joke about a bovine revolution. What they might do, if ever they knew their own strength.

And then something knocked me to the ground, and there were hooves thudding over my head. Thundering, thrashing. I sat up, gasping.

The cows have got out!

But it is only my mother I must round up tonight. Closer now, mischievous as a child. Saying something.

You won't get me!

For god's sake, Ma. You'll catch your death.

I was just going to the privy.

There hasn't been a privy in twenty years, since she finally agreed that an indoor toilet was a modern luxury even we Calverts could afford. I put my coat around her narrow shoulders. Chilled to the bone. She doesn't resist as I shepherd her back towards the farmhouse.

There were no candles, Pop. I got lost.

I switch on the kitchen lights. Put her in the chair by the Aga. She blinks up at me, her eyes pink and wet.

The light, she whispers. Jerry will see. Jerry will get us.

I peer at the dark patch on the front of her nightgown, wrinkling my nose. That tart, animal smell. She has soiled herself.

I sigh, undress her in the chipped, porcelain tub in the downstairs bathroom. She sits there, trembling. Taking care of her, I feel my age, and she is just a girl. It's after four by the time I'm back in bed.

I reach for Sandra, but I am alone under the covers. There are clanging crockery sounds from the kitchen, and the cows are bellowing impatiently. They know the time as well as anyone. I roll out of bed. Late for the school bell, late for milking. Echoes of my childhood shame, only now I am seventy-one and my old man and his disappointment in me are six feet under.

I pull on two shirts and a fleece. Ache and fumble through my ablutions. Curse when my fingers catch in my sleeve and the toothpaste plops off my brush onto the yellowed enamel of the sink. I am dog-tired. Sometimes when I move it is the floorboards that creak. Sometimes it is my own body. Breath escapes me like air from a dead thing.

The kitchen is steamy. Sandra turns from the Aga with a pot of coffee and thrusts a mug into my hands. Look at her: my wife, still young. Her hair is glossy mahogany streaked with grey. Dark bags hang below her eyes. I try to touch her, but she twirls out of my reach to wipe a splash of milk on the counter. She's listening to the *Today* programme, which never fails to put me in a bad mood. *Frankly, if you don't like big government, you're automatically very suspicious of Brussels, and I would never belong to a European union if I felt...* I'd prefer to have a conversation than to listen to all that bickering. Or some good music. Or even silence, so early in the morning. But Sandra needs the news like it's insurance.

Hallo, Georgie, says my mother, sitting at the kitchen table, the brightest of all of us.

I tell her how she got me up in the night, my voice rough. Her eyes cloud over. Sandra shoots me a disapproving look.

Sleepwalking? says Ma. Was I?

There's colour in her cheeks now. I let it go. She is a force of nature, my mother, nimble and resourceful at ninety.

You better go and help Harry, Sandra reminds me, gesturing towards the farmyard.

Give me a second.

The cows are making a racket, Elder Son down in the cowshed already. But there's no sign of Younger Son. I hesitate.

Have you seen Tom?

He graduated from Glasgow last summer and announced he was going vegan. Branded the farm exploitative, *dependent on the forced labour of the vulnerable.* The cheek of him. They're bloody cows, and I pride myself on the way we treat our animals. Still, there's no arguing with the young, something I keep forgetting as quickly as Sandra can point it out to me.

In bed? she says, taking a seat, gazing into her coffee.

Lazy sod.

He stopped joining us at the dinner table after I cooked the wrong supper one evening. You'd think I'd served him a plate of veal, force-fed him like a foie-gras goose. But I made a special effort for the little prima donna. There was no meat in the dish, just curried aubergine and a heap of steamed greens, tossed in melted butter.

What's this cooked in? he said, a mouthful of mangetout at his lips. Is it butter?

For god's sake, Tom, just bloody eat it.

He was halfway through before he got up, red in the face. Shouted something about respect. He has stayed in his bedroom ever since, apparently applying for jobs. I bristle at the thought of him. Our new deal is that he must pull his weight on the farm. I won't allow him to fester, do god-knows-what up there. Not under my roof. Time he acted like part of the family. He'll never make it in life if he can't even stomach his own flesh and blood.

I turn for the sitting room and the inner staircase that leads to his hideaway. But Mother taps on the kitchen window and stops me.

Who's that coming up the path?

The back door opens with a bang. Speak of the devil: if it isn't Tom, blotchy-faced, eyes smudged – I hope just with tiredness – saying, Dad, come quick.

Before I can question him, he turns and runs. I pull on my boots in the utility room, Dusty the collie licking at my face. Then I'm out under a leaden sky, gasping the cold reek of morning – silage and manure. I lag behind Younger Son, follow him down the hill and across the farmyard. Not to the milking parlour, but to the cowshed.

Harry is there to meet us. Elder Son. Lips bloodless under his patchy moustache, gelled hair standing to attention.

What is it? I pant.

14

There's people, Dad. I've told them to clear off.

He steps aside and I enter the shed, swallowing a strange taste. Bitter sloes. I blink into the gloom.

There are crooked shapes among the cattle, picking through the straw like giant black crows. At least ten, even twenty people, all wearing hoodies and anoraks, brandishing protest signs. Who are these strangers? The ground begins to list. I set my feet apart, my boys by my side, ready for a fight. The intruders shout when they see us, and I raise my voice to meet theirs.

What the bloody hell do you think you're doing?

I take a step. If these folk were cows, I could drive them by breaching the outskirts of their personal space. Apply just the right pressure to direct them gently, no fuss. Through the gate and off my land. But I have no authority now; this herd stands its ground.

Stop mistreating these defenceless animals! cries a bullish woman, her hair scraped back and tucked into a woolly hat, a quivering nose ring in her septum. I'm sure I recognise her from somewhere.

You're trespassing, I tell her, as if she doesn't know. This is private property.

Murderer, she spits.

I have to laugh. I fold my arms over my chest.

I'm sorry, but I won't listen to this rubbish. You're going to have to leave.

Look at them, says another protester, a man hiding behind dark glasses. Lying in their own filth. They're sick.

They're not sick.

He points at Bea, heaped on a muddy rubber mat. She lets out a husky groan. That one! he shouts. She can hardly support her own head.

I just stare at him. What does he know? Then Elder Son steps in.

This is a family farm, he says. Do you even care about that? Why don't you go and bother one of the big factories? That's right: take your signs, take your cameras, and fuck off!

What cameras? I say.

A tall man emerges from the crowd, slinking like a cat. He's clutching a camcorder.

You're filming us? I snarl. How dare you?

We're not filming *you*, says the man, in a clipped transatlantic twang. We're just documenting the conditions on your farm. We want to put customers in touch with the food chain so that they can make more informed choices. That's all.

He comes closer, towering over us. He's what Sandra would call a pretty boy, dressed like a pantomime prince in a military coat, a lacy shirt, and tight blue trousers. I weigh him up, not bothering to be polite. He looks like Adam-bloody-Ant.

I'm Luke Underwood, he says, extending a large hand and simpering.

I'm calling the police.

Luke drops his hand and lowers the camera. That won't be necessary. Really. We're about done here.

For now, adds the woman with the ring in her nose. And then I place her.

Every year, I welcome the public to Alderdown Farm in the hope of educating them about the dairy business. It was springtime, the scent of primroses and nettles and wet grass drifting up the hill, the sunshine warming my face as she started to interrogate me. *What happens to the bull calves, Mr Calvert?* Scratching as the sweat began to creep below my collar.

That's it, everyone, says Luke, turning his back on me. Let's leave these good people to their day.

The crowd begins to file out, bottlenecking at the door.

Well, shit, says Elder Son, watching them shuffle away, scot-free.

I turn to look at my girls, the state of their bedding. All this should have been clean; Tom was supposed to muck out yesterday, while Harry and I were busy with Maisy, who was calving. She's roaring now at the invaders. Protective of her little miracle.

As the last of them leave the building, they clump beside her cubicle and point their phones. They mutter and tut, and wring their soft hands. Then they are gone. I let out a long, anxious breath. Maisy continues to cry.

What were they looking at? says Harry, going to lock the back gate.

Looking? I echo, trailing him, a slow return to my body.

Dad, he says. He has stopped by Maisy.

Yes?

What? says Tom, who sounds guilty, and he should be – for never pitching in. What is it?

It is the relief knocked out of me.

Maisy is half-lying on her newborn calf, a lick of skin and bones just caught on camera. She must have collapsed, worn out by yesterday's long labour. Crushed her immense bulk up against the concrete corner of her cubicle, her little one hidden from sight. Poor thing looks to have been dead a while.

If only they'd broken in before, when we were there for Maisy. Her protectors, her farmers. The only thing standing between her and the wrack and nag of Mother Nature, who would have taken her life too when the calf wouldn't come.

Up you get, I say, as we lug the silly cow to her feet. Swivel-eyed, fluttering her long lashes and crying her heavy heart out. Stupid beast.

Son

I ROLL UP MY SLEEVES, READY to muck out the cowshed, and pop my earphones in. SOPHIE's siren song swells in my skull like a pink balloon, inviting me to be real.

Dad is talking to the police in the privacy of the parlour. Harry is in and out, seeing to the herd. I keep my head low and shovel the shit, my blood on fire. It's like blowing bubbles in a milkshake, the way the music rattles me. That loud, dance-it-off synth, round and round, that bouncy baby voice. The music sees me; it knows my secrets.

But I can't just plug in and escape to some fantasy world, not this time. I'm afraid that they'll hear the music too, and somehow read my mind. The bleating of an alarm, but I'm awake.

I kill the music and scrub at my guilt as Harry bags up the tiny calf that's died. He carries it out into the yard while its idiot mother grunts and looks for it. Animals die on farms all the time, even calves. But not usually like this; it's not something I ever thought the cameras would capture.

I pull my scarf tight and tug tools like prison bars. Cows stay in during the winter months when the grass is nibbled raw and the pastures turn to swamp. Lock them up and they will stand in their own waste until there are bugs up their udders and rot in their hooves. It's a farmer's job to save them from themselves, bed them down with fresh straw, clear them out to start anew every second day. But their mess collects quickly, perfect for LivestockAid to come and get some dirt.

Right into the corners, Tom, Dad warns, stalking in behind me.

I tighten my grip on the shovel. Like I'm not already on it, like the rules haven't been drummed into me a thousand times.

The problem with a family business is that you're expected to belong. It's a conversation we've done to death, a conversation we first exhausted when I decided to go away for uni to study Maths. *What do you want to do that for?* It never occurred to Dad, ruminating alongside his cattle, that Alderdown might not be for me. And Mum still likes to insist that I am a farm boy at heart, deep down, somewhere forgotten and far away.

You used to love the cows, Tom. We used to find you brushing them.

I have stepped back in time to an adolescence of free labour, rain or shine. The iron stink of winter mud. School holidays spent filling feeders and wiping pink teats with iodine, hands cracking in the cold.

But I have changed, and my waxed forearms reassure me that my time away actually happened: I am not the person I was before uni, before the messy world contaminated the clean calculations of the lecture theatres, before boyfriends and adorkable big hair and New Romantic sartorial experiments. Before the rows with vegan friends. Before I stopped drinking milk meant for babies, and before I realised that animals are kept as slaves – and dairy is a form of child abuse.

Before I realised there are other ways. Before long talks – long silences – with the university counsellor, where I was too afraid to articulate the problem. Before I allowed myself to look, and really see myself.

My phone twitches against my thigh.

I ignore it, finding an unexpected calm beneath the forkfuls of filth, in sanitising the natural world. I pack the mechanical bucket at the front of the tractor, and when it is full, pull up to the mountain of straw-thatched manure at the back of the farmyard. I unload: more fertiliser for the fields, for growing the silage to feed the cows to dump in the shed to make more fertiliser.

As I rake the dung and my conscience, it starts to rain. I head to the coop, where the chickens peck around my boots, and can't keep his face at bay: the queasy pleasure of holding it in my mind, reliving the way he looked at me, the way he took my hands in the predawn darkness. The way he winked at me as he disappeared, back into the digital realm, where all my fantasies reside.

I had waited so long to see him in the flesh. I have waited for everything, steadfast as a dog with an empty bowl.

Pigeons pack the farmyard. They launch themselves from one barn to another, then down to the ground. Past the barn and the cowshed, the men use familiar voices to chivvy the cattle out of the milking parlour. Hup, hup! Attagirl.

I shelter under the lip of a corrugated roof, the bag of dead calf by my side, protecting my phone from the drizzle. The cold has crept under my clothes, and my hands are trembling.

I am alone again, and when I am alone, I lose sight of the life I want. Without a job, a ticket off the farm, I too am its hostage.

So I allow myself to breathe. I read my messages.

It's another fifteen minutes before the knacker van arrives. The driver pulls down the ramp to reveal a sorry little hill of lambs, crested with a fat ewe, flung onto her back, legs splayed and eyes bulging. It is too cold for flies.

I lift the calf carcass, feeling its bones and death-stiff joints through the plastic bag. The driver takes it and throws it into the back. It's a callous end for a newborn, whose bereft mother will cry for days, asking her questions.

The man slams the door and shakes some papers at me. I scratch my hasty signature. It comes out wonky and stark, hardly recognisable as my tired old name.

Here you are, I say, and my voice is hollow, as everything I have been told I am just falls away.

The name Tom Calvert is a lie. That signature is a forgery, my old identity a theft. I watch the sputter of exhaust, the dissipating vapour of my breath. The ink lines of a skeleton, snatched away by the knacker man.

13 January, 1944

YOU WERE A GIFT ON Christmas Day. Humbled by my invitation to join the Edwards family up at the farmhouse, I attempted to make myself useful in the kitchen, where I quickly proved a nuisance. Mary advised me to take a seat at the dining table, which was gloriously festooned with holly, cut from the glossy hedgerows around Alderdown. After we had eaten our festive feast, I presented Herb, the man of the house, with a gift I had made for the whole family: a hare carved from a stump of oak. Just a small offering. He set it down on the tabletop, then sat back to survey it, an inscrutable expression on his face. I felt rather like a child, offering up his playthings to his parents, and pretended to be fascinated by my own fingernails.

Little Lizzie came to my rescue, reaching across the table to seize the hare in her tiny hands. 'You made this?' she said, polishing its wooden face with the end of one of her pigtails. 'Can you make me a kitty?'

Herb spoke from the side of his mouth, which, as usual, was clamped tightly around his pipe. Smoke escaped with his voice in little puffs. 'We didn't get anything for you.'

'I didn't expect you to,' I said, worried that my gesture was misfiring, that perhaps I had embarrassed my hosts. 'You have already been so generous.'

Then Maggie took the hare from her little sister, gripping it delicately by the ears, stroking them between her thumbs and forefingers. 'Is there nothing we could give you?'

I put up a fight, insisting there was not.

'There must be something. What do you miss from home more than anything else?'

She burned through to me with those piercing silver eyes of hers, and I felt the warmth in my cheeks, and told them all I missed nothing more than pen and paper. A sensitive answer, though not entirely honest.

I had never heard of a woman farmer before I came to Alderdown; my Emilia loathes to step outside if it is so much as drizzling. But it didn't take me long to recognise that Maggie – whom I have only ever seen wearing trousers, usually coupled with her muddy pair of boots – is in her element here, roaming with an independence and confidence beyond her years, comfortable with machines and animals alike, authoritative yet tender in her handling of the natural world. In short, the girl is the genuine article, whereas I am only playing a role.

And yet she has always made time for me, ever since my first day on the farm.

'Right,' she'd said, straight to business. 'Do you know how to milk a cow?'

I did not, but I was ready to learn, and she was keen to show me the ropes. With all the young men called up to fight, and the farm's dwindling workforce bolstered only by elderly volunteers from the Home Guard, and Land Girls from the city, helping hands are in high demand. We are feeding the country, heroes of the people's war. The locals wave to the Edwards family wherever they go, and they are starting to extend this same gratitude to me, though many of them know I am German. I credit Maggie's thorough instruction for everything: her father's high opinion of me, my permanent move to the farm, this rare and precious security in the most precarious of times.

Writing has made me mellow. With nowhere to put my thoughts, they have tended to gather, swirling like smoke, choking me. But this pen is cold between my fingers, and putting the nib to paper, I am a surgeon, and my mind is the patient.

Perhaps I will make a sketch of my room, then map out the scale of Alderdown, a happier prison by far than my last camp. Making marks on these pages, I could be back in my old life, limiting my worries to briefs and deadlines, smoking cigarettes at my desk with the blinds half-drawn.

Yet I cannot spare any longer this evening. I want to finish repairing a steam engine for Herb before I sleep. I must earn my keep, repay his kindness.

Until next time.

Father

WITH THE HELP OF MY boys, I place each of our cows in the great metal cage of the cattle crush. It's positioned in the middle of the yard to make the best of the chilly sunlight. We tease clumps of dung from winter-matted fur, yesterday morning's invasion on all our minds.

Can't leave the shed unlocked, I tell Elder Son, who is used to being in trouble, looks everywhere but at me. Anyone could get in, I say.

I could have sworn I locked it.

Well, it wasn't locked, was it?

I want to shake him. A grown man in his twenties. He has a wife to take care of now. Lauren thinks my late brother's old cottage down the lane is pokey, has her eye on the farmhouse. Before long they'll start a family of their own. But I'm not walking away while the fate of our business remains uncertain, and Elder Son is yet to fill me with confidence as its future guardian.

D'you think we're in trouble then? he says, his face rigid.

That's not the point. This is about attitude, Harry.

If he worked half as hard to earn his place as I did with my own father, things might be different. Self-doubt is a powerful motivator.

Younger Son takes advantage of the pause. I don't want to hear from him because those protesters were his sort. Guilty by association. Still, he says his piece.

I might have been the last out, Dad. It might have been me who didn't lock the gate, OK?

Harry turns to his sibling. A grateful smile. Ah, it's not your fault, Tom. I should have checked it.

It's not often I catch them acting brotherly with each other. Well, I say. We'll all remember for next time, won't we?

No harm done. After the incident, there are three normal days – milking, feeding, cleaning and bedding – until Friday arrives with a bite.

The levels in the drinking troughs have dropped more than usual. I suspect they are about to freeze, and we'll have to heat the pipes. Cows drink a lot throughout the day, can't be left long without water. Younger Son agrees to keep an eye.

Dusty at our heels, we beckon the herd into the milking parlour in the usual way. The cows talk to one another, hold their positions or swap places. They have their preferred order, their hierarchy. Maisy hesitates at the rear, unsure of herself.

She doesn't want to, Tom protests.

So Harry mutters and coaxes, stroking her back to cheer her up. Sweet-talked, she eventually does as she's told.

The animals get in line. Our parlour is the outdated layout: the cows stand abreast to be milked. Elder Son serves the cake, keeps the girls occupied throughout the process. Younger Son cleans their udders, plugs them into the milking unit. They're happy to let this happen. I check the samples for mastitis, then we're away. Milk pours down the pipes towards the cooling tank, and I am thinking of my rumbling stomach and the half-finished crossword I left on the kitchen table.

It is then that Dusty runs to the door, tail wagging, to greet a visitor.

Gran? says Harry, looking over an armful of plastic packaging.

I stride over to my mother. You look cold, Ma. Why don't you go back to…?

She doesn't listen. She's approaching a white cow, medium build, with a veil of dark markings across her neck.

What have they done to you, Nettie?

I frown. Nettie was her first ever cow, entrusted to her by her father when she was a little girl. She used to tell us tales of how she'd ride her, adventures they went on. She and that long-suffering beast. The boys are standing together, concerned.

Are you feeling all right? I say.

Course I'm all right, says Ma, with a flap of her hand. Stop fussing.

Gran, these are our purebred Holsteins, says Harry. You and Uncle Mike sourced them from the French Alps.

Do you remember? says Tom.

A flicker of hesitation before she nods. I'm a little tired, she says. I think… I think I'm going to lie down.

I supervise as my boys guide the herd back to the shed. Harry threatens Tom with a handful of straw. They carry on together, try to get it down each other's necks. Then Tom sees me watching. Moment over.

I send him to cut some new sticks for herding. He is best suited to these solitary jobs. He has patience, Younger Son, like his old man. Always waits until he's located exactly the right strength and straightness, a trusty feeling in the hand.

I watch him go. Wolf down a bag of salt-and-vinegar crisps in just a couple of mouthfuls. Perhaps I've got carried away with my worrying. He'll be all right. He's always been serious, not like Harry, and it's normal to do a bit of soul-searching in your youth. God knows I didn't settle down on the farm until I met Sandra, well into my forties. My parents must've thought I was a lost cause. Travelling the world with nothing but the clothes on my back. Tom is a dreamer too.

I suck the salt from my fingertips, get on with my day. It's two hours later when Elder Son gives me the news. I am driving across the yard, a case of silage at the front of the tractor. He waves me down. The water has stopped flowing from the taps. Tom's responsibility.

I climb down from the tractor. Your brother not back?

Harry just shrugs. At this rate, we'll be late for afternoon milking.

Bloody waste of time, I grumble.

I follow him and we inspect the troughs together. Then he stays behind to steep the plumbing in hot water, and I set off to find his straying brother.

I open the farmyard gate, knotted with bits of frayed string. Cross the first of our small fields, towards the meadow. The open space is untended, stubbly. Framed by heaped earth, run to the edge of the ditch and the hawthorn border by weeks of heavy rain. The hedge is studded with ash, elm and oak trees. Frigid and bare, though snowdrops are trying hard to break out of the dirt.

Younger Son is sitting at the other end of the meadow. Perched on a branch overhanging the running water. He is reading his phone, doesn't see me coming. I don't rush. I smooth my boiler suit a few times as I walk.

Got the sticks? I say, when I am close enough.

Tom looks up. Oh. Yes.

He points at a small pile of saplings at the foot of his tree. I step over the stream, take a stick in my hand. It's decent.

You taking a break then? I ask.

Tom goes back to his phone. Sorry.

No good you sitting up there. You said you'd check the water.

A fake smile. Yes, Dad.

It rankles, the boy's dragged feet. I take a deep breath. Well, it's too late now, I continue. It's already frozen. Harry's had to stop what he was doing to sort it out. And I've had to come find you.

Tom looks down. I hold fast to the stick, might throw it otherwise.

You still won't help? I say. The cows need water, Tom. I thought you cared about animal welfare, this ridiculous fad you're following.

It's not a fad. It's what I believe.

28

Even after you've seen what these people are really like?

I've told you.

And I've told you this isn't a hotel. You have to contribute.

Fine, he says, hiding behind his phone. Fine! But what if I did something else? What if I helped Lauren with painting the barn instead?

His sister-in-law is converting a disused barn into a wedding venue for simple people. Farms are working spaces, not fairytale backdrops. I was dead against it – my own father used to scoff at such schemes – until our accountant threatened us. *You need to diversify or, soon enough, you won't have a working farm at all.*

I put my foot down. No. Not while there's proper work to do out here.

The wedding venue's not proper work?

I drop my gaze, dangerous ground. I don't want this conversation to get back to Elder Son. But the thought of Tom taking shelter with his sister-in-law sets my teeth on edge. Her pretty influence on his soft clay.

So you'd rather be indoors, titivating with the women, I snap.

I'd still be contributing, wouldn't I?

I leave him there in the tree. Parenting is a war of attrition, father and son each trying to bash the other into shape. My old man made a quick impression on me, tore my first loose tooth from my gums with a piece of thread before it was ready. *It's for your own good, boy.* I hid my tears. Metal and salt taste of endurance. Of the parts of me lost over the years, of what it's taken to bear through it. And as I head back across the meadow – like I can't be bothered with him, conversation over – there's an unexpected spring in my step. I am going to win.

At dinnertime, I shut the back door of the farmhouse and enter the kitchen. Mother's in her easy chair by the window, Sandra at the table with Younger Son. They're hunched over the family laptop.

Harry's gone to fetch Lauren for dinner, I announce, peeling off my cold, sweaty boiler suit, rolling up the sleeves of the crumpled shirt beneath.

We've got a problem, Sandra tells me.

I am peering over the Aga. The blue tiles are dripping. A large saucepan of claggy rice scorches on a medium flame, pools of flecked, starchy water on the stove top.

What've you done here? This rice has boiled out…

Those activists are from an organisation called LivestockAid, says Sandra. They've posted about our farm.

The windows are all steamed up, I say, moving the pot to the sink.

They've published their video.

Just then, Harry and Lauren open the door. Hallo!

Lauren's cheeks are rosy. She unwraps her thick teal scarf, polished fingernails clacking. Her hubby helps her out of a pristine winter coat.

Sorry we're a bit late, she huffs. Phew, it's warm in here…

Hang on, I say.

I get behind Sandra and Tom, hold the backs of their chairs as I lean down to squint at the laptop screen.

What's up? says Lauren.

Those vegan protesters have shared their footage.

Sandra waves them over and the kids assemble at the table. Mother cranes her neck from her chair by the window to see what we're all up to.

Elder Son presses in beside me. Bloody hell.

It's quite bad, says my wife. Mostly misleading…

What's vegan? says my mother.

It's about rejecting animal products, Lauren explains, gently. Like meat, milk, leather. My friend Gemma went vegan for a while to lose weight, but she got terrible bloating.

Let's just watch it, says Tom. It might be… Let's just watch.

The video starts brightly. Cows roaming free in summery

green fields. A narration begins, the limp prophecies of the man who introduced himself to me in the cowshed, Luke Underwood.

When you think of a dairy farm, is this what you imagine? Blissful images of happy cows, and Victorian maids a-milking.

That's not our farm, says Harry, triumphant.

Well, the video continues, *that couldn't be further from the truth.*

Here *we* are. Blurry images of our farmyard. Putrid puddles, muddy with morning light. Then darkness falls around the animals, and we're in the cowshed. Straw scooped to the edges and smears of dung on the concrete.

We invested in that building just two years ago. I'm proud of the refurbishment – the smart, new cubicles and steel-framed roof – which we'll be paying off for years. The girls have free access to their own spaces, can rest whenever they like. And the passageways between the cubicles are cheerful and sociable.

Oh, for god's sake, I say.

One of the cows tries in vain to stand up.

Look! says Lauren, covering her mouth with a hand.

Well, that's just Bess, I tell her, my voice tight.

What's wrong with her?

Absolutely nothing. She's a strong, healthy cow. A bit clumsy.

Some close-ups: a drippy nose, drooping eyelids. A cow on her mat, presenting her hoof. What looks like a lesion.

Oh, damn, says Elder Son. Who is that? Did you know?

It's Sal, and no. I didn't.

Because she never let on, I think. *She's been walking happily enough.*

We'll sort her out, I say, shortly. It's nothing to worry about.

The video continues its condemnations.

Don't believe the lies that dairy sells, says Luke, huskily. *This is the reality. Babies snatched away, just days old. Their mothers raped, forcibly and repeatedly impregnated until they're no longer useful. Then slaughtered.*

31

Some sombre stills. Moody portraits of cows looking tragic. Maisy lying on her calf, the sound of the raw footage in the background. I make out the muffled voices of the activists. The word, *Holocaust*. The phrase, *kill someone*. The cows stare into space. Dreaming of the end.

We do look after them, Harry tells Lauren, a little defensively.

Idiots. How can people fall for this? Cows have sad eyes and flabby mouths. That's just what they look like. But humans will happily project their own feelings onto an animal face.

Then Luke appears. Sitting on a blanket in the dirty straw with an arm around Bess's neck. She's nuzzling into his chest – the traitor! – as he does a bit to camera.

We live in a speciesist society. You wouldn't lock up or kill a human being just for food. So it's time to take a stand for these wonderful, intelligent animals – our beautiful friends. Here at LivestockAid, we're committed to change, and it can't happen fast enough. If it takes putting ourselves in danger to accelerate the systemic revolution that needs to happen, then so be it. Alderdown Farm must close! Join us, and then we...

I snap the laptop shut. Bloody bunny-huggers.

It's all over our page, says Sandra. I'll keep deleting it.

Why bother? They look hysterical.

Well, we can't just...

They've hardly got anything, Sandra. The video's not even that bad.

She shakes her head. But that dead calf, and some of the images... It might look a bit grim. To the uninitiated.

I start to pace. Throw up my hands.

Why? Because it's winter? And they're inside, and the barn's not the bloody Ritz? They're just cows. That video tries every trick in the book to shock the public, but that's a normal video of a normal farm...

Sandra tries to speak, but I'm not finished.

...with a few issues – yes, fine! – which, of course, we will sort out as quickly as we can. But I'm telling you, this is over the top. They can say what they like. They can tell everyone that Alderdown Farm is Guantanamo-bloody-Bay, for all I care. We're one of the good ones. We're a family business. We're just… dairy farmers.

I sag with tiredness, voice fading.

Who's going to listen to them? I say.

Harry pulls Lauren in for a hug. Hey. Come here, baby.

The daft woman is practically crying.

Sandra sighs and goes to the Aga. Let's see if we can salvage dinner.

Smells delicious, darling, says Mother, who I'd forgotten was there. She stares out of the window at the pitch-black evening.

I knead my scalp, catch Tom's eye. I'm telling you, I mutter. Going to be a flash in the pan.

Son

I SHOULD NEVER. AS SOON AS I finish washing up, I fire shots with my phone.

You said you'd leave out the footage of the calf. Three dots – he's writing back, but I am quicker off the mark, tapping furiously in the corner of the kitchen. It was an accident, I insist again, a cow lying down in the wrong place!

You have to think of the animals, Tom, he replies. Does she have enough room?

I AM thinking of the animals, but it's still my dad and my brother.

I stuff my phone in my pocket and go to Gran, who has always been my safe harbour. She is in the sitting room, sunken into her threadbare armchair by the fireplace, the one Mum wants rid of. She is so small these days, a morsel in the jaws of the inglenook; I dread the day she's snapped up.

I sit down on the sofa, and we put the telly on. It's some holiday-home thing about New Zealand, which makes me think of Great-Aunt Lizzie, how we visited her there when I was thirteen. I try to concentrate, but I can't stay still, can't sit with it. Punishing my palms with my fingernails, I trace every blind step I've taken recently, with no idea where I wanted to go. How I reached out to Luke with a furious DM, never for a minute expecting him to reply to me, how I told him about Dad's lie, the butter in the veg. I wasn't ready, reeling from the braying faces of the people I love around the table. All of them, laughing at me. And Luke had a plan that might teach them a lesson.

34

Settle down, says Gran. You wriggler!

She puts her hand on my arm, and I remember all the moments we snuggled up here together, forgotten by the rest of the family. How I'd regale her with every detail about my day. I should spend more time with her. She was always patient with me, even when I insisted we watch American high-school dramas or the oversaturated music videos of pop princesses she never really enjoyed. I sink into the sofa, lean into her. But my phone won't let me go. It struggles for my attention until I finally retrieve it from my pocket.

Be brave, kid, says Luke. I'm here, no matter what. If there's anything I can do for you, don't hesitate to ask.

I just feel awful.

I know. But we're going to do great things together, you and me. I'm so glad we met, Tom.

My mouth is dry. I start to answer honestly. Backspace. It is too soon for that.

Turn it up, would you? says Gran. I can't hear.

I reach for the remote and up the volume until she cracks a lazy smile. She sits back, and my eyes rest on the slow rise and fall of her chest, and I long to be at peace with myself. I think of Glasgow: dinner on the stairs, vegan sushi with Dan, fingerless gloves and playlists on phones. My short-lived freedom.

I just want to get away from this place, I write.

But my family is not a place; they are not the farm.

My cup of tea goes cold on first contact with the morning air. I said I'd meet Lauren down at the wedding barn, a historic building tucked away from the rest, encircled by mature trees and looking out over the meadows. It's a vast, arched space, forested with beams and vaulted like a place of worship. Lauren has sprinkled it with ladders and splashed the floor – which needs to be sanded anyway – with paint. She's chosen one of those not-quite-whites with a strange name that takes itself far too seriously: *Scottish Summit.*

Not *too* dazzling, she explains to me. So the bride's dress pops in the photos.

Dad doesn't like Lauren because she has a mind of her own, which is exactly why I do. She wears her femininity with ease. She works in a salon in the village and knows how to talk to people. But I get the impression Dad wanted his Number One Son to end up with a traditional farmer's wife: a floral-printed vision, bearing gifts of homemade bakes presented with a sweet smile, her wellies caked in mud. Lauren could never live up to that, being a real person.

Funny though, because in some ways she's not unlike Mum. She too has always had her crafts: candle-making, bonsai, calligraphy. She wasn't made for the farm either; she once said she regretted not going to university, as so many of her friends had. Her dad was a solicitor, but the household was a traditional one, and she wasn't encouraged to follow in the footsteps of the man of the house. Instead, she worked part-time jobs at the local library, wrote short radio dramas, which she sent to the BBC. No response. Then Dad, the farm, and everything else took over.

Take your pick, says Lauren, brandishing a paintbrush and a roll of decorator's tape. Your choice. Let's go.

It's a fiddly job, decorating between the beams. Lauren has me line them with the tape, which I peel from the roll in long, soundless strips. It's soothing, clean as a calf's tongue, and I'm relieved to get away from the complicated aliveness of the animals. Once I've protected the wood, Lauren follows with the paint.

I don't know her too well, but we get along just fine. When we break for a cup of tea, she lets me in on a little secret. The barn is haunted: one beam at the far end is covered in hundreds of little scratches, a long-forgotten tally, like someone was trying to keep count of something.

Weird, right? she grins.

So weird, I say, pleasantly spooked.

Like, was someone held captive here? Was there some sort of abduction?

Maybe an unsolved crime?

Yes! We should make a podcast, get to the bottom of it…

We sit and talk in the middle of the echoing room. Lauren outlines her grand plans for the wedding barn. I can visualise it, the romance of it. Banks of seats, aisled into symmetry. Lilypad tables and petalled air. Lanterns hanging from the beams, like the university cloisters in Glasgow, glittering with lights at Christmas. Holidays in the snow, exchanging presents with Dan…

Gonna be awesome, I say.

Lauren takes a sip from her cup, studying me. Has it been hard, coming home from uni?

It's OK, I say without looking at her. Same old.

Your dad is always stressed to hell, isn't he?

My dad? He's just spent too much time around his cows.

But she's right. He wears his martyrdom like a medal. It can do that to you, physical labour. The strain of it becomes your natural state. These days, Dad practically vibrates with the sheer Sisyphean effort of living. He huffs and puffs, grunts and groans, even when the task at hand is simply to sit down at the breakfast table and eat a full English.

Lauren laughs. You're obviously very patient.

Nah. You're the one who's had to put up with him the past few years.

He's lovely, really. Just old-school, don't you think?

I nod, then set down my cup and go back to taping. I sometimes wonder if Dad's become more conservative now that both Grandad and Uncle Mike are gone, and the full burden of Alderdown has fallen on him. Even Mum spends most of her time avoiding him, volunteering in the village, or drinking endless coffees with friends.

Lauren is still watching me as I climb the ladder. Is there anything else the matter? she digs. I'm not trying to pry, but you just seem… I dunno, like maybe you need to talk about something.

I put a piece of tape between my teeth. She's not exactly progressive, Lauren. But still, she might be understanding, and I'm so tired of holding myself down.

Probably, I say.

I thought maybe you were missing someone. Someone in particular.

I blink. Not *girl*, but *someone*; it's like she knows part of the truth, if not everything. I turn to look at her, pulse racing, but she is preparing her paint tray. I pull myself together, determined to give her nothing. She'll only pass it on to my brother.

I clear my throat. Nothing like that, I say, and my voice is self-consciously deep, not like me at all.

There was probably someone else. Dan had always been too good for me; he just hadn't known it yet. Head down, hands in pockets, pulling his waistband up. The stiff mustard fleece cardigan that was so ugly, to wear it was an act of rebellion.

We barely lasted six months before I found I couldn't hold his interest anymore. He hardly looked at me in those final days, so I wasn't surprised when he ended it, right after graduation. It took me some time to make sense of my feelings. I didn't love him, but I loved what we had, watching him pluck at his guitar, listening to his diatribes. To me, even his scrapbooked collection of fortune-cookie fortunes – such a weird thing to keep, but just on the right side of ironic – was endearing in a naff sort of way. His quirks only made me want him more. Me *and* strangers. It was only ever a matter of time before one of them stole him away.

It's not Dan that I need. It's the feeling I had when I was with him – of being seen. Dan wasn't perfect. I didn't like his internet persona, the way he scoffed and sneered and trolled. But I liked the games we played together online, where he was a muscled warrior of fantasy cliché. And I… I was Tam, as our late-night co op games started to feel realer than reality. I am Tam.

The thing is. The thing.

Dan is the first person I ever told.

17 January, 1944

I AM GLAD TO HAVE YOU with me, little book. I am writing this by the light of my carbide lamp in the hayloft, in which I make my bed. I am used to being alone, with only my thoughts for company. I mark the days on the beam by my feet. At night, when I am too restless for sleep, loving and hating the home that sent me away, I descend the ladder to the cold ground, and there I stand on my head to quiet myself. Upside down, I rest my heels against the wall, performing set after set of push-ups. I exercise until my temples are throbbing and my eyes are bulging, the pressure forcing out the memories of the night I came to England. The night I almost died.

I had been conscripted by the Luftwaffe, training as a photo-reconnaissance pilot. I was never an avid Hitler Youth – too cosseted for that, comfortably disengaged from politics – and did not want anything to do with the war. If I was to be called up against my will, shooting photographs was a reasonable compromise.

My first expedition, I was piloting a Junkers Ju 188, and we were on our way to the industrial north of England, photographing the railway lines as we went. But just before two o'clock in the morning, there was a deafening bang, as if the whole earth beneath us had been cleaved in two. Then another impact. A cannon shell hit my instrument panel, dials and tickers flailing as the sky beyond the windshield filled with fire. A rod of metal struck me on the brow.

'The port wing?' I gasped, dazed and bleeding.

'It's spreading to the fuselage,' said Hans, my co-pilot, and then he was pulling me out of my seat by the arm. 'Stefan, we have to jump.'

I took my parachute and scrambled after my four crewmates. Not one of them looked back before dropping through the forward escape hatch, driven by fear as much as by courage. We were a fireball, a comet, several hundred gallons of burning petrol crackling across the sky, and it was only a matter of time before we crashed or exploded.

I left a part of myself in that plane. I haven't stopped breathing the fumes, and sometimes when I am walking, I can feel the heat of the fire on my back, and Hans's urgent grip on my shoulder. I see the flash of teeth behind his blond moustache.

'See you on the ground,' he said to me.

But I never saw him again.

I remember the moment I plummeted. My chest filled with the cold horror of the night. My one hope was for a safe landing, but there can be no safe landing in enemy territory. Twenty-four is too young to die, I thought. There are so many things I used to take for granted. I know that now. But I cannot go back to before. That is what war does to us.

There are new guests here at Alderdown. Herb introduced them to me just before midday, when the sun was bright and cold, and I was taking five minutes to smoke and clear my head. He fetched them from the gate where an officer had dropped them off, then led them across the farmyard, lugging their suitcases while they went empty-handed. He introduced them as Mr and Mrs Nicholson.

'And this is Mr Stefan Becker.'

I offered my hand for them to shake. Mr Nicholson pulled his chin beneath the collar of his coat, like a tortoise retracting into his shell. 'Stefan?'

'He's never a Jerry?' realised his long-faced wife, pulling on her husband's arm.

I let my hand drop and took a drag on my cigarette. Anything to keep my mouth busy.

'One of my finest farmhands,' Herb defended me, already pushing on towards the path up to the main house. 'He's been working here six months and moved in just before Christmas.'

I said nothing, but I was touched by his support. How readily it was given.

The Nicholsons trudged after him, muttering to one another, not wanting to let me out of their sight. I can't say I blame them. Herb told me they were coming, evacuees from the city and victims of last Thursday's bombings. They had emerged, blinking, from the London Underground, to find their home of twenty years reduced to rubble overnight. It was a senseless loss, and I could see a newfound insecurity in the way they looked at things. The throaty rattle of a nearby corncrake startled them. They had discovered, as I had, that anything could happen to them at any moment, that sometimes things just fall out of the sky.

Father

THE WIFE AND I ARE huddled on the old chesterfield, bits of paper everywhere. It's arctic in the sitting room. A draught whistles through the gaps around the windows. We are wearing our coats, Sandra with her chin tucked behind her hand-knitted snood, ruffled up to her earlobes. We pore over our accounts. Even the farmland has fallen in value, all the referendum uncertainty.

We're covering costs, I say, steadying my voice in the bitter cold.

But there's no wage left at the end of it.

Yes. Well…

I thought we were in a better position, George.

We will be. Next year.

Sandra lifts her glasses, closes her eyes as she pinches the bridge of her nose.

I reach out to comfort her. We'll clear our debts, I say. The cowshed's done, and the feed shed. And the new maize clamp.

You were going to get the parlour extended, weren't you?

Yes, but…

I trail off. It's not going to happen at this rate.

No rush, I say. No rush.

Sandra sucks air through her teeth. But what about this house? she says. It's only getting worse. If we don't get round to it soon, we'll have bigger problems on our hands. You know that, George.

I cast an eye at the ceiling. The pockmarked, bending carpentry, propping up our house of cards. It's hard to imagine that any of this was ever new. It's now the kind of house they'd put on telly, that a celebrity architect would 'read' like a medium.

Here's where the windows were blocked up to avoid the eighteenth-century window tax, they'd say, reaching into the past, unearthing misery after misery. *As for these floors, they've been restored, but sadly not in the most historically sensitive style. The owners of this house were clearly strapped for cash.*

Sandra pulls her fingers through her hair.

If the chimney is still leaking, she begins.

It's just condensation, Sandra.

But if it's still leaking, those roofers should come back and look at it for free.

They're not going to do it for free.

Well, we can't afford to pay them again. Besides, if they didn't get it right the first time, who's to say they'll be able to fix it this time?

I stand and take a couple of steps towards the fireplace. Swallow down the old soot musk. I can hear the scathing voices of my father and brother.

This house is part of the family legacy. Built in the seventeen-hundreds, tenanted to our ancestors by the village squire. I brush my fingers across the wooden beams. There, distant members of the family have documented their allegiance in faded etchings, their names and initials carved into the grain of the wood.

In his retirement, my grandfather, Herbert Edwards, traced our roots almost six centuries into the past. For over half a millennium, our ancestors have called this place their home. If that isn't a mandate to take care of it, then I don't know what is.

I picture the leak around the chimney. It spreads from the roof, down to the decaying timbers.

Maybe I can fix it, I mumble.

We need cash, fast, Sandra says. Thank goodness for Lauren. There's just enough on the mortgage extension to finish the barn conversion. If we can get some weddings booked in, maybe that will finally get us out of this hole.

I glare. Lauren can't be the one who saves us.

Yes, I say. Well… Let's not be dramatic.

The house phone is ringing, so she doesn't argue. Just makes a face and goes into the kitchen to answer the call.

I stand there, alone. When we first met, a whole lifetime ago, she was a happy young thing, about Harry's age. I'm sixteen years older. My father never approved of the gap between us, thought it wasn't proper. But I was in the prime of my life. I'd just returned from a stint in Spain, working for a building company. And Sandra begged me to come home, to stay – for her. She called me her Don Quixote, always off on adventures. Neither of us knew he was supposed to be a figure of fun.

I wish I could hold her again. Have her love me, and yield to me as my wife. But we both know I'm not the man she fell in love with. A man with a plan, the man with the answers. The things you come to learn in life through the slow and exacting passage of time are always the hardest to forget.

There's the creak and clatter of the back door. Elder Son kicks off his wellies with a couple of light whumps, greets his mother. Then he appears in the sitting room, dressed in his muddy boiler suit and sweat-stained socks.

It's always so bloody freezing in here, he says. Still doing the accounts?

Afraid so. We can go and sit by the Aga if you want.

No, it's all right, he says, dropping into my mother's tatty armchair, rubbing his hands together. Used to it, aren't we?

I scowl with shame, take my seat on the sofa. Swipe the pile of receipts on the coffee table into their dirty supermarket bag-for-life. I can't look at Harry, his grim smile.

I'm aching all over, he says.

I flare my nostrils like a bull. It is the only answer I can muster. Don't we deserve better? After this, we'll be back out there. Pollarding trees, nurturing the hedgerows – those hideaways and winter hampers, where birds and rodents can take shelter, live off nuts and berries when food elsewhere is scarce. Every winter, we take the time to cut back the maple, the hazel, tend to

44

the hawthorn. It is an act of devotion. We stake the saplings with bamboo. We watch as the rooks drift in to nest.

We will honour this ritual, this thankless work. I used to fight about it with my brother. He found solace in the natural world. He honoured and cared for it and, even then, it took his life in the most brutal way. Sometimes I think he would not have minded had he known this.

I'm sorry it's been so rough, I say, thinly.

Elder Son winces. Dad, come on. We're doing OK. It's commodity pricing. Everyone's in the same boat.

Then he looks to the door, where Sandra has reappeared.

You good, Mum?

No, she says, flopping down beside me. Not really.

I put a hand on her knee, rising to the occasion. It's all right, darling.

You don't understand. We've just had a very peculiar phone call. Some animal rights nut who's seen that ridiculous video.

I sit up straight. And?

It was a man, saying… I don't know. *You've got an evil business, history won't look kindly…* That sort of rubbish.

Fuck's sake, says Harry.

They've got no right calling here, I proclaim. How'd they get our number?

Anyone can get our number.

Clearly a very lonely person. Starved of connection.

Probably, says Sandra. I told him not to call here again, and then I hung up.

Harry is looking at his phone, swiping. Mum, Dad, he says.

You should have handed him over to me, I tell my wife, my voice rising.

Why? What's the point?

Harry waves. Hey!

I would have told him where to go, I say, practically shouting at her.

Listen, Harry is saying. It's gone viral. It's gone…

What?

The video. This is really bad… It's almost at a million views.

Sandra takes his phone. A million? You're not serious.

Haven't people got anything better to do? I growl, my anxiety like those million views, snowballing into an avalanche. I dig my nails into my thighs.

Sandra lets out a low moan. Listen to this, she says, reading: **The disturbing footage captured inside Alderdown Farm reveals horrific scenes of animal neglect: extreme overcrowding, filthy living conditions, sickly and dying animals dumped in gangways with no access to food or water…**

No access to…? I slam a fist into the arm of the sofa and shout, That's libel, that is. That's bloody libel.

This could ruin us, says Sandra, quietly.

It's not going to ruin us.

What about the wedding business?

What about it? I demand, having to calm myself with every breath.

Well, we were counting on it, weren't we? Who's going to book us after this?

There's no such thing as bad publicity, I bluster. Isn't that the phrase?

Harry snorts. I dunno, Dad.

Once more, the phone starts to ring, pealing through the air like a burglar alarm. I lurch from the sofa, heading for the door. Sandra is right behind me.

Don't, she says.

What?

I agree with Mum, says Harry, from the armchair. Let it ring. If it's a proper call, they'll leave a message or try our mobiles.

I don't care. If it's him, I'd like to give him a piece of my mind.

No, says my wife, taking my hand. Not when you're angry. It'll be worse if we react.

So we just ignore it? Let them get away with it?

Mum's right, Dad.

Fine, I say. Fine!

I won't allow Sandra to lead me back to the sofa. Free my hand from hers, drop down with an angry groan. Sandra sits next to me, but keeps a space between us. Her arms and legs are crossed, tucked away from mine.

A clatter and a beep next door. Tom, answering, Hello?

Son

IMAKE OUT A VOICE, BUT the words take a second to follow. Don't hang up on me, you bitch.

I clutch the receiver to my ear. What?

Your horrible business is not long for this world. You hear me? You're not going to get away with it. People are waking up. And we're coming for you.

Who is this?

Drinking milk from the udders of another animal; that's sick. That milk belongs to their babies.

I swallow. Look, you're talking to the wrong…

How dare you? How do you sleep at night?

My brother enters the kitchen, his fingers worrying the scruff on his chin. I gulp at him, eyes wild. Then Mum and Dad appear, pale and pink-nosed. Mum shakes her head, gestures as if she's cutting her own throat. *End the call.*

They said not to hang up, I explain, my vision swimming.

But Harry prises the phone from my grip and sets it down.

A blood tint seeps through the kitchen windows. As the sun sets, our curdling thoughts fill the farm, spirit behind hedgerows and through the skeletons of trees. We gather around the laptop at the table, beckoning our attackers in, extending the masochistic invitation I am responsible for granting in the first place.

There are thousands of comments under the video now. Some of them pose reasonable questions. Most of them call for the guillotine.

Sick practice. Shame on them. I will never drink milk again.

Please do something! Somebody has to stop these monsters.

Spread the word. This farm must be brought to justice. I'm willing to do whatever it takes.

Dad makes an optimistically litigious note of the usernames behind the more threatening comments, jotting them in his spiral-bound notebook. He looks so vulnerable, earnestly engaged in this futile endeavour; he doesn't have a clue.

I tap a message to Luke. People are threatening us. Someone called the house. I didn't sign up for this.

Who are these people? Mum keeps saying, over and over.

Bloody inbreds, Dad replies. Probably all know each other. Got their prat mates to join the pile-on.

Mum takes Dad's notebook and starts scribbling a generic critique of the accusations levelled against us.

So we can reply to comments, she says. Copy-paste.

She writes with her tongue between her teeth. Her bracelets rattle. The table shakes.

See how they like that! she mutters, stabbing a full stop.

It's sticks and stones, all right? says Harry. As long as they keep it virtual, they're just keyboard warriors.

Exactly, says Dad, nodding at the laptop. They're cowards. They can talk the talk on *there*.

Fucking losers. Who's gonna listen?

I'm not sure about that, says Mum. Think about it. Most people spend half their time glued to their phones. Just because you're always out there in the fields. This is the world we live in, whether you like it or not. If something takes off on the internet, it spills into reality.

Yes, all right, Mum, says Harry.

I read Luke's reply under the table: Shit, you ok? There are a lot of crazies out there, Tom, but I promise they're not with LivestockAid. Call me?

*

49

The night draws in, and the faces of my family sicken under the halogens. They bounce worst-case scenarios off one another, wondering how we might be made to suffer, competing visions of our inevitable downfall. Their fears spiral creatively. They talk of invaders hiding in the hayloft, spooking the cows, flooding the parlour. I picture a pool of rancid yellow milk. Shit posted through the letterbox, trade blockades on country lanes, bringing the struggling business to its knees.

They're used to my silence. Thank god they let me be. If I had to speak, I'm sure they'd hear the shame in my voice. Perhaps I should let them. Isn't that what I'd wanted so desperately: to be heard, to be seen? This has gone far beyond that. In highlighting our differences, I have waged war, and now the battle lines have been drawn.

Dad is ready to take up arms.

We've got a lot of sharp tools to hand, he says, elbowing Harry, who looks alarmed. We're not afraid, are we?

It won't come to that, I blurt. I won't let it.

You'll stop them, will you, big man? mocks Harry, and he's right about me, all empty threats.

We go in circles, arguing. Mum leaves the room, then stomps back in to have the last word. She distracts herself with household chores and throws the laundry in the washing machine, overlooking – in her agitation – a bright-green sock, which whizzes around with the whites, sluicing them a watery cow-pat colour.

I read the comeback she drafted and left on the counter.

This is not true and not fair. Here at Alderdown Farm, we prize the well-being of our animals, regularly choosing the more difficult, costlier paths so that we can guarantee our customers the most ethical product. These activists are spreading a slanderous misinformation campaign, and anyone who endorses or shares their video doesn't know the first thing about farming, the challenges involved or the benefits of our approach. Nowadays, we have to compete with intensification, with the mega-dairy system from the US. That's what's coming if you put us out of business with your ignorance. That's the industry you'll be left with. And it will be on YOUR HANDS.

The note swells with emotion, ending with a furious, blue zigzag; the biro has torn right through the paper.

I have to do something.

I'll take over, I propose. I'll run the emails, the social media. Then you don't have to worry about any of it.

Maybe I *want* to worry about it, says Dad, puffed up.

But the others are nodding at me.

Probably more your thing, anyway, says Harry. Sitting at the computer.

Yeah, I say, doesn't bother me. I'll do some – what's it called? – crisis management. Saves you having to see it, waste time worrying when you can be getting on with the... with the real work.

Are you sure, darling? says Mum, putting a hand on my shoulder.

Yeah, of course. There's a difference, right, between raising awareness – engaging in debate and so on – and all of this. I don't want you to see this crap.

Raising awareness? huffs Dad. Raising awareness of what, exactly?

I sit in bed, soothed by the gentle chirping of my electropop playlist. It is impossible to argue with Dad. I used to play the long game of dropping provocative but irrefutable facts into our conversations, until one day, when the topic arose, he'd offer them up like they were his. But that's not happening this time. I tangle my fingers in the bedsheets. There are cartoon stars on midnight dark, the comforts of childhood all around me. I take my phone from the bedside table, where I like to place it on top of the case of smoothed glass I once combed from beaches: whites and browns, pinks, aquas and cornflower blue, all honeyed by amber lamplight.

Luke's name flashes on my screen. He needs me. Alderdown Farm, with its verdant watercolour meadows, bluebell woods and historic house, is of a type – the dairy farm as timeless Eden. This is the image that LivestockAid needs to taint in the eyes of the public, not the much-maligned factory farm, so easy to despise, but the bucolic idyll of British dairy: cruelty and exploitation, sanitised and packaged up on the lid of a chocolate box, pretty yet hollow.

But Alderdown is also my home, and this bedroom has been my sanctuary. My crumbling yellowed walls are papered with celebrities, layer upon layer of beautiful heroines checking in on me, their backs to the wide world. Peeking between them is the solemn comfort of my 'Entropy' print, regimented molecules at the top of the page losing their certainty, devolving into a glittering stardust that represents heat death. Why did I love that nihilism, the inevitability of it all? I trace my jaw, the prickle of stubble I can't keep at bay. *Nothing matters*, I used to repeat to myself. *Don't fight it.* I still haven't sorted the heap of clothes spilling from the bottom of the wardrobe, lapping the foundations of my manga towers, comic books stacked by genre and piled high because the bookshelves are holding my game collection: *Cluedo?* from the sixties, *Enchanted Forest* for digging up treasure in the roots of trees, and *Ghost Castle* – because it's easy enough to escape from a playset. It's just a game.

I turn my phone in my hands and read Luke's last message. I get it. What you've done is really tricky, but I know you have your family's best interests at heart, and I truly believe that we can lead them, and the farm, into a new era: one that doesn't depend on animal exploitation to survive.

He can be so pompous.

I shut him down with a terse response. This was a mistake. We're too close to violence.

He won't leave it. His anxiety vibrates under the covers, where my phone is pressed between the mattress and my left thigh. I gave him special access, long before I unlocked the shed door for him. Ever since I agreed to our first video call – to prove I was serious. He was so kind, so understanding. And then I couldn't stop myself checking in for a daily fix. It was a bridge away from Dan, from the farm, lifting me up to some imagined place. Luke never had to try before; I was ready to give him everything, and he doesn't want to let that go. But this way round, our dynamic is intoxicating.

Let him beg.

I go deep now, and dive into LivestockAid's past campaigns. I scroll with my left hand; with my right and more dominant hand, I buff a light, matte foundation into my skin, tucking the soft brush into the peaks and crevices of my jawline.

A link leads me to a newspaper article about a month-long protest, last year, outside a village butcher's. There are photos: a mass of do-gooders, changing the world with uncompromising placards about murder, and dripping with red paint.

Passing parents picked up their toddlers and crossed the street. Elderly customers kept their distance; they were outnumbered three to one. The owner of the shop, an old man himself, ventured out in his apron, hoping to ask them politely to let his customers through. They called him the Village Ripper.

How would *you* like to be butchered? one of the activists asked him.

But the Ripper, according to the article, had a productive conversation with Luke.

He is quoted: We discussed that I wasn't some corporation – just a small, independent business, run by family and friends, and part of the community for years and years. He completely understood where I was coming from, and tried to ensure everything stayed civil.

Maybe. But Luke could have called off his goons, surely? I tense as my phone rumbles against my leg.

Perhaps I'm not giving him enough credit. I have always been afraid of conflict, though I realise a certain amount of conflict is unavoidable when you take a stand. More than that: it's necessary. And Luke knows this, for sure. He's said as much. How else will anything change? How else are rights and freedoms won?

I scroll down to a photo, a portrait of his inhumanly lovely face. I put aside my mascara to examine him. He is beautiful. In his cold, dispassionate expression, I see complete self-confidence, an all-consuming self-regard.

I would give anything for this. My body pulses with fear and desire.

I stick my phone in the bedside drawer, open the camera on my laptop, and yank the gooseneck lamp clipped to the headboard, angling it to shine on my face.

There I am on the screen, transformed. Smoky eyes, glitter tumbling.

I apply a kiss of lip gloss. Smack. Then a spritz of setting spray. My cheekbones shimmer as I check my angles.

Examined in isolation, each part of the image seems right, painted to perfection. But when I zoom out, when I take in the whole, I see someone strange and ill-formed. I haven't yet worked out how to externalise the discoveries taking place inside me in a way that is fully satisfying.

I let out a lungful of breath. I mouth my name.

Hands trembling, I search for an anonymous chat site and give it permission to access and stream my webcam. A few clicks. I type.

Tam.

I am live, instantaneously matched with a stranger. My video takes one window, and a young woman materialises in the other, fiddling with her collar, chewing gum. It says her name is Lacey.

Hi, I say, but she is already gone.

I'm given another encounter. Someone joins my room, but there is only a heavy pair of breasts, pressed close to the camera, pink and wrinkled around the nipples.

I click away.

A purplish tumescent prick.

I click again. Now my partner is a mystery, screened black. I assume they can see me; that's the point. I myself am used to being hidden, but I come here to be seen. I sigh. There's a feeling I cannot name.

Hello, I whisper, and I wonder exactly who I'm expecting to meet in this sea of strangers, lonely and liminal, and always far-off enough for there to be a safe way out.

The stranger in the dark is typing.

I wait, lighting a cigarette, calmer now, settling. My limbs suffuse with warmth as the shame begins to ebb, and there: that's what I wanted, what I crave, the queer pleasure of existing, of watching and being watched.

A message appears in the chat box.

U a tranny mate?

I blow my lungs clean. Take a second, my face hot. Type back, **I don't know**, and click away.

24 January, 1944

TODAY I MET MAGGIE IN the creep, where the new calves are housed and fed, at the lane-side of the farmyard. She'd come to bed them in, but I was already finishing up. So she invited me to accompany her and Lizzie for an afternoon of twig-picking. As we made our way to the hay meadow, Lizzie rushed around us, playing, keeping close. The girl was rather nervous: a ribbon had come loose in her hair, and one pigtail was frayed, trilling about her ear.

'Watch it!' said her big sister. 'You'll trip us up.'

Lizzie fell behind, hanging her head. 'Peggy said some planes landed behind her house.'

'What planes?'

The girl didn't answer. Instead, she looked up at me, disturbed and wary.

'German planes?' said Maggie. 'Peggy's pulling your leg.'

'But what if she's not? What if they came to our farm?'

'Then I'll protect you,' I ventured, because she was looking at me like I meant her harm, and I couldn't bear it.

'Of course,' said Maggie, 'but they won't. If there's an invasion, they're not going to start here. All right? We're not that important, Lizzie.'

She was no longer listening. She came up and slotted herself between us, seizing our hands. Hers was small against my palm, and as I held it, I knew that I would indeed defend her, like a daughter or a sister, if ever she needed me.

There was a disturbance in the trees, squabbling magpies. Lizzie squeezed my fingers. I looked at Maggie. I thought she might object to her sister holding my hand. When some part of your identity marks you out, I suppose it is inevitable that others may see that first, and above all else. My instinct told me there was no harm in it, but there are rules. There are laws.

Yet she said nothing, and in so doing, said everything.

The three of us worked in silence in the field, crouching on the cold, wet ground and gathering bundle after bundle of fallen branches. It felt good to serve in this way, like we were a brood of fur-picking apes, only we were grooming the land.

The weather has turned, and now the cows are free to roam in the open fields once more. It is essential that I can control them, but I haven't the knack. I've been trying to build my relationship with these stubborn beasts for the best part of a year, and I am working harder than ever, afraid of outliving my usefulness. Lizzie sat on her father's knee on the bank at the side of the field while he repaired the long, split handle of a scythe. The evening drew in. I was trying in vain to direct the cows from one field to another. I spoke to them in English, then in German, then in some wordless combination of barks and hisses. I waved my arms, scattering the animals like seeds from a dandelion clock.

'No, no,' said Maggie, with a short laugh.

My incompetence on full display, I was on the verge of begging the dull-witted creatures: don't do this to me, not now.

'Stop all that,' said Maggie, shooing me.

I retreated, allowing her to take over. The cows began to settle, chewing sedately. The grass shone like wire under the winter sun.

'Approach them calmly,' said Maggie, closing in. 'You want to be about twenty paces away. All of this' – she stopped, stretching out her arms – 'is their space. That gap between us, right now, they want to maintain it. So, if I step into it like so' – she demonstrated for me – 'they'll start to move, just enough to regain the space again. Do you see?'

I couldn't believe how simple it was, how elegantly and precisely Maggie could assemble and direct the herd, without saying a word, without breaking a sweat. There was such understanding between them. The more she closed the gap between her and the cows, the faster they moved to reopen it. And she could control their direction just by adjusting the angle of her approach.

'Try it with me,' she said. 'Close in around the back, and we'll steer them towards the gate.'

I went to her side, stepping in, stepping out. Start, stop. It was a dance, Maggie leading, a natural rhythm emerging.

The cows clumped into a neat column; they moved at a manageable trot. I looked to the bank to see Herb standing beside Lizzie, watching us dance together.

So, now I can commune with the cows. That was the missing piece of my Alderdown puzzle, but at last I have it. I have proven my usefulness, and Herb has seen it: the moment I became a farmer, under Maggie's expert tutelage. I owe her my continued security and must find a way to thank her.

Father

HOLD ON A SECOND.

I am pulling on my duffle coat at the back door, Dusty desperate to be let out. Ma is talking to me from the kitchen table as she pours milk into her tea.

Go easy on George, she tells me. It's getting to him.

Ma? I say, and she looks startled. It's me. *I'm* George.

She twists her mouth like she's just eaten a lemon. Then she clears her head, smiles. Georgie! she beams. You wrap up warm now.

Yes, Ma, I say, as I realise I have put the toggles of my coat through the wrong loops.

I take the tractor out over the grey land, mount the chain harrow. It trails broadly behind the wheels, its black teeth clinging to the ground. An annual chore, gouging and spreading the grazing and silage fields in preparation for new life.

Green spikes of daffodils are sprouting in the woods beyond the stream. These first signs of growth reassure me. Spring is in the air, and the cows know it. They stomp and bellow in the shed, impatient for the end of their enclosure. But they must wait a while longer. The grass must be cultivated, won't last with the whole herd stampeding over its vulnerable shoots.

I rock in the seat of the tractor, check the clean, dark strip I leave in my mirrors as I turn the soil. Everything is released: the dead grass, the molehills and clods of manure. Ready to be rolled flat, come to rest in a fine bed. Redwings flock to the churn of worms.

I am finishing up when Elder Son comes striding through the corner gate, waving.

I give him a nod and climb down. A stick of KitKat hangs from my mouth like a cigarette. A robin hops around my front wheel, hunting. My work delivers a feast, helps the birds through a hungry time. We eat together in peace and quiet until my boy interrupts.

Dad, he says. It's Brenda.

I nod. Brenda has been marked for almost nine months now, a blue stripe on her tail. Her first calf has been due for several days.

She's sprung? I say.

She is.

It's a rite of passage for our heifers. From two years old, we keep them calving every twelve months. They're bred for this. A hard life, but wild cows face a similar workload. They give birth over and over until they're spent and old. Then they're carried off by predators, ripped apart to feed the feral hungry.

Her whole life, we've housed Brenda in the lower shed with the other heifers. We keep them there until they're productive, separating them from their older sisters. Yesterday, she was anxious. Tossing her head, groaning. So we isolated her, moved her to the upper shed for the space to rest and roam as she pleased. And now she is ready.

I'm a bit worried, says Harry, it being her first. You think she's roomy enough?

She might want a hand.

Not sure she'll want it, but she might need one. She's nervous.

He's nervous, more like. I roll my eyes, can't help it.

We ride the tractor back to the farmyard, past Mike's old, steam-powered Fowler engine – left lifeless too long, and now speckled with rust – then across the way to the upper shed.

Brenda is at the far end. She stands with her back to us, blocks out the world. Her udder is ballooning, slime roping a second tail where the calf will crown. A puddle beneath her feet. Her muscles bulge as she strains with the life inside her.

We'll approach slowly, from the side. She's always been a challenge, Brenda. It annoys me no end when people make out that cows are all dozy meat-bags, without a thought to share between them. They can be wily and selfish, courteous and mild. Brenda is a born leader, with a fiery temperament to rival any bull. No sooner had she hit the pasture than I'd catch her head-butting her elders. Don't I know what that's like.

Now I whisper and woo, while Elder Son keeps his distance. I tell him to make himself useful, prepare the cattle crush inside the upper shed. We will coax her into it and hold her fast, for her safety as well as ours. This is the tough love that outsiders wouldn't grasp.

Brenda kicks out when I touch her back.

I know, I whisper.

She looks me in the eye, and understands: I have come to help her. She walks all the way into the crush. Harry makes a halter, lassoing her.

Keep her still, I say.

He fastens a cord over her nose. I fetch a pail of nuts and silage. Brenda dips her head, more interested in eating than birthing her calf. We give her a minute to settle. I lead Elder Son back outside.

Lauren and Tom carry paint tins across the yard. The pigeons rise like a round of applause, fill the sky before descending again behind one of the steel-framed barns. There is an abandoned paddock back there, piled high with scrap. Nettles and thistles have sprouted all over the metal and the plastic, a reminder not to let our guard down against the wild.

Elder Son greets his wife. Her long hair looks damp and messy, a smear of paint on her pink cheek.

Brenda's calving, I say, gruffly.

The hens surround Tom, stretch and burble for attention. He flinches as they peck at his laces. Animals appear to disgust him.

They like you, laughs his brother.

They want to join in, Lauren giggles. *Buk-buk-buk.*

I head back into the upper shed, preferring to check on Brenda than humour the kids. She moos, softly. Presses herself against the side of the crush.

You're all right, girl, I say.

Harry, Tom, and Lauren follow me in. Harry comes to my side, while Tom and Lauren hang back, wide-eyed. Hopeful for some drama. The cows in the main shed all know what's afoot. They add their mournful chorus to Brenda's cries.

Flushed with suspense, Elder Son looks between me, Brenda, and his wife. It's showtime.

Let's get her secure, I tell him. She doesn't seem to be pushing.

He fumbles with the headlock, and she allows me to steer her into place. Then I stand at the back of the crush and pull on my gloves.

I'm going in, I announce.

Why does she have to give birth in a cage? says Lauren.

I reach inside Brenda, take her tension in my arms.

What? says Harry.

Well, says Lauren, it's just... After everything that's been happening, you have to wonder how it might look.

I block them out, feel for the calf. My fingers stroke the hard ball of its scalp. Easiest if the head comes first.

So? says Elder Son. It's not hurting her.

I'm just thinking of LivestockAid, says Lauren. I know you mean well, but is there really no better way to do this?

I agree, Younger Son pipes up. Maybe for our own good we should consider...

You keep out of it, says his brother.

I interject now: I know what I'm doing, I say. I've done this hundreds of times.

I disappear up to my elbows. Brenda and the calf are hot, pulsating.

I was just going to say we should remember other people's perspectives, says Tom, with a timidity that only riles me more.

Whatever for?

I pull on the unborn calf.

Harry turns on his little brother. You're so bloody patronising, Tom.

Brenda wriggles and roars.

I can see it! gasps Lauren, clapping her hands together.

There are reasons we do it like this, says Harry. And anyway, things can't just change – he clicks his fingers – like *that*.

It doesn't matter, guys. Look! says Lauren, overcome with sudden feeling.

I get what you're saying, Tom continues. But there's no reason people won't eventually stop using animals for business altogether, and what would you do then? Maybe lab-grown meat will take off. I don't know.

The calf is coming. I imagine it is a shapeless lump of artificial flesh, incubated in an amniotic sac. The thought is so unappetising that I clench my stomach as the calf slips free. I carry it to the straw. Ungainly and wet.

Male, I say. Baby boy.

He's disgusting, says Lauren, appreciatively.

My sons aren't even watching anymore.

Tom, says Elder Son. There's something like seventy billion farm animals in the world. It's big business. You really think we need to pay attention to what a bunch of fucking snowflakes have to say?

I help the calf to his feet and instruct Harry to deliver the placenta. I have to ask him twice.

I get that it's not going to change overnight, says Tom. I'm really just agreeing with Lauren that maybe this is an opportunity, you know, to take stock of the situation. Because the world is going to keep changing, whether we like it or not…

I don't give a shit about the woke brigade, mate, says Harry, finishing up and removing his gloves.

Tom clears his throat. I'm only saying this because I don't think it's going away, he says in a low voice, almost a whisper. I'm not trying to make… You don't have to bite my head off.

Harry frees a relieved and quiet Brenda from the crush. She comes to investigate her calf. While she licks him, I go to milk her, break the seal on the golden beestings. Harry holds the groggy calf up to her udder, and he lifts his head by instinct. Sniffs. He knows what to do.

Lauren crouches to get a better look at him taking his first drink. Aww, she says. Clever baby.

I put my arm under his body, support his spindly limbs. He sucks and gulps, blearily. Tom stands with his arms folded. Looking down his nose.

I know what he's thinking. In the wild, calves suckle from their mothers for up to a year. Brenda and her firstborn will have just a few days before he's taken away, before he's shipped off to mainland Europe, to a country where they have a taste for tender veal. That's the business. And Brenda is a bright young thing. She will remember him.

I glare at Younger Son. Yes, I know what he's thinking – and it's no word of a lie.

What, Tom? I snap, the warm little calf weighing on my arm. What?

His mouth drops open. I didn't say anything!

If you don't like it, you can go and find yourself somewhere else to live. And don't pout. You look like a bloody girl.

George! says Lauren.

Tom uncrosses his arms and lets them fall to his sides. Now I've done it. He looks disorientated, doesn't know whether to fight or flee.

All right, Dad, says Elder Son. Leave it, yeah?

I turn my face away, fix my gaze on the suckling newborn. That connection between parent and child. I picture my wife at the hospital. Weepy and glowing, and perfectly exhausted – our babies, who would be Harry and Tom, cuddled to her breast. To my horror, tears start to prickle in the corners of my eyes.

*

I clean myself up, then retreat to the small office adjacent to the milk storage area. I'm recovering there when Steve arrives in his tanker for the afternoon collection. He honks the horn, calls me outside. Normally, he doesn't need me. Knows his job well, tends to get on with it by himself. I approach with interest as he climbs down from the driver's seat. The great cylinder on the back of the vehicle shines through the mist.

Hallo, George, he says, removing his cap. Did you know someone's written on the road outside your entrance?

On the road? Written what?

I think it's just chalk, or chalk paint. Wouldn't rub off, but I'm sure it'll be OK if you wet it.

Right, but what's it say?

He smiles, meekly. Ruffles the spines of his moustache. Err... It says 'Welcome to Hell'. Someone's got a wild sense of humour.

I try to laugh. Oh, for goodness' sake.

Yeah, I'm sorry. I know you've had some grief recently.

Not sure why they've chosen us, but there we go.

They're just nutters, mate. There's more around than you'd think.

Thanks for telling me, Steve.

Any time.

He dons his cap and starts back towards the tanker, ready to grade and pipe the milk, and then be on his way. I stand and watch him go. I'm so tired that I want to lie down on the concrete and blot out the world.

Son

MY MORNING ROUTINE: I WAKE at ten, and clasp my phone before I even open my eyes. The outside cuts into my bedroom, finding ways around the curtains, and my duvet is so cold that it feels wet against my skin. I switch on the lamps and they illuminate my breath in sleepy cloudlets. Then I dress, pulling on the old, oversized hoodie I'm using as a painting overall, while flicking through the previous day's hate mail on my phone. I like to get this – my atonement – out of the way first thing, when I'm not yet awake enough to give myself a hard time.

The numbers are finally falling, which is a relief. There are under ten emails today. Four of them are so nasty they are borderline unreadable. The rest are earnest attempts to school us: on sustainability, on the environment, and on animal exploitation. I read these ones, as we share a common cause. All the same, I don't reply. I've agreed with Mum and Dad that the best response is no response, and that does seem to be working.

Just as I'm leaving my bedroom, one more email drops into the farm inbox. The subject is 'Greetings from Germany'. Stopping in the dark at the top of my windowless staircase, I start to read.

Good morning,

I hope you don't mind that I am writing you this message. My name is Friedrich Becker, and I live in Berlin. My grandfather, Stefan, who passed away last year, lived and worked at Alderdown Farm as a prisoner of war between 1943 and 1944.

While he never talked about this time when he was alive, he tells the story with an astonishing clarity in his journal. This he has left to me, as I am a linguist and amateur historian. I think it is clear that Alderdown meant a great deal to him, and I was hoping to connect with you to share this very special history.

I do not know if the Edwards family, who made him feel so welcome in spite of the infelicitous circumstances of his stay, is as yet living and working on this farm, but I am hoping.

I am planning to visit the UK later in the year, as I have friends to accommodate me in London. If possible, it would be so wonderful to visit the site my grandfather has described in such detail, and if the Edwards family still lives at Alderdown, we will have many things to discuss.

Best regards,
Friedrich

Gran's talked a bit about wartime on the farm, but she's never mentioned working alongside German prisoners, and I'm fairly certain I've never heard the name Stefan Becker before. Part of me thinks this might be some sort of trick, connected to LivestockAid's campaign. But I don't see how.

I read the message twice, finding pleasure in my curiosity. I have good news for Friedrich: we are the Calverts now – Edwards was Gran's maiden name – but we are still here, for better or for worse, all these years later. I hurry downstairs to share the email with the rest of the family.

Days on a farm start before the sun, and Mum has been up for hours. She is sitting in the kitchen with her laptop, some papers, and a pot of coffee. There is a crystal vase of freshly picked snowdrops on the table. I stare at them; she never stops trying.

Aren't they pretty? she says, barely looking up from the spreadsheet she's studying. They're flowering on the verge.

I try to read Friedrich's email to her, but as soon as she realises it's not another threatening letter, she loses interest and tells me to show my dad; she's sure that he will want to hear all about it. I am already late to meet Lauren in the wedding barn, but I head down to the yard with the email. Dad and Harry are marking all the heifers born during the winter so that they'll be identifiable upon their return to the fields in March. Harry puts them in and out of the crush, and Dad deals the freeze-branding.

I was told, once, that this does the cows no harm. Dad creates the identification marks by cooling an iron in a mixture of alcohol and dry ice, a couple of hundred degrees below freezing, and then pressing it against the cows' rears for about a minute while they grunt and complain. I creep over, trying not to wince at the squirming of the animals.

What do you want? says my brother.

Once the iron has destroyed the pigment cells in a cow's hair follicles, that's her turn over, and then the next cow is brought in. The hair will grow back white in the shape of a number. I think of the protesters' comparisons of our farm with Nazi death camps, entry numbers tattooed on human skin.

Here, I say, listen to this email we just got.

I read Friedrich's message all the way through, pausing occasionally to allow for Dad and Harry's comments to one another as they brand a skinny heifer they call Darla.

What's that? says Dad, when I'm done.

Didn't you listen?

We're right in the middle of something, says Harry.

OK, I say, disappointed. Then I'll let you read it for yourselves, later.

Just tell us quickly, barks Dad, and I resist the impulse to argue.

It's from this German guy, Friedrich, whose granddad worked here as a prisoner of war.

Dad has his back to me. Really? he says.

He died last year, but apparently he was here in the forties, during World War Two. And Friedrich wants to meet us.

He looks around, now. Seems a little odd, doesn't it?

Why?

I don't know, Tom. Could be anyone.

I shrug, and hear myself say, Well, I'm going to reply to him.

You can do what you like.

He wants to come and visit in the summer.

Dad has turned away again, back to his branding. Not now.

I stuff my phone and my hands into my pockets. I expected a bit of traction, a chance to connect. No, I say, not now. In the summer.

It's not a good time, Tom.

Neither Dad nor Harry are listening anymore. They talk to each other, over each other, swapping instructions. It is clear our conversation is finished, and my feet are itching to walk away. All the same, I make one last remark as I turn to go, watching a branded cow wriggle and stamp her hoof.

They're pretty tolerant, aren't they?

You should see the way your gran used to do it, says Dad. She used a red-hot iron. Now that was cruel.

That evening, I shut myself in my bedroom and turn to my computer like a friend. The LivestockAid video continues to find new viewers all the time, and the comments section below has become a destination for saints and trolls alike. Whenever the two collide, their conversations quickly escalate beyond all reason.

Just ate a big juicy steak. Mmmm.

Maybe eat some human flesh next. Youd like that too wouldnt you.

You want me to eat you slut. Wait your turn bitch.

Bet you cant get it up, all the hormones in your meat.

It's just too easy to ambush and derail even the simplest of conversations. All it takes is one person to engage, to allow themselves their righteous anger. Then it doesn't matter how hard anyone else tries to bring the discussion back to the video, or the issues it raises. And no quantity of teary emojis can compensate for the palpable hatred on display, coming to a head in the dark and anonymous no-man's-land of the internet. I try to tell myself that it's all for the best; their fights tend to deflect attention away from Alderdown itself, and my family.

I apply my make-up as I write back to Friedrich Becker.

My name is Tam. I was so interested to read your message. I'm afraid it's actually kinda hectic here, so I can't promise you a visit anytime soon. But let's stay in touch. I'd love to hear more about your grandfather and his experiences at Alderdown.

I click send.

My night routine: I confront myself. I draw a new image, layer upon layer, and yet I feel light, bare, as if I have stepped into the shower and washed myself clean of the day. Gazing into a compact, I stretch my cheeks, pucker my lips. This is not a defacement, it is truly me, this mask of my own creation, for don't we all choose how to present ourselves to the world?

I set aside the mirror and take my laptop again. I am about to put my webcam on when something under the farm video catches my attention. Luke is there, his name in the comments. I read his words, biting my tongue.

Love, he prescribes, and respect for all. <3 You never know what truths reside behind someone's words. Let's keep it civil and be kind to one another.

A call for compassion, for humanity.

I've ignored his flood of messages, every attempt at reconciliation left unread. But he has managed to communicate with me all the same, indirectly. Where nobody else can even see how I've been injured, he is reaching out to say he understands that we are all in pain. And he has hurt my family. He has hurt me. Collateral damage. I will not be drawn in.

The people's prophet, he's sent them scrambling. The commenters below are in raptures, but I do not want to read their contributions. This is between me and Luke. I click through to his Insta feed.

His bio: **Vegan. UK/UAE. Pan.**

I survey the photos I studied for months before I had to block him out. He appears all over the world, oversaturated, larger than life. Reflecting by an infinity pool in Dubai, geocaching in downtown LA, cavorting with farm animals. He strikes a pose, cuddling a stressed-out chicken, kissing a hairy pig on the snout, stretching his arms around a fat Limousin cow. Scrolling through the thirsty comments left by his followers, I think of those softcore calendars showcasing Hot Guys with Baby Animals.

I stroke my fingers over my made-up face, smack my lips against the back of my hand. I must not indulge that familiar flicker of sad green fury. Luke is a star, and I am yet to play myself in my own story – don't even appear as an extra, my portrait conspicuously absent from all my social feeds. My gallery depicts me only in absentia, by association with a slideshow of seashells, sunsets and elaborate Ukiyo-e.

Now, here is Luke at Pride, half-naked, shoulder to shoulder with happy, celestial mates, laughing with a rainbow-bearded friend, posing with another, a glittery someone, bald and graceful and enigmatic in broad daylight, smiling in the sunshine.

I want.

This is everything.

Some paused part of me awakens like muscle memory. I go to my DMs. Luke's unread messages are right at the top.

Tom, it's OK if this is the end of our story together. You love your family, and you are now being hurt by the work LivestockAid is doing. I understand. But just know I never set out to cause you pain. I believe we can live in a world where everyone is treated with respect, regardless of species. Whatever happens, I will be here, working towards a kinder, fairer existence, and if you ever need me, you know where to find me. Peace.

I picture him writing this. Perfect, beautiful, and – somewhere out there – thinking of me.

More than anything, I want someone I can talk to, someone who thinks deeply, someone who believes we don't have to accept everything the way it is. *The way it's always been done.*

Someone who won't bollock me for looking *like a bloody girl.*

I can't help wanting Luke, his better world. And now he is asking for nothing in return. I sit up straighter in bed, tuck my hair behind my ears, and start tapping a new message into my phone.

Sorry for the late response. I've been taking care of things here. But please don't think I've given up on fighting for change. In some ways, it's more important to me than ever. I've just got to work through some stuff.

A second chance at a one-time offer. I lie back and put the phone upside-down on the pillow, next to my head. He will not reply, I tell myself. I left it too long.

My eyes are closed when I feel my phone buzz.

Welcome back, Luke's written. I've missed you.

I hold the screen close to my face, so close that the text starts to move.

I've been thinking of you, he continues. I shouldn't have started something like this, leaving you to pick up the pieces.

It's OK, I reply. He's still typing.

I want to help you. I want to work together – more closely.

Srue, I tap, and my muddled letters are autocorrected. Sure.

Sorry if this is too little, too late.

But I am lonely – and it isn't.

8 February, 1944

THERE ARE OWLS OUTSIDE THE hayloft. Beyond the scratching of ink against the page, I hear them screeching, hunting, just as I used to hear them in the woods when visiting Emilia, my beloved, at her parents' house in Bavaria. Thirteen long months we have been apart. Countless times I have wondered if she thinks of me, the way I'd light up when Frau Schneider opened the front door and, over her shoulder, I saw her, my love, descending the staircase; our chaperoned walks beneath the spruce trees, where a look could quicken my blood, when so much was left unspoken; the heat of our bodies moving to music in the dancehalls of Munich. Back at the camp, I sent letters home via the Red Cross, one letter every month. I do not know if these letters reached her.

Again and again, I return to the night I plunged towards England, leaving behind our doomed Junkers and my ticket home. I do this because a part of me doesn't believe the present and expects to wake up in the shock of the night sky. I am reminded of the Baltic Sea, in which I almost drowned as a child. There were currents in the air. My life compressed into that moment.

I panicked when I remembered where I was. Yanked the ripcord. Then the ropes pulled tight, my legs jerked, and my spine thrashed the clouds like a whip. I couldn't breathe, cold water in my lungs. I fell back to early mornings running circuits at school, little boys complaining in the mist, half-walking, dew soaking through our socks.

The parachute guided me towards solid ground. My cheeks were wet, my eyes streaming. The world had vanished around me, pitch-black and silent. A chilly breeze whistled in my ears. My voice was hoarse as I tried to call to my crew, to Hans, to Max, Emil and Jonas. But we had drifted apart like a flurry of snowflakes, and the land was lurching up to me and white with frost.

It was the end, and yet I am still here.

A church steeple snagged my parachute and I hit the wall hard. That was when my ankle cracked, a reminder I was alive, of everything I'd yet to lose. Maybe it was the pain – it still gives me trouble when I walk downhill – or maybe it was the sense of terror that overwhelmed me, but I lost the next few hours, coming to in the morning light. I was suspended from my parachute, dangling above a couple of middle-aged women in winter coats. They shielded their eyes against the bright mirror of the sky, gazing up at me in bemusement.

'My Geoffrey is calling for help,' said one of the women. 'You'll be down in a jiffy.'

And the other said, 'Would you like a cup of tea?'

Despite all the kindness I have been shown, I cannot forget that I do not belong here, that my freedom is a privilege that might be withdrawn at any time. There are black patches sewn onto the backs of my legs. At the camp, my fellow prisoners said these were targets, something for the British soldiers to shoot at, if ever we tried to run away.

I would not dare. I've always had an instinct for these things. The best escape is not retreat, but the transcendence of circumstance. I escaped suspicion and surveillance at the camp because I was a model prisoner. In this same way, I will be indispensable at Alderdown, and keep my distance from the Nicholsons. That is how I will rise above my enemy status. That is how I will make my way back to my family, and all that is lost to me.

Father

N O SOONER THAN THEY'RE READY for planting, the weather sabotages our fields. Elder Son and I have just finished fertilising them with a nutrient pack, the culmination of months of muck-spreading. Then the deluge begins, and the rain pours for two days straight. All we can do is watch, stricken. Watch as the waterlogged meadows begin to sink, as the enriched topsoil runs to the margins. This is why we farmers struggle with trust.

Whenever the brook bursts its banks, it makes a lake of the dell. Now there are gulls swimming serenely on its surface.

Smug bastards, says Elder Son, as if they're mocking us. Fuck off!

I tell him to watch his mouth.

Dusty the collie leaps into the deep pools, tongue lolling. The birds are unfazed by her doggy paddle, pay her little attention.

I am at Harry's throat. Where is the boy's initiative? I must point everything out to him, line up every task. Doesn't he realise he's not the only one who'd rather be doing anything else? We check the fences around the fields, water lapping the tops of our wellies. I indicate a post that needs replacing.

And that one, I say. You'll sort it.

Sort it how?

It's just a bit of rot, Harry. Can't you handle a bit of rot?

The ground is unveiled in slivers over the next week. We concentrate our efforts elsewhere. Sandra takes the Land Rover to the garage, returns with a headache and a huge bill. Lauren and Tom beautify the barn.

Elder Son and I see to every preparation for the cows' release.

When the work is this relentless, you find yourself fixating on the milestones. I am beyond tired, but I refuse to rest. Liberation day is imminent. We had some lameness at the end of last year's winter, and I don't want to give LivestockAid any leeway if they return. All the more reason to keep the cows' feet trimmed, their bedding clean and limed.

It's all right, I say, as the floodwater recedes. We're ready. The land is ready. We'll do it tomorrow.

I step outside the next morning. The air is so frozen I can taste it. Smoothed over by the breeze and crusted, the lawn dazzles, heaped with sunlit snow. Sparrows and wrens alight by the trees on the far side of the garden. Pecking, curious. Mother Nature provides, but she can also be cruel.

Sometimes, all you can do is wait. For the sting of grief to deaden. For the crops and cows to ripen. For the snow to melt and the land to drain. For your children to grow out of it.

Elder Son scoops a powdery handful off my wife's fussy Victorian bird table, squeezes it into a snowball.

Don't you dare, warns Tom, preparing to dive for cover.

Harry turns to Dusty instead. Catch, he says.

He hurls the snowball and Dusty springs into the air. Blitzes it with her snapping jaws.

I come across a hedgehog, half-buried.

Look at this, I say, and Younger Son wanders over.

I nudge the hedgehog free, turn it with the edge of my boot.

Oh, I say. What a shame.

It has been killed and eaten. Hollowed out by a fox in the night, judging by the telltale tracks in the snow. All that's left is the tawny casing of spikes that were supposed to protect it. Tom crouches to get a closer look.

It's almost surgical, he says, apparently fascinated.

A civilised eater, I agree, wondering if the phenomena of food chains and predators offend him.

I talk logistics with Elder Son. We'll have to clear the way for the cake lorry, scheduled to deliver the cows' pelleted feed this afternoon. And to make sure we can be reached by the milk tanker. Not to mention the herd's winter quarters still need two cleans a day. I can't be this tired before we've even started.

All hands on deck, says Elder Son, pointing a finger at his younger brother. I am pleased when Tom puts his head down and gets to work.

I leave my boys gritting and raking, follow the cake lorry back to the farm. By the time I've hobbled into the yard, the delivery man is blowing cake down a pipe, into the bulk bin. He notices the old Fowler.

Haven't seen one of them in a while, he says.

Oh, it's knackered.

Yeah?

I should probably let it go, but my father swore by steam power. If you want to get the best from the land, you have to use the right tools.

The delivery man replies politely, but I'm distracted by Dusty. She's barking at something at the other end of the yard. I call her, and when that doesn't work, I excuse myself to investigate. She licks her chops, presses nervously against my legs, lets out a short whine.

There's a breezy hush in the air. A cow breaks it with a low, curious bellow.

I peer into the shed. A trio of strangers clings together in the shadows.

I squint, my eyes adjusting. There are two girls, a lanky boy sandwiched between them. Sallow, wearing a necklace shaped like a wolf. One of the girls has acne, the other orthodontic braces. They're just kids. They shrink away from me as I approach, huddled in their coats and scarves.

My voice sounds strange to me, like a recording. How long have you been hiding in here?

They back into the metal gate halfway along the shed. It takes me a second to realise they've chained themselves to it.

Are you from LivestockAid?

The girls guffaw, delighted by their own bad behaviour. The boy struggles to hold my eye contact.

Dusty decides it's safe and approaches them. Tail wagging. All three of them lean away from her.

You're going to get yourselves in trouble, I say.

Outside, wheels crackle on the gritty drive. The cake lorry sets off down the road. Leaving me alone. Sandra's at Harry's cottage with Lauren. My sons will keep clearing the snow until they're finished.

But I can handle this. It doesn't need to go any further.

How about I let you go, I say, and we can forget the whole thing?

We're not going anywhere, croaks the boy. Not until these cows have been freed.

I stop in front of them, pat my thigh to call Dusty back.

Then I suppose you'll have to stay here and live with them. I think you'll find it's not so bad.

This isn't a joke, says one of the girls.

Isn't it? You think I'm going to release my cows into the wild?

I smile, cheerlessly. Why have we lost sleep over this? These activists are dropouts and children, looking for something to follow. I make myself small, sink into a crouch.

Not many of you, are there?

There are more, says the boy. Just not today.

Probably put off by the snow, I remark – small talk.

He lifts his chin in defiance. Cows are ruminants, he tells me. Do you know what that means?

I raise my eyebrows. Do *I* know what that means?

They should be out in the open, so they can choose what they need to eat and where they want to go. It's for their physical well-being.

And for their mental health! adds the girl who spoke before. Her friend stays quiet, bites her lower lip.

They're only in for the winter, I say, jerking to my feet. And they'd be out if it hadn't snowed. Look.

I point at the cows. A few of them have gathered, curious. Most of them are lying in their cubicles, chewing the cud.

They're happy, healthy cows. It's not crowded. It's well-ventilated. These cows have control over what they do, and how, and if you want to come back in a week or so, you'll see them out in the fields, just as nature intended.

The girls turn to look at the boy. Their resolve is fading.

Look, I say, you must be freezing. Why don't you come up to the farmhouse? I'll make you a cup of tea and then you can be on your way.

Then the quiet girl interrupts. As if we'd go anywhere with you, you stupid twat.

I stare for a few seconds, taken aback. Then I clap my hands.

Fine. Are you going to do the sensible thing and get off my property? Or do you want this to get serious? I'm about to call the police.

Call them, says the girl, with a quiet intensity. We don't care.

You don't care?

Your cows are scared.

Scared of you, probably!

Fuck off.

I shake my head, appalled. That's it, I say. I'm calling them now. You'd better be gone by the time they get here.

I can't go too fast. Our footprints have compressed the snow, and I slip on the icy path on my way up to the farmhouse. Dusty trots ahead, turns back every few seconds to encourage me.

I pick up the phone in the kitchen. Is this an emergency? I hesitate, don't want to lose my nerve. Maybe I've put them off, and they'll leave by themselves. I don't want the whole day to turn.

What service do you require? says a faint, tinny voice.

I'm tongue-tied. Don't know how to explain myself. I'm angry that a bunch of kids can put me in this humiliating position. I'm transferred to the police.

Ah, hello. I need some help. I'm calling you from Alderdown Farm. There are three… youths… trespassing in my barn.

A long pause. Is anyone being threatening? Is anyone hurt?

Err, no.

And is the property damaged?

No. They've just chained themselves to a gate.

I see.

But it's not good for my cows. They're used to me. They're used to being handled by me. But those kids could get hurt. I don't know. The cows could stampede, or…

I'm going to send someone as soon as possible.

Will you tell them to bring something to cut the chains, just in case?

Ah. I'm not sure they'll be able to do that.

Why not?

It needs specialised operatives who know how to cut lock-ons. But I'll see what I can do.

Righto. I understand.

If you could just give me your details…

I already regret involving the authorities. I answer the questions and end the call. Shouldn't have bloody bothered. They were little help last time I rang for advice. My shirt is damp. My skin prickles with a strange heat. The wife will be back shortly, no doubt unsurprised I can't even take care of some kids. But if my boys had been with me…

My mother enters from the sitting room, her shoes scraping the tiles.

Nothing to worry about, I tell her, gingerly.

She ignores me, moves over to the window. What's Sunshine doing out?

The sun? I frown, going to stand beside her.

I look out the window. We can see the corner of the yard from here. Muddied, greyish-white. And that's Maisy, free. Skipping jubilantly, like a kid let out of Sunday school. She flees across the yard, towards the road. I'm already hurrying to the door.

I run like I haven't in years. The girls appear. They're holding the main gate to the shed open. Shriek when they see me coming.

Then I am thrown off the ice. I fall onto my back, cry out as the pain crashes through me.

Barney, look! shrieks one of the girls.

I clamber to my feet. I won't let this happen.

The girls get out of my way. I find the boy inside. He's trying to free the rest of the cows. Bess is running around him, mooing in anguish. Going everywhere but out.

I pause at the threshold, breathless. Maisy is probably safe for the moment. The road is quiet. Besides, she is more interested in finding her way to the fields, and the snow is disorientating her. I enter the shed, heave the gate shut behind me.

I've called the police. You're in serious trouble now, you little shit.

Something slams into my right side. Throws me to the ground.

I graze a wrist against the concrete. Put my hands in a streak of dung as I raise myself up. Despite the cold I am soaked through. A terrific pain shoots up my right arm. I use my left to stand.

The cows are running wild.

I pat my pockets. Where's my bloody mobile? I can hear Sandra now: *No good having one if you've never got it on you.* It's probably in the glove compartment of the Land Rover, or maybe charging back at the house.

Barney tries to dodge past me. I seize him one-handed, tackle him to the ground. He manages a couple of straining steps before I get him.

Then he starts to scream, and I am shouting, You little idiot! and kneeling on his bones, smearing cow shit on the shoulders of his denim jacket. Stop bloody struggling, I say, aware that the cows are stamping. It's dangerous down here on the floor.

I shift my weight. Heave the boy, turning him onto his back. He thrusts out an arm and I flinch. But he isn't trying to hit me. He's holding his phone up like a weapon.

Leave me alone, he stammers. You're on camera.

Then one of the girls shouts, Get away from him!

The other one kicks me, her foot colliding with my ear. I fall back, try to stand. The pain in my arm is excruciating. I am dizzy. And there's the boy, still tracking me with his phone.

Barney, is it? I say from the ground. Is that your name?

The cattle stir and huff and hoof the straw. I make it onto my hands and knees.

I got it all on video, he tells me.

All what, you little punk?

I lunge to my feet, lumber towards him. I have lost it.

All fucking what?

I have never been a violent man. But the urge to harm this nasty brat has risen suddenly, uncontrollably. Like bile.

If you ever try something like this again, I'll take the gate off its hinges and drag you to the road myself, I threaten.

But they are already gone. Not quite running, satisfied perhaps with a job well done.

I fall to my knees. There's a throbbing lump under the skin of my forearm. My knees are torn and red. The pain rips through me. I try to lift my arm and it fills with fire. I am too cold, too weak to stand.

Maisy! I shout, crumpling.

To my great surprise, she pokes her head around the barn door.

Good girl, I say, shuddering.

She rumbles with bemusement.

That's the thing: my cows know where they're best off. Maisy's friends greet her, gather around her in a gossip ring to hear the whole story.

How'd you get out? says a voice outside, closing in.

That's when Elder Son appears, and sees me.

Son

HARRY IS DRIVING US ALL to the hospital; Dad is pretty beat up. I'm sitting in the back of the Land Rover behind the driver's seat, and from there I can see his pained face, alternately pink and white. All my senses are heightened: the sky cuts into the car around the stencils of trees, the seats are like sandpaper, and the air is stale as a tomb. Cold waves of panic crash through my body. Gran is sitting beside me. She peers gloomily out of her window, and at one point reaches out with a shaking hand to grasp mine. Mum is going to make her own way from her friend Clare's house.

It's a stop-start sort of journey; Harry and I managed to clear and grit the stretch of our lane, and he sticks to the main roads as much as he can, but there are still a few places where the snow and ice are lethal. So I make myself ill, glued as I am to my phone, queasy with guilt and motion.

Promise you didn't send them, I say again.

I've told you, comes Luke's response. LivestockAid had nothing to do with this.

I don't know what to think.

Tell me – what actually happened?

Dad was attacked! They tried to free the animals, and then they attacked him. That ellipsis, message pending. My heart drums a warning as my silent words overflow on screen. If my family ever finds out, I type, but I don't know how to finish the sentence.

*

We sit for forty minutes in the A&E waiting room. A nurse has a quick look at Dad, who insists that he's absolutely fine, even as a bead of sweat on his brow betrays him. The nurse peers at his arm, which continues to swell. She smiles doubtfully.

Looks like it's fractured, she says. We'll get to you as soon as we can.

The police arrive before Mum does, a couple of dozy-looking officers with their hands on their radios. Dad asks me and Harry to go and find something to eat while he gives his victim statement. He hasn't stopped smiling since we got here, gazing magnanimously at the hospital's other visitors, as if he's only come to provide moral support to the less fortunate. We walk side by side down the warm, numb corridors of the hospital, until we reach the busy food court.

I guess they'll put his arm in a cast, I say, as Harry and I join a long queue for sandwiches.

He shrugs, not meeting my eye, not looking at anything. We fit right in here, all the worried faces.

He'll be OK, I press, picking at my sleeves, wanting to know what my brother is thinking.

Mm.

Maybe they won't come back, now that the police…

I called a couple of security providers this week to see about upping our protection.

I shut up. Harry is blazing with quiet fury.

Fifty grand, he says. That's the best quote.

Geez. That's…

Impossible money, yeah.

I nod, hollowed out by fear. This is what I have done. These are the consequences.

The other day, we got a letter from the Environment Agency, Harry tells me. Regulations about water courses changed, and we didn't realise, so we might be looking at a fine.

A fine? What for?

Waste offences.

How much?

Up to twenty grand, apparently. I gave them a call yesterday. I told them… He gives a short, bitter laugh. I told them we'll have to pay it in cows.

You haven't committed any waste offences though, I say, helplessly. Have you?

Harry shrugs. Here's hoping.

I fall back on empty reassurance. I'm sure everything's gonna be all right, I say.

Are you now? He looks at me, then, and I tense with shame. Tom, he says, you can't possibly agree with these people?

It's like he's shone an interrogation lamp in my face. I blink hard. Obviously not. Not really.

He moves in close to me as he lowers his voice, his eyes wild. I almost take a step back.

Not really? he says, and I can smell the farm on him. They must think we're pretty fucking evil, eh? How can you take their side against your own family?

But it's not about sides, and I hate seeing him like this, old and young at the same time – tired of it all, yet scared like a boy. I want to roll over, to put my hands up.

Harry, come on. Just because I'm vegan, doesn't mean I agree with every…

He jabs his finger into my breastbone, his nostrils flaring. Look what's just happened. Can't you see these people are weirdos? They're freaks.

We're almost at the front of the queue now, and people are turning to look at us. There's a whooshing in my ears, and the sickly aroma of beef stew, cleaning fluid and coffee catches in my closing throat.

That's not fair, I say, almost whispering. They're not all freaks. You know a third of people now cut meat out of their diets to some extent, and animal products are just…

You think you're so clever, don't you? Are you proud of yourself?

My breathing is shallow, my anger rising, but we are at the front of the queue now, so we have to stop.

I grind my teeth as I excavate a buried memory. I was about twelve, and my brother was probably fifteen, and already helping out on the farm with Dad and Uncle Mike. Mum and Dad were in the village, and Gran, who'd been left in charge of us, was watching telly. Harry had a girl in the utility room, and I walked in on them, doing it, right there against the washing machine. And Harry couldn't put a foot wrong by then, but still he wanted to make damn sure I didn't grass on him. He'd barely pulled his trousers up and he had me by the throat, threatening me, telling me what would happen if I said anything. The girl was pleading with him to stop. She tried to prise us apart as he choked me.

Harry has always done this, bullied me into submission. I walk a few paces behind him as we follow the long white corridors back to the waiting room.

By the time we emerge in A&E, Mum has arrived, and Dad is reporting what the police said to him. Harry and I take our seats and hand out the sandwiches. Mum immediately puts hers aside; she is tense with concern, unable to keep still. She paces, fidgets, moves her bag from the floor to a chair and back again. I notice that the hair around her ears is mostly grey. I know I am a hypocrite for wanting to help my parents. My phone buzzes in my pocket.

They sent someone to look down the back lanes, says Dad, but the whole area is snowed in, and the kids are obviously long gone.

Mum stoops to examine the cut above Dad's ear, spearing his hairline.

Those little bastards…

I check my phone. **LivestockAid may not have been involved today, Luke says, but I am going to take responsibility anyway, OK?**

It's fine, says Dad. I'm fine, Sandra. Stop fussing.

Mum finally sits down. They have to keep pursuing them. They can't get away with this.

I type. This is because of your video. That's what inspired these kids. While the video's up, my family is in danger.

I don't know, says Dad. I might not press charges.

What? says Mum. Why?

I fought back, didn't I? I could get in trouble too.

What do you mean, you fought back?

Can we go now? says Gran.

I tackled that Barney kid to the floor, says Dad.

That's self-defence, says Mum. Nobody could hold that against you.

No problem, Luke replies. I'll take the video down. And I'll post something new, making it clear that LivestockAid is against violence, and urging people to back off. What do you think? If you've got any other ideas about how we might de-escalate this, just tell me. OK?

Dad makes a face. How's it self-defence?

You were defending our business, says Harry, flatly. What are we supposed to do? We're meant to be sending our barren stock for slaughter this week. It makes you worry about retaliation, doesn't it?

Exactly, says Mum. We shouldn't be having to look over our shoulders all the time.

Dad rubs his forehead with his good hand. Mum strokes the back of his neck.

My phone buzzes again. I want to be there for you. Are we still on for Friday?

Are you all right, Tom? says Mum.

Fine.

You look a bit pale.

Do I? Yeah... It's just worrying, isn't it?

My phone lights up through the fabric of my trousers.

Dad sighs. I'll admit, I'm worried about the video they took today. I acted like a nutter.

Mum talks into her fist. They wouldn't post it, she mumbles. They'll want to protect their identities after what they did.

Dad would be the only one on camera, Harry points out. The kids wouldn't have to give themselves up.

But they could be traced, couldn't they?

Mum looks to me for help.

Couldn't they be traced?

I don't know, I say. Probably.

That's not going to be a priority for the police, says Harry.

Mum slaps her hand on the edge of Dad's chair, startling him. Why not? she says. Trespassing, assault. It's absolutely outrageous. Is there no common decency anymore? For goodness' sake, when did it become such a taboo to milk cows?

There can't be too many local kids called Barney, I point out. They can probably do something with his name alone.

The others stare at me. My phone keeps on in my pocket, like a trapped fly.

Tom, says Mum, who's so desperate to talk to you?

21 February, 1944

YESTERDAY WAS MAGGIE'S EIGHTEENTH BIRTHDAY. I met Herb at the shippon first thing for the morning milking. It was steamy in there, the warmest place on the farm, and the smell of the animals was sweet and comforting. We took our seats and started filling the pails. Soon, the volunteers, Gerald and Billy, joined us from the village – they are good men, though too frail to work as they would like – and then Maggie emerged from the farmhouse, head down, trying to keep her special day a secret. But her father went to kiss her, and then Gerald led a rousing rendition of 'Happy Birthday', to which I attempted to contribute, slurring along to the English words for the very first time. Maggie threw a handful of straw in a vain attempt to make us stop.

It was a good start to a day that ended rather dismally. I'm writing this by candlelight, waiting for the sun to rise, knowing I will not sleep. Birds flock around the hayloft like an air raid, ready for the morning chorus.

After milking, Herb led the old boys out to the fields. I stayed behind to give the cowsheds a thorough cleaning, and Maggie got to work grooming the herd. I couldn't help but watch her. She seems to know every beast by name, and they appear to know her too, greeting her with a nuzzle or a low moo or a toss of the tail.

'Attagirl,' she said, patting ointment into the tired legs of an old cow. She caught my eye. 'This is Nettie. Have you two met?'

I said we had not.

'She was my very first charge. Pop gave her to me when I was six, so I could learn to look after the animals.'

'You're fond of her?'

'We've grown up together.' She packed her creams and brushes into a box. 'I used to put a saddle on her and ride her around the garden, at least until she got a whiff of the bulls. Then she wouldn't suffer that kind of treatment anymore.'

'If I'd grown up around animals,' I laughed, 'I expect I would have done the same.'

I can imagine her as a little girl: her wide eyes, daydreaming, and her mouth twisted in mischief.

'You know, Ma's making me a birthday dinner tonight,' she said, looking up at me as she fastened the clasps on the box. 'I'd like you to come. We'd all like you to come.'

I normally take my weekly rations down to the barn, where I keep them in a chest up in my hayloft. When I need to cook, I light a stove outside the barn doors, next to a veil of trees, and a shallow ditch, which borders the path out to the fields. It is quite private, and I have my choice of table and chair from the tower of haybales in the barn. I appreciate the simplicity of the whole arrangement.

'That's very kind,' I said, 'but I doubt Mr and Mrs Nicholson would like me up at the house.'

'I thought you'd say that,' said Maggie, as we stepped out into the silver farmyard. 'They don't eat with us. They take dinner in their room.'

'They do?'

'Keep to themselves, these city folk. They won't even know you're there.'

'In that case…'

I wanted nothing more than to go. Sitting at the dining table and sharing the company of my hosts, I thought I might be able to wish away the war, if just for a night.

As it got dark, we walked around the house together, tapping on the windowpanes wherever any light was escaping. I knew from my pilot training that a lit farmhouse in the middle of the dark countryside could serve as a calibration point or a beacon, guiding planes to their target destinations. Inside the house, Mary and Lizzie adjusted the curtains until everything was perfectly contained.

Mary had prepared a delicious dinner. Although food regulations prevent farmers from slaughtering livestock for their own use, we were having beef.

'The poor cow fell down a pothole,' Herb explained. 'Injured herself.'

Then Maggie winked. They'd found a way around the rule to make her eighteenth birthday supper suitably special.

'Bad luck for her,' I smiled. 'Good luck for us.'

'And for Mr and Mrs Nicholson, upstairs,' said Mary, with a wry look at her husband.

He sniffed. 'Yes, well.'

'Fussy eaters,' Maggie told me. 'They don't like the taste of game. So I suppose this is their lucky night, too.'

It is obvious that nobody much appreciates the Nicholsons' behaviour. These are trying times, and it won't do to waste food, particularly on a farm where everyone is working so hard to provide it.

Mary brought out a birthday cake: a dark, cocoa-flavoured sandwich with treacly black icing. There was a single candle burning on the top. But before we could sing, Herb drummed his hand on the table, calling for quiet. We listened.

There was the unmistakable drone of planes in the sky, closing in fast. We all leapt up, rattling the tableware.

'Get down to the cellar,' said Herb. 'Quickly now.'

Mary thrust candlesticks into our hands, lighting them swiftly with the birthday flame. 'Come on. Chop-chop. Take your cups and plates.'

The entrance to the cellar was a trapdoor in the heart of the farmhouse, at the foot of the inner staircase. Our candles flickered as we went. Herb had climbed the steps and was talking to the evacuees on the landing above. Mrs Nicholson was wailing at the sound of the bombers.

Little Lizzie led the way, clutching her ragdoll to her chest and whimpering.

'It's all right,' said Maggie, taking her by the hand.

The cellar was large enough for all of us: about twelve feet squared. There was a circle of old chairs already down there, a wooden crate to be used as a table, and a scattering of damp cushions on the stone floor. On one side of the room were two barrels Herb used for cider-making. There was a dank, cold smell, like the interior of a dripping cave, and our candles streaked the walls with orange light and long dancing shadows. Subterranean spaces bring to mind our ancestors, their past conflicts. I felt on edge. The droning came and went as planes passed overhead.

'So many,' said Maggie, staring up at the cobwebbed ceiling.

There weren't enough chairs, so I left them for the others. Mr and Mrs Nicholson watched me as they took their seats. Herb and I stayed standing, leaning against the wet walls.

We could just about hear the doleful herd in the cowshed at the bottom of the hill. They knew something was afoot. Then a new sound began to punctuate their lowing. The arrhythmic thudding of the bombs, falling on poor old London.

'Oh, Lord,' said Mrs Nicholson, her face lit severely from below. 'Lord have mercy.' She gave me an accusatory look. 'Shame on you. How can you just stand there?'

'What do you expect him to do?' said Herb.

'She's right,' said Mr Nicholson, uncanny with shadow. 'You invited him into your house, Mr Edwards. What can you be thinking?'

'Maggie can invite whomever she wants for her birthday dinner. And Stefan is a model houseguest.'

I was far away, my mind fixed on my aunt and uncle, and my cousins in Hamburg. I was remembering what I had been told of the airstrikes there, and I wanted to say that I was sorry, that I am sorry for all of it. But I couldn't quite find the words, nor was I entirely convinced it would do any good, trying to placate the Nicholsons, who had clearly suffered and were still waist-deep in their pain.

'It's not appropriate,' Mr Nicholson said to me. 'You should leave.'

I made for the ladder. The buzzing was at its loudest now, a bomber flying almost directly overhead.

'Don't go anywhere,' said Herb.

'It's fine,' I whispered. 'I'll be quite safe.'

'You're not any safer just because you're German,' said Maggie, sharply.

I paused at the foot of the ladder, turning to look at her. She was sitting next to her mother, who was stony-faced and disapproving. I was unsure what to do.

'I can go to my hayloft,' I suggested.

'What if they use the farm as target practice as they're passing over? What if they decide to dump the rest of their ammunition on their way back home?'

Mrs Nicholson let out a splutter of angry laughter and folded her arms.

I put my hands on the rungs of the ladder. 'It's all right, Maggie.' She sprung to her feet. 'Then I'll go with you.'

At this, Lizzie started to cry. 'Maggie, no!' She looked to her parents, wild-eyed.

'That's enough,' snapped Mary, speaking up for the first time. 'Nobody is leaving this cellar. While you're under our roof, you're one of us, all of you.' She glowered at the Nicholsons, who scowled back at her obstinately. 'We must sit this out together. It'll only be a few hours.'

Some of the longest hours I've ever lived through. I will admit, I have never before felt so despised, and just for being who I am. In this way, up until now, I suppose I must have been fortunate.

Father

I GRIN AND BEAR IT WHILE they check me over, then set my arm in plaster. It is one thing to be ill, but getting hurt by some children and my own cows is just embarrassing.

The doctor looks twice at the hand on my broken arm as he weaves the bandages between my fingers. For most of my life, I've been missing the fifth digit.

What happened there? he asks me.

I was fifteen, and bothering Pa. He didn't trust me to help him pollard the yew trees bordering the yard. But I had nothing to do. It was either make myself useful down on the farm, or make life harder somehow for everyone else. So I stood there, at a loose end. Crooning an old song, trying to get a rise out of him.

I say, he snapped, halfway up a tree in the corner of the hedgerow. Would you cut it out?

It's been going around and around in my head.

I had to make myself heard. My mother was busy with little Michael, her new arrival. And Pa had never had much time for me.

If you want something to do, he said, you can fetch me a cider.

Can I have one?

He didn't even bother to say no. Just scowled at me, then dropped down from the tree. He tossed his saw onto the pile of felled branches. Sloped off towards the farmhouse to get the cider himself. Another job I couldn't be trusted to do.

I'll wait here then, I said.

I don't know why I did it. I doubt I genuinely wanted to work. Maybe I wanted to prove myself. Whatever I was thinking, I took the saw and wobbled up the ladder.

Pollarding is harder than it looks. After a few smooth strokes, the saw would catch at either end. I turned my body to the side, tried for a better purchase. Probably a knot in the wood. The saw jammed and I half-hung on it, heaving, pushing against the branch with my left hand.

The blade had its teeth in the wood. A fierce grip. I tried to free it, clenching everything with the effort.

Then the saw whooshed through the cut and I let go. Even before I felt the gushing pain. My pulse was in my hand, my finger attached only by a small hinge of flesh.

I didn't cry out. I was more concerned with the failure, the shame. *Keep quiet*, I thought. *Don't tell.* I gaped in horror as blood fountained from the wound.

Maybe I could wrap it somehow, take myself off to see the doctor. Nobody would have to know. But my clothes were already spattered red. The blood had streaked the sawblade orange. It patted the ground like falling raindrops.

What have you done? Pa came running as soon as he caught sight of me. You stupid boy.

There was nothing to say. My father tried to close the wound, wrapped the finger in his shirt. The farm turned dark. Our trip to see the doctor is all a blur. I just remember it was too late. My finger was gone forever.

It is strange to think of it now. A part of me, decaying long before its time to die. Perhaps just a bit of bone and nail somewhere.

Life is the process of being broken down. The years go by, the ages take their toll. Little Mike became a man, green-fingered, and now he is in the ground in the churchyard, buried close to Pa. But I am still here, imagining that I am bending my phantom finger.

*

Harry drives me home. Sandra takes my mother and Tom in her Volvo. Dusty jumps up at me as soon as I walk into the house, panting a greeting. I shout at her, send her scurrying for cover. Sandra tries to scold me. But my arm is itching under my cast and my hip is sore, and I am too tired to listen to her. I drag myself into the sitting room, park myself on the chesterfield. My family stays in the kitchen, nattering. Lauren comes up from the cottage to join them. She pokes her head around the door, says hello.

You poor thing. You must have been so frightened.

They were just kids, I tell her.

Sound like a right load of idiots. Do you want a cup of tea?

I do, but no sooner has she gone to fetch it than I have fallen asleep. When I open my eyes, the tea has gone cold. Sandra is sitting next to me.

George? she says. That boy's video is up on the internet.

Already? I rub my eyes; I'm still in the grip of sleep, and this is like a nightmare. Oh god. Let me see.

You don't need to see it, says Harry – so it must be really bad.

Lauren is perched on a frayed footstool in front of the inglenook. My sons are sitting in the chairs at either side. Younger Son, in Ma's old armchair, has the laptop open on his knee.

What time is it? I say.

Lauren checks her phone. Just gone five.

You should have woken me, I protest, sitting up straight.

Tom is typing something, his pretty hair curling over his face.

What are you doing? I say, a little too forcefully.

He's taking our social accounts down, Sandra explains, before Tom can reply.

Is that a good idea?

I don't want all our details out there. Not right now. And there's no point having social pages if people are going to keep covering them with their horrible messages. It's bad enough what they're doing in real life.

We'll have to rebrand the wedding venue, says Lauren, pulling on the buttons of her shirt. We can't just take it down or we won't get any clients.

No, I say, raising my chin. We don't have to do this. We're not going to let ourselves be hounded off the internet. Tom, you've been deleting the negative comments, haven't you?

He nods. Sure. I can keep doing that if you'd prefer...

Leaving everything up is just asking for trouble, Sandra insists.

I know, I know, says Tom. I'm deactivating everything. You can always reconsider at a later date.

I nod, slowly, chewing my cheek. That seems like a reasonable compromise. Sometimes you have to put your problems on hold. Sleep on it, and wait to see how things pan out. Besides, I am not thinking straight right now. My mind is as frozen as my hands and feet. Outside the window, the occasional thump of melting snow, falling from the roof. I ask Harry to light a fire. He slides off his chair, onto his knees by the hearth. I am like a carcass, catching flies. The beams across the low ceiling are fragile as a rib cage. Lauren talks about the new management at her salon in the village, while her husband builds the fire. The kindling starts to crackle. Then Tom speaks up.

The LivestockAid video is gone.

What do you mean it's gone? says Harry.

They've taken it down.

You mean the first video? says Sandra, scooting forward beside me. The leather cushions creak like the snow has reached indoors.

Harry shuffles over the scuffed wooden floor towards Tom, who swivels the laptop for him to see.

Yeah. It's down. That's weird.

They've released a statement, says Tom, taking the laptop back again. Basically, they're condemning what happened today. That's good, isn't it?

Must be trying to distance themselves, says Sandra.

Good news though, Lauren chimes in. She tangles her fingers in Harry's hair as he settles on the floor, leaning up against her. It can only help.

Exactly, Tom smiles. And Luke Underwood wrote the statement himself. Something to celebrate.

Don't be naïve, I say. There's nothing to celebrate here.

His smile fades.

Yep, says Sandra. Those people are not our friends. They didn't do this for us. Probably just reclaiming the moral high ground now that those little squirts have made them look bad.

Tom stares down at the laptop screen, frowning. The fire's first breath reaches my hands.

It's true, I say. Or they're afraid of a lawsuit. Either way, they're not getting off the hook that easily. LivestockAid are to blame for all of this.

That Luke character can say whatever he likes, says Sandra, her eyes shining. He's as bad as the rest, and we don't forgive any of them.

I smile at my wife in solidarity, nodding and nodding as the warmth returns to me. Looking between my wife and kids, I feel like a general.

This isn't over, I affirm. They can't ever take back what they've done.

Son

I GO TO MY ROOM, FIND the half-full bottle of rum I haven't touched since Glasgow, and take a swig. The liquor burns through my panic. The first time Luke tries to video-call me, I can't bring myself to answer; we've gone beyond words now, and people are getting hurt. Mum is crying downstairs in the kitchen. Dad is in plaster and a sling, his face bruised and swollen. I shut the curtains, snuff out the lights, and sit swaddled in my bedclothes, self-medicating. The bottle is almost empty by the time I muster up the courage to call Luke back.

Tom, he says. I can't see you.

My face materialises from the darkness of the screen, lit only by his image. He is bathed in light, his hair golden, the frames of his Wayfarers flashing on his head.

Are you OK? he says, after a second.

I let out a long, throaty breath by way of an answer.

Stupid question, says Luke. What's been happening over there?

It's pretty hopeless, I tell him. Everyone's really upset. Scared.

I'm sorry. About all of it.

I think we have to stop talking. For good this time.

Luke leans in. Wait a second.

It's gone too far.

I know. I know. But we can't just pretend this never happened and hope for the best. We have a responsibility now. Don't you think?

He gazes into the dark window of the call, as if looking into my eyes. As much as I want to hide, I appreciate his concerned expression, his care. Though I remain invisible, sitting in the dark, it starts to draw me out.

Are you there? he says.

I'm here.

He pauses for a second, frowning. Have you been drinking?

Couldn't have fucked this up any more, could I? I mutter.

It's OK. Let's take our time, yeah? And then we can regroup and decide where to go from here.

Take our time? I shake my head, needing more from him, wanting him to address the elephant in the room. Have you seen what those kids uploaded?

The blur of a struggle, then Dad's teeth, bared, and the dark ceiling. *You little shit*, he repeats, again and again, and there are girls, shrieking, *Let him go! Get off him*, and Dad is snarling and panting like a wolf until the camera rolls again. *I've got this on video*, says a boy's voice. Then the camera swerves, and Dad is climbing to his feet and surrounded by cows. He lunges, and the boy cries out in fear, and the next few seconds show the girls running ahead of him, away into the farmyard, past a roaming cow, and down to the path that leads to the fields. One of the girls is wearing a sky-blue jacket. The other has a multicoloured scrunchie in her hair. They run and run through the snow.

Yep, Luke admits. It's bad. But they were kids, getting carried away.

They made my dad look unhinged.

He half-shrugs. People really care about animals.

That doesn't make it all right.

Of course not. He sighs, dropping his gaze for just a second. Then he looks at me with renewed determination. We need to de-escalate for starters, he says. Did you see the statement I made?

Yeah.

And I took the original video down. Did your family see that?

They saw.

He smiles as if I've just thanked him. *Least I can do.*

I lean back against my pillows, thinking that it's time to say goodbye. Well, maybe that's it then, I say. I'm sorry this didn't work out.

It still could. Why are you so quick to give up?

I'm not. I don't want to give up.

Then don't. What do you want, Tom?

I open my watery eyes and the laptop screen streaks across the dark. I hold on to my voice.

I want to feel like I belong, I say. That's all I ever wanted, really – to feel like I could belong with my own family.

Luke frowns; this is the wrong answer. What does that mean, though? he says. If you don't fit in with your family, that's not the end of the world.

It feels like it.

My words are stiff, locking in the flood. Luke takes a moment. I bite hard on my knuckles, as if my sorrow might step aside for the pain. My dingy, familiar bedroom has become a strange place, every book, toy and trinket ghostly in the laptop light and tinged with unreality. Like the hours I spent with these things never happened, or maybe my childhood was another life altogether.

Then why not keep trying? says Luke, finally. To change their minds?

Please... I don't know.

You don't know what?

I fill my lungs and force myself to look back at him. My mouth tastes of tears, but I refuse to cry.

I just... I think, if they can't change, that's the end. The end of me having a family.

Luke rests his chin on his fist. You're never going to agree on everything, he says. I know this is a big argument. It's your family's livelihood; I get it. But they'll come round.

No. They won't. And then that's it: I won't have anyone.

Tom, they're not going to discard you just because you have

different beliefs from them. Come and meet me on Friday, and we can talk about…

When I was ten, there was a talent show at the summer fair.

Luke narrows his eyes. OK.

I sang Dolly Parton. And then Dad disappeared. He went back to the farm.

Sorry, I don't… I don't follow, Tom.

Luke is rubbing his temples like I'm giving him a headache. And maybe he can't follow me, but there's no stopping the memories now. They are spurting like blood from a wound, thudding with my heartbeat. I talk over him, and he falls silent.

I always played with the girls, I say. I sat behind my friend, Ellie, on the carpet at primary school, and I'd get in trouble for doing her hair. I used to cry when Mum took me to get my haircut.

He just listens now.

I continue: I used to think about long hair, how it would feel, how it would fall. Sometimes I'd play with towels, putting them on my head like wigs, and tucking them behind my ears.

I cup my ears now, and the warmth of my hands is comforting. I push my fingertips into their junctures, massaging in small circles. I close my eyes. And then Luke speaks again.

So, what are you saying exactly?

I swallow, my head fizzing with drink, my eyes still closed. They won't want me, Luke. As soon as they find out.

Find out what, Tom?

They won't want me. I always knew. But at least this will be the reason. This will be the reason.

He sounds faraway. The reason? Instead of… what?

I open my eyes, and he is staring into my darkened room, looking solemn, but not stern. He wants to know, and I want to tell him.

Instead of… me, I say. Who I am.

And… who are you?

The truth begins to rise in my throat, urgent and frightening. I swallow it down, and whisper, I can't meet you on Friday. It doesn't feel right.

Luke lowers his voice, like I'm a frightened animal he doesn't want to spook. You're upset.

This is too much. I lift my hand to shut him down. Let's just leave it.

He lunges at the screen. Don't hang up, he urges. Think about it, Tom: if you're right, and we can't do anything to make this better, then you'll need somewhere to go, won't you? You told me you couldn't stay there, around all those animals. Not if nothing changes. And it sounds like there's even more to it. To all of this. Right?

I look around the room at my little life, its numb comforts, the safety of a dead end. I used to drift off here, curled up to the reassuring voices of my parents downstairs, the frenzied laughter of Saturday-night TV. Wasn't I happy then?

It's complicated, I mumble.

I'm sure it is. It's family. But it's OK if you need someone to talk to, and if things go south, Tom, you'll need a friend. I want to be there for you.

I'm sorry…

Come and meet me on Friday, yeah?

I am quiet, sensitive to any glow of hope, no matter how faint it is.

I don't know, Luke, I say.

Give me a chance to help you. I finish what I start, Tom, and I'm not ready to let you go yet.

15 March, 1944

I'M SORRY I HAVEN'T WRITTEN, little book. I have been addressing my words instead to a life with which I've lost touch, spitting bitter bullets of paper, scrunching them up and burning them on the embers of the cooking fire I light most evenings by the door of the barn.

The primroses are in bloom, but the bombs continue to fall. It is strange on the farm, far as we are from the front line, the war a whisper in the trees. The Nicholsons have approached the constabulary about my status here as a German prisoner, their beloved Officer Jenkins having been of little help. I know their enquiries have attracted attention from the locals. Yesterday, Gerald the volunteer asked me how long I could expect to stay at Alderdown, a question I did not know how to answer.

There is much I must answer for, it appears.

Two days ago, after we'd finished milking the cows, Herb summoned me across the farmyard and handed me a damp bundle of letters. I took them with trembling hands, four envelopes that had of course been opened already, in order for the documents to be checked and censored. Herb gave me leave to read them in private, so I went down to the riverside and sat on the bank, and the gargling water carried me away to the sea and the mainland beyond, and the ditches and waterways webbing a path to the place I call home, and to Mother and Emilia, whose love I felt I was holding in my hands.

There were two letters from each of them.

Stefan, my darling son.

Mother, in her nervous style, fixed her gaze on the past.

These long months apart, I have only my memories to comfort me.

She had received word of my arrival at Hayes Hall, where I had started writing home, and where I had first demonstrated that the guards could depend on me – could even pass the time with me, talking and joking – all because my mother, an excellent teacher, has spoken to me in four different languages ever since I was a child. Her writing was strained with relief.

It has been agony, she had written, *not knowing, desperate for news. I lock the door to the workshop, for Susanne and Ilse, our little guests from the city, cannot be trusted with the ships in bottles you have left half-made on the table. But, at night, when the girls are upstairs in bed, I let myself into the room to view these delicate works of art, your works in progress beckoning you back, with the hushed reverence of a gallery visitor at the opening of a long-awaited exhibition.*

Reading her, hearing her voice, I was not alone. I pulled my knees up to my chest, hugging them for warmth.

Come home, my son. We are waiting for you, and these ships in their glass display cases are your promise, renewed each time I look at them, that you will find your way.

I will. I will.

Then I tried in vain to read about my father, whose world-class medical expertise makes him valuable cargo, to be shipped all over Europe, and used however the war requires. My mother had given some detail, but all this had been obscured by the censors under great black bars, blotting out whole paragraphs. Still, if there was news enough to hide, then he must be alive and well. I continue to comfort myself with this thought.

In her second letter, Mother took me back to Coburg, the national gymnastics festival in which I once won silver. She recounted the memory in some detail, so that the scents returned to me – chalk and rubber, wood and sweat – and then my mind was awash with blue and green, and the English countryside was chattering with German, and my parents were standing behind me, the pommel horse ahead, and my legs were tight in anticipation of the flares and splits I'd practised night and day for a year.

Afterwards, as I took my medal and the cheering surged, a breeze unfurled the swastikas on the festival banners, and my victory became a part of something greater, and my pride was in my country, and its resilience and ambition.

My mother chose this memory with care. To her, every story is a parable or fable, and while the moral here had been omitted, I did not need it explained to me. Her final words were, *Caution, Stefan. There is foresight in distrust, and prudence in loneliness. Do not become too comfortable, for we will soon have you home. I love you, son.*

I reeled, reading and rereading the letter until its language turned foreign.

I am conflicted, but why? Have I betrayed my family, making myself amenable to the English? I spend all my hours on a farm so that the enemy of my country has enough to eat and drink, but I am not sorry. We are all human beings. I love my home, but I never wanted to fight. Besides, striving for the glory of the Fatherland is not how to survive here. There is safety in fellowship. Mother has not lived the days I have lived, and these have changed me. I have changed.

They cut me loose from my parachute, brought me down from the church spire, then carried me in the back of a car to the local doctor's surgery. There, a quiet, no-necked man sat close enough that I could see the thread veins on his cheeks and the speckle of dried sleep under his eye, so that he could stitch closed the wound on my forehead. He sucked in his mouth, concentrating, caring for me as if I were any other patient.

'That should do it,' he said.

Then he stood up and gave me a polite nod before leaving the room, and I pulled at the handcuffs tying my wrists behind my back and concentrated on the soothing burn of the alcohol on my sealed skin. My eyes had finally stopped streaming.

A bickering pair of old Home Guards drove me on to a hospital, where I was reunited with Emil, who had broken both his wrists on landing. A couple of nurses bound and plastered our injuries, and then we spent the next night at a holding camp, separated, and put in solitary confinement.

I got little sleep, for my enemy had all the power, and I was unsettled. But I had a bunk to lie on, and I was given food and water, and told where I was and what was happening. I felt almost thankful, like a guest, but guarded myself against this instinct to trust. After all, the enemy must have had designs.

Sure enough, the next day, I was brought into a windowless room, and there I was interrogated. A middle-aged man from the British Army sat opposite me, addressing me in perfect German, though I made it clear we could speak in English if that were easier.

'It's just to make you more comfortable,' the man explained.

He wanted to know what I'd been doing when I found myself in trouble, the nature of my mission, and the larger scheme of which it was a part. I gave him only my name and rank.

'I'm sorry,' I said. 'My head injury… I can't remember.'

'What happens to the intelligence you collect?'

'I don't know.'

'You were travelling along our railway lines. What was your destination?'

I held fast to my training, though it helped little with my nerves. I was afraid that they had methods to make me talk, that the soldiers in the hallway would be called in as reserves. But the interview concluded cordially, and I couldn't believe how easily I was dismissed. I lay on my bunk, looking at the cracks in the plaster on the ceiling, imagining prising them open wide and running free, expecting to be dragged back into the interrogation room at any moment.

That never happened. We boarded a train to another transit camp, a large factory building on the edge of the city of Sheffield. An English crowd had gathered to watch our arrival, standing on the other side of a mesh fence as we filed through the entrance gates.

'Hard luck,' a woman said.

'Not so hard,' a prisoner replied.

There were over a hundred of us there, including Emil and Max, and we waited while they considered what best to do with us. I appreciated the anonymity. During the day, we were trusted to roam freely around the vast factory yard. We traded food and cigarettes, barely watched by the British Army soldiers stationed at the perimeter of the camp, trusting the padlocks and the wire to do their job and keep us safely contained.

After three weeks at the transit camp, I boarded a heated passenger train with comfortable seats, tables, and curtains on the windows. It carried a group of us south towards Hayes Hall, newly opened as a centre for prisoners of war. A German soldier in the next carriage had somehow kept hold of a Nazi flag, which he boldly displayed in the window, and we were stopped for half an hour while the British investigated. The soldier was escorted off the train. I don't know what happened to him, but I resolved then and there to keep my head down and stay out of trouble for the sake of my family.

We arrived at Hayes Hall, a grand stone building set in idyllic countryside. If it weren't for the spiralled barbed-wire boundaries and the nightly floodlights, you would never know it was a camp. We were fed generously, and slept in hostel beds, each with a pillow, a bolster, and four blankets. There was an oak-panelled dining hall and a large library, in which we had a ping-pong table. Some of the naval officers complained that we had no cigars. We were wanting for little else.

Yet it was still a prison. For me, the real cells were constructed by time, and furnished with boredom. So, when I could assist my captors, I did. I helped prepare our midday meals, carried out inspections, and led the cleaning detail, which performed weekly maintenance on the rooms we used. And I felt my family would have approved, for I was going to find my way back to them.

I toiled hard. One thing led to another.

Soon, I was offered the opportunity to leave the camp, and labour – with supervision, of course – out in the community. I was flattered. This was a privilege, and one for which I had worked, so I felt no guilt in leaving my fellow prisoners behind. I had set an example, after all, and they knew what they needed to do if they too wanted to improve their situations. They had to work with the English, to make themselves fit. They had to become more English.

I swallowed my shame, folding the letters from my mother, and slipping them back into their envelopes. Then I turned to the letters from Emilia, fluttering with anticipation.

I read them in the wrong order. First, I opened her farewell: a shred of a letter, calling off our engagement.

I cannot live my life through dreams, Stefan. I cannot lie, night after night, wondering where you are, and when this war will end.

Face falling, all sinking.

I loved you once, but you have become a memory. I am no longer sure of what I once felt so strongly, and it is not fair to encourage your feelings for me under false pretences.

So sudden, it could not be real. I sat there, alone on the bank. The chill of abandonment rippled through me.

Stefan, I set you free. Look forward, and survive, and one day I know we will see each other again, in happier times, and you shall remain in my heart forever, my dear friend.

I mouthed a response. Free from the past? I am caught between two times. I don't like to ask myself when the war will end; it does not bear thinking about. But I'd known there was a life waiting for me back home, that there were people who loved me, and that their prayers surrounded me.

For a few minutes, I must confess I did nothing but weep, drowned out by the steady burble of the water. Finally, in disbelief, I tore open the last envelope. My fingers quivered. This was the earlier letter, sent three months before. In it, Emilia affirmed our love.

When we are married, we will have a dog, and I will grow vegetables in the garden. Do you remember that little lost puppy, the adorable dachshund that trailed you for a whole afternoon in the Englischer Garten? You fed her pumpernickel, soft touch that you are, and I didn't tell you at the time, but that was the moment I saw you as the husband you would be one day, and perhaps the father, too.

I blinked, full of perverse hope. How could her feelings have soured, when I had not been there to change her opinion of me?

It is so strange, this forced distance. I cannot see you. Hear you. I cannot speak to you, or touch you. But every day we are kept apart, my longing for you grows, and I appreciate what we have, and I believe in the days and years to come.

I heard a faint voice and turned, trying to compose myself.

It was Mr and Mrs Nicholson, walking arm in arm. They miss the city, and had not shown much interest in the countryside, but Herb and Mary have encouraged them to go out and explore so that they might come to appreciate something of their temporary home.

'What are you doing there?' said Mr Nicholson, as he and his wife slowed to a halt.

'Shouldn't you be working?' said Mrs Nicholson. 'I doubt the Home Guard would be too impressed if they knew this was how you spend your days.'

'Don't start,' I said, for I was not in the mood to spar with her. 'What's that?'

I stood up, wet-faced and raging. 'Just move along.'

'How dare you talk to us like that?' said Mr Nicholson.

'Rupert,' said his wife, shrinking from my thunderous expression.

'You should think about who you're talking to. What your lot have put us through...'

Then I was marching towards them, and there was German on my tongue. 'You think you're the only ones who have lost something?'

'Get away from us!' shouted Mr Nicholson, fists raised, and I stopped, and remembered myself, and stumbled back down the bank to the water's edge. I thought of my family, and heard my mother, urging caution.

The Nicholsons hurried off, triumphant, making for the farmyard.

Afterwards, Mr Nicholson said I was brandishing a stick. There was no stick.

In my misery, I almost threw the letters into the river. I imagined them being carried away on the current, floating like little boats, heading out to sea, and there was something comforting in that. But they are all I have of home. I will keep them close to my heart.

Father

IT HAS BEEN A CHALLENGE, adjusting to my broken arm. It helps to keep busy with tasks I can still manage. This evening I get to work in the paddock behind the cowshed. I clear pieces of scrap, hack at the weeds that have been trying to claim them. The hedges enclosing us were planted by Pa. This was to be the new site for the muck pile, a disused corner of the orchard. But the new becomes old. The land will always remake itself, everything changing but the coordinates on a map.

Elder Son and I build a great fire of pruned foliage, offcuts, and deadfall. Then he heads home to see the missus. I prefer to stay for a while and stoke the flames. It has gone eight by the time my wife comes down to find me, sitting alone amongst the nettles and the smoke.

Still burning? she says. I've kept your dinner warm. I already had mine, and I took your ma's to her in bed. I hope you don't mind.

I give her a faint smile, grateful for her patience since my injury.

Thank you, darling.

She doesn't look at me. Her flickering face is fixed on the flames, her coat zipped right up to her chin.

George, she says, with a strange softness. I've been worrying about something.

Tell me.

I had a look at our emails the other day, the farm account.

I thought the whole point of Tom running it was that you wouldn't have to see it.

113

No, no. I'm not talking about the death threats. That *is* why I first looked, to see if the numbers really were falling. But then I came across something else.

What?

There are emails back and forth with that German man, the one whose grandfather was a prisoner of war. And I noticed Tom signed off with a different name. Tam.

Tam?

Like a girl's name. Tamsin, or something.

It's not a girl's name. Tam o' Shanter?

Well, Sandra snaps, it's not *his* name.

I consider this for a moment, then shrug. Must be a mistake, I say.

I don't think so. He's done it three times. You don't do that by accident.

I fold my arms, narrow my eyes at her. Sandra, what exactly are you trying to say?

Well, nothing. But it seems odd, doesn't it?

It's odd, all right.

As if he's leading some sort of… double life.

I wouldn't be surprised, I say, carried away with my galloping pulse. With ideas about the kind of double life this 'Tam' might be leading. I picture dark alleys and neon lights, hospital gowns and syringes. I want to confront him. I imagine his mincing smile, the nerve of him. Always pushing my buttons. Don't I have enough to deal with already?

There was one time in a bookshop. He'd just turned ten and wanted to spend his birthday book token. He picked out an illustrated biography of Audrey Hepburn, offered up the book to me, all flutter-eyed. He'd been watching her old films with his mother. The shop's papery smells soured with my embarrassment. The title was written in a spindly pink typeface. In the photograph, Audrey Hepburn was looking demurely at the camera, her sinuous arms crossed and elegant. It could have been the cover of a women's magazine. Not a book for a boy.

You don't want that, I told him, my voice hushed.

There was another man standing nearby. I snatched the book away before anyone could see, couldn't stop thinking of my father, what he would have said.

I *do* want it, said Tom. Why can't I have it? It's my token!

I took him by the wrist and yanked him out of the shop. It was Sandra who returned with him, later, to make the purchase.

There's certainly something wrong with him, I tell her now.

Don't say that.

Well, what do you want me to do about it? I've tried and tried with him. You're the one he likes. You're the one who's had an influence on him.

For goodness' sake, you're not blaming this on me.

Harry never gave us any trouble like this.

Sandra laughs. Harry? There wasn't a week when we weren't hauled into the school office over some scrape he'd got himself into.

I just look at her. She's missing the point. Harry was predictable, a charming little scamp with his slingshots and Tarzan antics. Leaping off walls and breaking into neighbours' barns. He got average grades. Girlfriend at thirteen. He would drink too much as a teenager and pass out on our bathroom floor. None of that ever worried me. I knew he wouldn't stray far, Elder Son, Number One Son. Never had to push him to join the family business. He had his eye on the surefire beer money. He's a normal lad, our Harry. Easier than I ever was.

But there's always been something about Tom.

Maybe he's gay, Sandra is saying, readily, shiftily. Like she's always had a hunch. And I am alarmed to hear my own suspicions in someone else's mouth. Whatever it is, she continues, he's been acting strangely, and we've got to prepare ourselves, in case he needs us.

I swat the air. I don't want to know, I say. I just don't want to know.

He's your son too.

Yes, well, he's never wanted to be. But I'll tell you what, he could have had it a lot worse. He's had a roof over his head, a business to learn from and take pride in, good values to lead him in the right direction. That's what this family stands for. And he just throws it back in my face, every chance he gets.

That's not fair. You're blowing this way out of proportion, George.

My eyes burn. The fire sheds sparks and ash, lifting in a vortex over our heads.

It doesn't matter if it's not what we wanted for him, Sandra says. We need to show him that we're there for him, no matter what.

I wish he'd moved into Harry's old room, I say. We could have kept more of an eye on him.

Yes, but we gave him the option. He probably wanted privacy.

I wipe my face. Privacy is the last thing that boy needs, I think. Who knows what he got up to at that university? Every year, he turns further away from the family. I've been losing Tom my whole life.

If my dad were still alive... I say.

What's your dad got to do with this?

And Mike. If they could see what's been happening.

I press my temples and groan. Mike wouldn't have said anything, just given me one of his serene looks, which did all the talking for him. At least it's not me; *of course* it's not me. Mike, who didn't rise to anything, who would turn away from conflict to tend the earth, hardly registering our father's grateful pats on his back. He never competed with me, his wayward older brother. He pitied me too much for that.

Tom... I said. The farm...

You're catastrophising, George.

All the times I left Mike to pick up the slack, I say. Now he's gone, and I'm letting everything go to the dogs.

Sandra shakes her head, angry now. Rubbish, she says. You're not *letting* anything happen. And if Mike had started modernising the business earlier, we might not have been in this mess.

I don't look up. Mike wasn't perfect. I do know that. He wasn't interested in new ways of working. Like our dad, too caught up in the romance and nostalgia of his youth. The proper tools for the job, the good old days, make your father proud. Right up until his death. But my wife is being unfair. There's no denying he was good at what he did.

How am I meant to keep the farm going, I mutter, when I can't even keep my own family right?

Sandra raises her palm, silences me. Shuffling around the fire, she looks towards the gap between the shed and the barn at the back of the paddock.

What is it? I say.

She just shakes her head, moves close to me. Her eyes are bright with fear. Then I hear it.

The gravel crunching. Someone is creeping towards us.

With my free arm, trembling, I reach slowly for my shovel. The only tool I've got to hand. Sandra wrestles it away from me at once. I am in no state to defend her. She raises it to her shoulder like a bat. I freeze, a cornered animal.

Who's there? she says.

A pair of eyes appear at the end of the path. They glow with the fire's reflection. I frown, my chest thudding. Then my mother steps out into the light, waves her hands.

What do you think you're doing? she hisses. A fire, at this time?

Ma!

You scared us, says Sandra.

Ma holds her bony fingers to her face. Put it out! she cries, her mouth gaping and pink like a baby bird's. They'll see us from the sky. A light that bright, you'll be the end of us all!

117

We are already by her sides, coaxing her back towards the house. What are you talking about? I say. What's going on?

Hush, says Sandra. Nobody's coming for us. It's OK.

No lights at all, Ma is ranting, her long hair escaping its pins. You know the rules. We have to be careful.

And this is it, I think. This is how we feel now, on our own land. Like we cannot hide.

Son

ON MY DUSTY BEDROOM FLOOR, I keep company with internet galleries of mistreated animals. Lambs nestled in the mulch of their decaying mothers. Dead horses, hollowed out in an abandoned paddock, their hooves like clown shoes on shrunken limbs. Pigs biting into their fallen brethren, eating them alive.

When I was a child, Dad took me and Harry to the park to play football, and invited some passing village boys to join in. I was not a natural. I stood there, stupefied, shivering in the heat of the midday sun. Dad asked me, *Are you a man or a mouse?*

Pigs in cages trample their young to death. Why must I think of such things, the incremental humiliations that built my early life, the stray balls and goalless kicks that tripped me up, that made my brother shout and the other boys jeer? And if we can't even count on parents to care for their children, what hope is there for our animals? We live in a time of industrial slaughterhouses and battery chickens, and Dad has become the crazed face of animal cruelty, red and roaring in a flickering mobile video. He is many things, and only a part of him is my father, who loves me. No wonder I am angry, pecked raw.

In this day and age, the way we treat each other. I click and click. I self-soothe to visions of hell.

Mum drives me to the station the next day. She tells me a small cheque has arrived from a charity that helps struggling farmers, only she doesn't want me to tell Dad, who is proud about such things.

It's just, if we lose the EU subsidies... I don't trust the government to cover us. It's not like they bailed out coal or steel when they were in trouble.

I respond to this confidence with a guilty lie, telling her I've got to the next round for a phone interview I did two mornings ago, an entry-level data analyst job, from which I haven't yet heard back.

That's so exciting, she says, eyes on the road. I've always seen you working in a nice office somewhere, getting a coffee on your way in, taking conference calls and whatnot.

D'you think? I say, ruefully.

Absolutely.

I look at her, and watch her smile begin to fade. What's up, Mum?

She brightens the smile at once. What? Nothing. Nothing at all. It's just nice to be driving you. I feel like we haven't talked in ages.

There's an ache in my chest. I sink a little in my seat.

You know you can talk to me, don't you? she continues, as she pulls up in front of the train station. About anything?

If only I could, I think. But I tell her, Sure, and get out of the car.

I board the train to London and walk to the end of the carriage, where I tuck myself in by the window. We pull away from the platform, and the land curves around us in silver-green.

I pull my compact mirror out of my bag and prop it up against the back of the seat in front. I will be myself to meet up with Luke. I toy through my make-up bag. Just a cover for the roots of my close-shaven stubble, a softening of the complexion, a warm smoke to bring out my eyes. I purse my lips and tweak a thick curl of my hair, pulling it down over the side of my face. My hometown blurs. The windows are dappled in droplets, but the April showers give way to bursts of sunshine, and Alderdown, with all its suffocations, recedes. I feel like I have got away with it – with everything. I fumble an earring – a sharp shock, back to myself – through the closing hole of my lobe.

I am afraid every time we come to a stop, and the door bleeps open and closed, wary of fellow passengers and their unbent normalcy, their jarring straight lines and repetitive angles. Then the train steams on once more into the breathy quiet of the countryside, and there in the heart of it are the animals: the cream blossom of sheep, the speckling of cows, and the wildness of horses. It's like when I left for Glasgow. With a little distance, Alderdown is less real, and safer, and then I wonder if it's actually so bad at home, and I ask myself what the hell I'm doing – what the hell I've done.

I exit the station and cross the road at the roundabout before climbing the hill into the old town. Luke and I are meeting at the Humane Bean, a café just off the beaten track. Even to me, it sounds aggressively woke. On arrival, I check my appearance in the window, stretching my face as I smudge the brown lines of my winged eye make-up. Luke materialises through my reflection, on the other side of the glass. I jump and redden as he waves at me.

A bell jangles as I come through the door, and a barista looks up. Luke greets me, taking my clammy hand in his.

Tom, so glad you've come. This is cute.

He nods at me, grinning, and I realise he's complimenting my appearance. I smile back. He leads me towards the counter.

What can I get you?

Oh, no. That's OK.

I insist, Tom. It's my pleasure.

Right. Thanks.

Dazed, I turn to the self-consciously casual menu, scrawled on a blackboard behind the counter. The barista says nothing, watching us. He is bald except for a long horse's tail, sprouting from the back of his head and twisted into a top knot. Impressive.

Just an americano… is fine. Please.

Milk? says Luke.

There are so many kinds – with dairy the one pointed omission.

No, I say. Thanks.

We take our coffees. Luke leads the way back to his table, slap-bang in the middle of the room, practically spotlit. But that's his scene. He moves languorously, long-limbed and easy amid the careful set design: industrial glamour, honest brick and leafy foliage, the aesthetics of the ethical. It's like he comes with the space. He points me into my chair, a gracious host. My knees bump the edge of the table, wobbling the water in his glass.

Sorry.

You're all right, Tom.

He sits back, arms hanging lazily by his sides.

I'm so glad you agreed to come out here, he says. It's good to see you again. See you properly.

You too, I say. I tidy my hands away under the table as he gestures at my face.

Is all this what it's about then?

All what?

The stuff you're afraid to show your parents.

I sip my coffee, which is just too hot to drink, and gather my thoughts. Sort of, I say. But it's more about me, and how I feel – how I feel is faintly ridiculous, I think – deep down, or whatever.

Sure.

If that makes sense.

Luke sits back, sizing me up. Of course it makes sense, he grins. I wanted to check. What pronouns do you use? I'm *he* and *him*.

It's the first time I've been asked, and I've only ever volunteered the information once before – with Dan, who hesitated over his guitar, mid-strum, and asked me why I was being such a poser.

What do you mean? he'd said. You don't get to be special. I'm not some manly-man stereotype either. There are lots of different ways to be a man, Tom. Sounds like you're reinforcing some weird-ass, gender-conformist bullshit there.

With a hallucinatory excitement, I hold Luke's gaze, and tell him, *They, them…* But I don't mind. People call me what they like.

122

Well, they shouldn't, he says, smoothly. You're the expert on you, right? That's why I always ask, gives people the opportunity to be authentic. I like authentic.

He sits up straighter, leaning towards me.

So, are you non-binary?

I just nod, breathless.

Sorry, says Luke, if I'm being intense. I want to get it right, Tom. After all, I hope we'll be seeing more of each other. I'm going to need to know these things.

In that case, it's not Tom, I tell him, emboldened, intoxicated.

It's not?

Tom never fit me. I've been trying a new name.

His foot touches mine under the table. Go on, he says.

My family don't know any of this, obviously.

Sure, not yet. But most people will happily call you whatever you ask them to. So, what's it going to be?

I offer my name up shyly. Tam...

Luke smiles. Tam. That's nice.

D'you think?

Yeah, I like it. Tam. Really nice. It suits you.

I shield my face with my coffee, veiled in its aromatic steam. I have been recognised, the way I never recognised myself – in the mirror, when I looked at my peers and felt terrified of growing up, being like my father, working on the farm. My body running away from me, out of control.

So you don't think your folks will get it? says Luke, cutting to the chase.

They're pretty no-nonsense. My dad in particular.

Well, how did they react when you told them you were vegan?

I laugh. I might as well have admitted to being an alien, I say. I'm not sure they were even disappointed.

No?

I think they were just shocked, or angry, like I only do things to rock the boat.

Luke frowns. Yeah, well, veganism is a rational position, isn't it? And if people keep turning away from dairy, they can forget about their farm. The industry itself won't survive it.

His point is punctuated by the whine of the coffee-grinder, the whirling rattle of the beans as they're blitzed to smithereens.

Well, precisely.

How's your dad doing?

I clear my throat, picking at my fingernails. Not great. It'll probably take about six weeks for his arm to be back to normal. I dunno. He's not young, my dad. I feel kinda terrible about it, what happened. That's the truth.

It's not your fault, Tam. Nobody was meant to get hurt.

I know, but what was the point? I reached out to you because he tricked me into eating butter, and now he's got a broken arm. Hardly feels proportionate.

It was an attempt at humour, but Luke doesn't laugh with me. OK, he says, but that's not the only reason you got in touch.

I guess.

You know it's not right, the dairy industry. And the end is coming.

A band of teenagers enters the café, all dressed up like grandparents – in cardigans, pinstripe patterns, and corduroy – and all talking at once. I'm struck by a blast of cold air.

Maybe, I say with a shiver.

One day, they'll realise you were just looking out for them. People are wising up. On my channel alone, views are up this quarter by two hundred per cent.

Yeah, I saw your Christmas campaign. About the turkeys.

He sits up straight. And what did you think? he says. It's shocking, right? Millions of birds slaughtered every year, and for what?

I just nod. It's almost morbid how Luke lights up; but it's the injustice that animates him, not the scandal.

We wanted people to ask themselves if it was really worth it, he continues. When they were eating the flesh of that turkey, was it worth the violence, the birds being crated up, bruised and grazed and loaded into trucks, carted off to their deaths with no way of defending themselves?

He's smiling now, a sour, angry sneer, and his indignation is infectious.

Exactly, I say, giddy with horror. Exactly.

Was it worth it, just for that one meal, for those beautiful animals to suffer the stress, the shock, the suffocation, and finally to have their throats unceremoniously slit on a production line?

Dad doesn't even like turkey! I splutter, like I've caught my father in a lie. He says it's dry.

What he likes is tradition, Tam. People like your dad, they're afraid of change, and losing their familiar comforts.

Definitely, I say, nodding ardently.

The group of kids have taken a table in the corner of the café, and they are watching us. Watching Luke. Their eyes are pressing in, all over his perfect face. I try to block them out. If only I could have him all to myself.

It's the playthings and safety nets they've had since their childhoods, he is saying. And they don't want to see other people doing their own thing. It's threatening, even if they're not doing them any harm.

Yeah, but I *am* doing them harm, I argue. We can't sugar coat this. I've been part of an attack on my own family…

It's been hard, says Luke, his eyes wide and beautiful. This week must have been terrible.

He reaches out – not for me, for his coffee, but I want him to touch me. I swallow.

Still, you're here right now with me, Tam, and you have a friend on the other side of it all. OK, Tam?

We loosen up, and chat like friends. He is a generous conversationalist, and the depth of his voice makes me tingle. He freely gives away his past, eager to let me know him, and talking with surprising self-deprecation, cringing at his mother's aristocratic roots, putting his success into context.

It would be very easy, Tam, just to walk away from all this. Sometimes, I wish I could just back down and make myself comfortable.

But he isn't as straightforward as that. He takes pride in subversion, and his wide-ranging and eccentric interests might have been chosen to raise eyebrows. Is he really this much of a nerd? He does competitive lock-picking, whatever that is, cycles everywhere, frequents antique shops where he selects pieces according to the principles of Feng Shui, something I admit to knowing nothing about, but don't admit to prejudging as a load of bollocks.

When you come to my place, you'll see, he breezes, and I begin to sweat.

The scar on his elbow he got from a parkour accident in Melbourne. He'd been clumsy on the catwalk, back when he used to model, living in fear of the next humiliating stumble. And, like me, he's never got on with his father, a fossilised fat cat who helms a financial holding company in Dubai. His words.

Nah, we couldn't be less alike. But he still holds out hope I'll change. He has a knack for investments, Tam, and he's expecting a good return on me.

He pauses for a sip of water. The blip of his Adam's apple clenches under the skin of his long, sinuous neck.

That's just it, I say. My family sees me as someone who's gone wrong. Like I've got lost – or lost my mind.

Yep.

They don't understand how anyone could disagree with them.

He smiles, his tongue bulging between his teeth. So, Tam, what are we going to do with you?

The throb of my desire is torture. I shrug, and sip my coffee, and try to cross my legs.

3 April, 1944

I CAME TO LAST NIGHT – I'm not sure I was ever truly asleep on account of the noise – to discover that my hayloft had sprung a leak.

The pattering on the roof and the rumble of the wind had been joined by a more insistent sound, a steady trickle of rainwater falling from the ceiling, where a shingle had slipped. I groped around in the dark and found a puddle growing just to the left of my knees. It was draining through the slats and dripping down to the floor of the barn, but not fast enough to prevent it from inching towards my bedding, which I bundled out of harm's way. I'd fix it in the morning. At that moment, I needed a bucket.

Stepping out into the murky darkness, I made a run for the milking parlour, where I knew I could find a pail. It can't have taken me more than a minute to reach it, clutching my jacket over my head. But the rain was falling diagonally, coaxed by gusts of wind into erratic surges, and by the time I'd crossed the yard I was soaked through.

I was dismayed to find the door was locked. Of course it was. But there must have been other buckets left out in the open somewhere. Or perhaps there was still some way of getting into the parlour. I pressed myself under the lip of the roof, though it provided little shelter, and my exhaustion and the exposure both combined to make me quite ill-tempered.

What I really needed to do was knock on the door of the farmhouse and ask for the key. That was the obvious solution, but it was also the last thing I wanted to do, given recent events and the tension they had stirred.

Then I saw something strange. There was a bobbing yellow light, moving through the garden: a candlestick, trembling against the elements. I couldn't see its carrier, but someone was heading back towards the farmhouse, passing through the grove at the top of the hill, and I had to reach whomever it was before he or she had got back inside and locked the door.

As I ran, I saw the candle snuffed out by the wind and the rain – its bearer must have failed to shield it – so, having lost sight of my target, I picked up the pace. The ground was slippery. My clothes were sticking to my skin, my face tingling with the cold.

She appeared to me suddenly, materialising in the shadows. It was Maggie. I forced myself to a stop, staggering. She turned around.

'What on earth…?'

She held up the candlestick, though it gave her no light. For a second, I thought she meant to strike me with it.

'I'm sorry,' I whispered, alarmed. 'It's just me.'

'Stefan?' She dampened her voice to a whisper. 'Blooming heck. You scared me, you bloody fool.'

'I'm sorry.' I spoke up just enough to be heard over the weather. 'I wanted to catch up with you before you got in.'

Maggie backed into the porch, beginning to shiver. 'What are you doing running around in the middle of the night? In the middle of all this!'

I explained my predicament. Then her shoulders dropped a touch, and from what I could see, her expression softened into one of sympathy and faint amusement.

'I'll get you the key,' she said. 'But you're drenched, aren't you? Come on in and let's dry off.'

I tried to make excuses. I had to stop the water before it flooded my bedding. But she simply said I could do that and then return for a cup of tea. 'Stefan, you'll get pneumonia if you don't warm up.'

I looked at the ceiling, thinking of the other occupants of the house. 'I don't think I should.'

Maggie shook her head. 'Nonsense. Don't worry about them. We'll be quiet.'

'The Nicholsons…'

'Come on. You're not going to insult me, are you?'

I didn't have a choice. She handed me the key to the parlour, and I did what I had to do, going back to the hayloft to catch the leak. Then I dragged myself back up to the farmhouse and entered the kitchen.

The room glowed red, illuminated by two industrial-looking table lamps. Maggie was squeezing her long hair out over the hearth and dabbing her neck with a dish towel.

'Here,' she said, tossing it to me. 'Have a seat by the stove.'

I sat down and made an attempt at drying myself as she brewed the tea. In such close quarters, I could smell the rain in our clothes. It was warmer than outside, but the cold was in my bones, and I was trying not to shiver. Maggie handed me an enamel mug as she took her chair.

'Is everything under control, then?'

She smiled at me, and all the tension left my body. I have been quite alone of late, especially over the past couple of weeks. To me, any small act of kindness is a grand gesture.

'Yes,' I said. 'Thank you.'

'It's horrible out there.' She quivered, and I saw her arms turn to gooseflesh. 'I feel foolish, getting so nervous going to the privy at night, carrying a light in the blackout. You'd think I'd be used to it by now, all the years it's been going on.'

I just listened, holding her eye. She sipped from her mug.

'I wanted to say I'm sorry.' The change of direction caught me off guard. 'Sorry about your sweetheart.'

'Oh…'

I had explained all about the letters to Herb when the Nicholsons waged their vendetta against me.

'Pop told me. But there was never a chance to say anything, what with the row. You know...' She pointed her eyes upstairs, in the direction of the Nicholsons. 'Anyway, we've all felt quite dreadful about it.'

I only nodded, too proud to divulge my private situation in any more detail.

Maggie ploughed on, unperturbed. 'I've had my own saga to deal with, actually. My old friend, Jim, has asked me to the dance at the village hall. You know the one on Saturday night?'

I didn't know. I am not welcome at such things, so I pay them no heed.

'I hope you don't mind me talking about it,' said Maggie.

'Not at all. Are you going?'

'I haven't decided.' She chewed her thumbnail, a habit she shares with Emilia. 'I can't say I'm particularly interested in these gatherings. Too busy with the farm.'

I took a drink. 'It can't hurt to have some fun once in a while.'

'It was a little peculiar, though. I hadn't seen him in ages – Jim – and then he turned up to borrow some chemical sample or other from Pop, and he jumped the fence to come find me with the cows. He came strutting over, and said he needed my help over on his farm. I thought this was rather out of character.'

I gripped my mug, sensation returning to my cold body.

'But I went with him, and he had a gigantic Hereford bull, called Earl, tied to a wall. He asked if I could give him any advice about breaking the beast. But as we stood and watched Earl, struggling to free himself – you know how they pull and strain until they lose their pluck – it became quite clear that everything was fine. There was no need for me to be there after all. I don't know if Jim had wanted to flatter me, asking for my help, or what.'

'You might be right.'

She sucked in her cheeks. 'Well, I wasn't about to embarrass him by pointing it out. He insisted on walking me back to Alderdown, leading me through the woods. The bluebells had just bloomed.' She smiled. 'It was rather nice, actually.'

'Well, I don't think he can take much credit for that,' I said, hiding my envy behind my cup.

Why was she telling me all this? If she'd wanted to protect this young fellow's pride, she would have done better not to talk about him at all.

'This is the last thing I need,' she said, watching me, appealing for comment.

'Don't you like him?'

'He'll always be my friend. I don't know. Perhaps when a boy and a girl reach a certain age, only one thing can come of their friendship.'

'I don't think that's true.'

'Don't you?' Her look held tight. Perhaps there was some message hidden inside it. 'I'm really not too keen on going with him.'

I was suspicious that she was playing with me. 'I'd go to the dance if I could.'

Maggie nodded. 'Anyway, I think Nora has her eye on him.' I know her: one of the Land Girls, shy but warm. 'So maybe I'll suggest he goes with her.'

'I'm sure he'll appreciate that,' I lied.

Maggie slumped in her chair, and stared at the blacked-out window like she was looking right through it. 'I think courting is more trouble than it's worth.'

Without warning, Herb appeared in the doorway. He was rubbing his eyes, dressed in a two-piece set of pinstripe pyjamas. 'What's all this?'

I jerked to my feet, setting my cup down on the table.

'It's nothing,' I said. 'There was a leak in the barn, and I came looking for a pail.'

'Then what are you doing in here?'

'It was me, Pa,' said Maggie, flushing. 'Stefan was soaking wet, so I thought he should come in to dry off. I insisted.'

'I'll go now,' I said, heading for the back door.

Herb followed me with his glare. 'You can't do this again,' he said. 'It's inappropriate, meeting like this in the middle of the night. And you certainly can't sit down here in the kitchen, what with our *guests*' – he emphasised the word, in case we had any doubt to whom he was referring – 'sleeping right upstairs.'

'No. I understand. It was thoughtless of me.'

'I stuck my neck out to keep you here. I mean, bloody hell, Stefan!'

He was right: I was only here because he'd stood up to the Nicholsons and made a strong case in my favour to the Home Guard. He'd advocated for me, said I was his best farmhand, that he needed me, and the evacuees were only prejudiced against me because of the terrible loss they had suffered back home. But I was no bother, and there would be no more trouble from now on.

It was an account the Home Guard had been reluctant to accept. As far as they were concerned, I was a loose cannon, given to chasing the Brits around with sticks.

'Pop,' warned Maggie, 'you're not being fair.'

'No, no,' I said. 'I've been careless. I won't come up here again.'

Herb said nothing as I made my exit, but I didn't need him to talk. I can see the line now – the boundary I must not cross.

Father

M Y MOTHER WAKES US ALL at dawn. She bangs on our doors, sounding the alarm.

They won't take us alive!

She's seen them, I think: more invaders, here to honour their threats.

I burst out into the soggy garden with one arm in my coat, pulling on my second boot as I go.

I almost trip on the damn thing. A cow skull left on our doorstep. It's been placed right in the middle, facing us. Its empty eye sockets have a horrible stare. This is what Mother has seen, what's set her off. But there are no intruders today. Whoever left the skull has come and gone.

My wife emerges, her arm wrapped around my mother.

It's all right, Maggie, she says. It's just an old cow skull.

I pick it up, hold it at arm's length. The message is clear. We are being watched.

Where'd they get it? asks my wife, as I return to the house, the skull bagged for disposal.

God knows.

Are you going to wash your hands?

I shrug and go to the kitchen sink. The grouting in the splashback needs doing. My mental list gets longer and longer.

At least it was just a skull, I say, and not an actual head.

Oh, don't. You'll give me nightmares.

I dry my hand on my trousers and turn to my mother. She's

sitting at the kitchen table. Moving her fingers back and forth over her chin.

You gave us quite a start, Ma.

I'm sorry.

Sandra is filling the coffee pot. I take three mugs – two of them chipped and at least as old as Elder Son – from their hooks under the cabinets, and set them on the counter.

Are you all right? I say.

Ma nods. It's just got to me, I think. All the talk. The danger.

I sit down next to her and sigh. It's nothing for you to worry about, OK?

Yes, I should have faith that everything is going to be all right.

It is.

But when the whole country is talking about it…

Sandra takes a seat opposite her and reaches across the table. I wouldn't say that, Maggie. Not the whole country!

My mother stands. Her chair cries out against the stone floor. I'm going to go back to bed, she says, smoothing her upswept curls. I'm not well today.

All right, says Sandra. I'll come in to see you in a little while.

We watch her go, stooped and small. We haven't reassured her. I should do better. They have infiltrated our home, turned our son. How far will I let this go?

I drag myself up and go to the Aga to pour the coffee.

Maybe someone from the press will be interested in our story, I say, passing a cup to Sandra. We could put some feelers out.

That's a good idea, she says, holding the coffee close, taking in its heat.

I start to pace, make slow circles around the kitchen table – an unshakeable habit that drives my family mad.

The skull's a nice touch, I admit. It's morbid and sensationalist. They're trying to scare us.

Yes. It's about time we stood up and said something.

My wife puts her head in her hands. Perhaps I should go back to bed too, she says. I haven't been sleeping.

Why don't you?

I almost take her in my arms. Instead, I squeeze her shoulder, just as the crunching gravel outside announces a vehicle on the drive. I go to the window as Sandra stands up behind me.

Who is it? she asks.

The police, I say.

It's the detective I met at the hospital, Sergeant Russell, and a woman who introduces herself as Constable Wicks. We sit in the kitchen to talk, but they won't accept tea or coffee. They tell us that they've identified the kids, Barney Hamilton-Jessop, Henrietta Shannon and Amber Peters. All seventeen years old, all local.

We interviewed the boy, says Sergeant Russell, and he gave up the girls. Honestly, he was quaking in his boots. Never been in trouble like that before. He agreed to delete the video, no bother.

So it's offline? says Sandra. Thank heavens.

Yep, we advised him to take it down and get rid of any copies of it. Told him that you were within your rights to press charges. And you're still welcome to do that, Mr Calvert, if you'd like to go ahead. But I doubt the lad'll do anything now. He just wanted to impress his girlfriends.

I'll think about it, I say.

Sergeant Russell adjusts position in his chair, leans his elbows on the kitchen table. The thing is, he says, there's no way of knowing if they've kept any copies of that video. If you provoke him, he or his mates might be able to use it in retaliation. Keep sharing it, or re-upload it, or whatever. Do you see what I mean?

I nod, grimly. The sergeant waves at my broken arm.

I understand, he says, that this has been really difficult for you and your family. But I don't think you need to worry about these kids anymore. Barney seems like a decent lad at heart, with a nice family around him. I think he's suffered enough. This whole experience has scared him straight.

I glance at Sandra. She looks back at me with tired eyes.

Fine, I tell the sergeant. We're happy to take your advice on this.

We start arguing as soon as the police are gone. I don't know what points I'm trying to make, just batting away Sandra, who is intent on controlling an uncontrollable situation. I want to escape, to block it all out. I go into the sitting room and play Jethro Tull full volume on the stereo. I hold my broken arm with my other hand, sway in the middle of the room. I nod my head to 'Locomotive Breath'. We used to listen to this when we first met. But now my wife comes in and turns it down. We are not young anymore.

I release the cows. They stampede towards their fair-weather home in the wide green fields. And I remember. There is always joy in the world.

Leaning on the gate in the chilly sunshine, my mother remembers too. Watching them, prancing like calves. There is clarity in her pleasure. It's impossible to see such a thing and not feel proud. Farming owes more to the rhythms of nature than it does to the man-made world. We are meant to be here, and that calling is stronger than any attempt to remove us.

Swallows are back, says Elder Son, pointing to the sky.

It's just a few birds, tireless after Africa. The first of the year, they carry the summer between the continents.

You've done well, my mother says, gazing out at the happy herd. What a slog, eh? But you've come through it, as I knew you would.

We are not young anymore – it's true – but I feel it, just for a moment. The light comes round, no matter how dark the winter. The scent of mustard floats up the slopes from the woods. Behind the clouds is deepest blue.

Son

I T'S SATURDAY, AND I AM the last one downstairs. The farm marches on at weekends, like every other day of the year, even Christmas. No rest for the wicked. This morning, there is a scraped-out pot of porridge on the side and sticky bowls in the sink. The air is cool and still, and smells faintly of damp, though a pale sunlight streams through the kitchen window, where Gran is standing, her face pressed to the glass.

Busy bees, she says, and I realise she is listening to the distant drone of the plough.

On the table, there is a china saucer with a splodge of cloudy, grainy sugar water. A large black beetle is crawling towards freedom, leaving a scratchy wet trail in its wake. I glance at Gran, baffled.

He was dying, she explains. He needs to keep his strength up. So he can fly back home.

Gran, this is a beetle.

She doesn't seem to hear me. I scoop the beetle back onto the saucer and take it outside. Dad's left his slippers in the hallway, so I move them to the back door, where he likes to be able to step straight into them once he's kicked his wellies off at the end of the day. Then I go and find Mum, who said she'd give me another lift to the station. She is beside her bird table, refilling the feeder with nuts.

Your Dad's coming too, she tells me.

Why?

We're going to see our accountant. That's all.

The sun is shining, and a cool breeze rustles my clothes and hair, carrying colours of the meadow and the bluebells in the woods beyond. Mum and Dad think I'm going to another job interview, but I am not worried about lying this time. Luke and I will find a way to make everything right.

So, I say, sitting in the middle of the back seat, that Friedrich Becker guy emailed me again. He's seen all the trouble we're having on the farm. He's still pushing to come and see us; he seems really keen.

Keen? says Dad.

He says he has something to share, some information he doesn't want to just send, which is fair enough, I suppose.

Strange, says Mum.

Yeah, it is a bit. He says he's been translating his grandfather's memoirs into English so that we can read them for ourselves.

Nice of him, says Mum, and Dad gives a quiet grunt from deep in his chest, and looks out of his window.

There's something going on. From where I'm sitting, I can see both my parents, Dad in the passenger seat, Mum at the wheel. He is tight-lipped – he's never liked being driven about by Mum – while she tries to talk. I shrink back and fold my arms, fiddling with my seatbelt.

Tom, says Mum, I'm worried about you. Is there anything you need to tell us?

I press my fingers into the plush of the back seat. Luke's messages light the screen of my phone through the fabric of my trousers. What does she know? My voice comes out in a rush.

What? Why are you being weird?

Dad jerks his head towards me, giving me a dangerous look.

I know you're not a child anymore, says Mum. We can't make your decisions for you.

OK.

But we're always here to talk.

Sandra, snaps Dad, and she falls quiet.

I just sit there, knocked about in the back. I don't know what she is asking me. I'm sure she doesn't know I'm going to meet Luke. I gape, my mind churning with questions. Dad keeps sniffing, releasing tension with little coughs. He always does that when he's stressed.

Anyway, says Mum.

I look numbly out the window. Should I open up to her? The steel web of a pylon disappears as the road sinks into a holloway. The car is latticed in the shadows of trees. She's invited me to unburden myself. But that isn't like her, and we haven't had that kind of relationship for years. And yet, I am beginning to thaw, turned over like a hedgehog, spines prised apart.

We arrive at the station and Mum pulls into the drop-off zone. Dad turns to look at me as I unclip my seatbelt.

Who is Tam?

My hackles rise. I get the strangest urge to hit him. I have to get away from this ambush.

I don't know what you're talking about, I mumble, and then I flee, leaving him and Mum sitting there in the car with their questions.

I am afraid to put on my face, as if they're watching me on the train. I must have written my name down somewhere. Mum used to search my satchel and read my schoolbooks and planners. I close my eyes and focus on my breathing. Why wasn't I more careful?

When I'm ready, I pull my make-up case from my bag and start to come back to myself. Thinking about it, Dad said my name like it belonged not to me, but to some stranger. *Who is Tam?* I begin to relax; there is no reason to imagine I have been outed, not yet. But I don't know how much longer I can sit on this tower of secrets before it collapses. More to discuss today with Luke.

I meet him at the food market, but he's not alone. He kisses me on the cheek, a shock of intimacy. Then he introduces me to his friend, Varsha, a food writer.

Tam, Varsha. Varsha, Tam.

She is tiny and dressed in bright yellow dungarees, her black hair scrunched up on the top of her head like an enormous flower. I'm unsure of myself. How can I tell Luke that my parents know my real name, that Dad confronted me in the car?

I almost take against Varsha, this interloper. But then she smiles broadly and asks me my pronouns, and it's easy as dreaming. There's no quibbling, no fuss. I feel for the first time almost as if the world was meant for people like me.

We walk and talk, taking in the various vegan offerings in the market, sushi burrito rolls, *tofish*-and-chips, Buddha bowls and blackened tempeh sandwiches. Luke is wearing aviators with reflective lenses, and I am too warm, not knowing when he's looking at me. Varsha is incredibly intense.

My point, she is saying, is that it's a simple scientific fact that animals have minds, with thoughts and feelings of their own. If they didn't, animal agriculture wouldn't even need to play at animal welfare.

It's staggering, right? says Luke.

It really is. We know that animals can think and feel – that's no longer up for debate – and still we let them live these nightmarish lives.

I guess people disagree on the extent that it's nightmarish, I say, the contrarian voice, as usual.

Seriously, Tam, says Luke, if you saw some of the slaughterhouses I've investigated… It's just a mess. Full of workers who've hardly had any training and don't know the first thing about animals. People turning up to work drunk, or on drugs, probably just trying to cope with the horror.

I've never been, I say, my mouth dry. I couldn't.

These places have on-site vets, don't they? says Varsha. You'd think they couldn't stand it and would end up quitting.

Nah, I reckon they're the worst, says Luke. They end up brainwashed. They can't admit to themselves that it's fucked, that the whole industry is fucking evil, or they'd lose their jobs. It's a basic conflict of interest.

And I suppose the industry can hide behind its vets and claim they're there to ensure standards are high, I say.

Exactly, says Luke.

It makes me so angry, says Varsha. The animals we farm are no different from children. They're dependent. They're totally helpless. They need us to take care of their needs. They trust us.

We decide on chilli non carne with brown rice and corn chips, and Varsha gets a box of cruelty-free doughnuts she needs to sample for an article she's writing. We take our food to the park and sit down on the grass. I have little appetite, so take in my surroundings as Luke and Varsha tuck in. Skyscrapers gleam beyond the treetops, and the path is a fray of people travelling in all directions, living their lives in heady freedom.

Watching them pass us by, I find myself remembering a night when I was still at school, and went to a friend's house party, a chaotic free-for-all over three vast storeys. Some men, friends of the host's considerably older brother, showed up in the early hours of the morning. The party was still limping on by this time, but many of us had settled down on the floors in our sleeping bags for a bit of shuteye. The men gathered around me on the landing, where they opened the window and started to smoke. They told me to move, gave me a faint kick in the side. I pressed myself into the wall, shrinking out of their way. I was half-awake when I first heard the sound. One of them hawked and spat. For a moment, there was nothing but the wheeze of suppressed laughter. Then more spitting, more wheezing. I was afraid to raise my head until they were gone, an hour or so later, when I was wide awake, and discovered my sleeping bag was dripping with loogies.

I don't know if that was the moment I became afraid of people, of hanging out, of being the butt of the joke. But it doesn't matter anymore. I am safe here today. I am with my own kind.

Varsha asks me about the hate mail and death threats we've been getting at Alderdown Farm, so I show her some examples on my phone.

People are pigs, she declares.

That's offensive to pigs, I joke.

It's got to stop, says Luke, placing a startling hand on my ankle. I'm embarrassed by the way I jump.

There are arseholes on both sides, though, says Varsha, almost defensively. I had a successful blog – I know, I know – and I was almost driven offline because of the abuse I was getting. Apparently I'm a lonely, miserable cunt with nothing better to do than write about cabbage.

Luke snorts.

I mean, yeah, Varsha sniggers, but what's wrong with sharing recipes and lifestyle tips that are ethical and globally conscious?

It does sound a bit irritating, Luke teases.

Maybe I was getting too big for my boots. I'm sure that's what they thought. So they had to take me down, and my inbox and DMs were just flooded. I couldn't sift through it all to find the emails I actually needed. I was getting smeared by the tabloids, opening work messages only to find they were decoys carrying disgusting animal murder gifs. It was carnage, honestly.

That's awful, I say.

What is it about us? We make people so mad.

It's the guilty conscience thing, isn't it? says Luke. People looking after their own egos by refusing to listen.

Sure, I say. It's easier to mock than try to understand.

And that's why we have to force people to listen to us. There is no other way.

Varsha leaves when it starts to get cooler, and I reluctantly suggest I take the train home. Luke asks me to stay, to catch up properly, and invites me back to his place. I have thought about this so many times. We hop on a bus together and sit at the back, our knees touching.

You've been distracted all day, he says. I wanted to get you alone.

I look out the window, the heat of his eyes on my face. Something's happened, I say.

He lowers his voice. On the farm?

No, with my parents. My dad.

What did he do?

I take a deep breath. He asked me about the name Tam.

Shit. When?

This morning, when they dropped me off at the train station.

Luke puts his hand on my thigh. He knows, then?

My face is hot. I'm not sure, I say. I don't know how he could know, really.

Are you ready to tell him?

I don't know. I don't think so. I didn't like the way he asked, like it was a challenge.

OK, well, don't worry about LivestockAid. All right? I'm here. And you should take all the time you need. Yeah?

He gently cuffs my knee, then jumps to his feet.

He lives pretty centrally, on the second floor of a modern building, on a street lined with boutique cosmetic and fashion shops. Of course this is where he lives: his flat is something from a movie, decorated like a New York loft. One wall is bare red brick. Past the entrance hall and the bathroom, there's a minimalistic white kitchen with a bar, then a couple of steps up into the main living area, which is partly walled off by a bookcase lined with old tomes and a round glass table.

Bloody hell, I say, and he shrugs off my reaction, clattering cupboards in the kitchen.

I climb the steps into the enormous lounge area, with its sprawling corner sofa upholstered in dark faux leather, and a metal staircase leading up to the mezzanine, Luke's bedroom. My eyes linger.

Let's have a drink, he says.

He makes us mojitos, the kind of thing I would never normally have. It tastes medicinal to me, too much mint, but I knock it back, grateful for the liquid courage. Luke takes off his jacket and shoes, stripping down to his white T-shirt and a pair of navy chinos. Uncovered by his shades, his eyes never stray too far from mine.

You OK? he says, sitting close to me on the corner sofa.

I'm good.

You know I'm going to help you get out of there.

I smile, shyly. I don't know what the solution is, and I'd prefer to try to sort things out than to run away, which I see as little more than a last resort. But I want to soak up all of Luke's attention, his warmth. I lean in.

Maybe I should talk to your family on your behalf, he says, stopping me in my tracks.

About what?

About everything, if you'll let me. I can explain about you, give them some space to think about it before they talk to you.

I dunno. Maybe that's something I need to do myself.

Right. But I'm here.

I do want to move out. As soon as possible.

And I can help you with that. We're in this together, Tam. OK?

He pours me another drink, then scoots in even closer, putting his hand on mine.

You comfortable? he says, softly.

I clear my throat, awkward. OK, why are you so nice to me?

He grins. What's wrong with being nice?

I dunno. Maybe this sounds paranoid, but you must… want something from me?

Don't you want something from me, too?

I fidget, embarrassed. I don't know what you mean.

He swirls his drink, watching me. You know what I want; it's how we met. I want access to Alderdown. I want to revolutionise it. I want to make it the model for a dairy-to-vegan farm transformation.

Right, I say, disappointed.

It does happen, Tam. A whole new business model. Send the cows off to a sanctuary. There's precedent. And now the spotlight is on Alderdown, I think we can make a real difference. And the hate mail is dying down. If we don't try, then won't all this have been for nothing? Wouldn't that be worse?

I've told you my dad won't go for it, I say, wishing Luke would take his hand away.

That's where you come in, Tam.

I'm not in any position to be helping, I argue. I thought you understood.

I put my drink down on the coffee table and sit back, hunched, crossing my arms over my chest. Luke puts his drink down too.

What's the matter? he says. Did I do something wrong?

No, not exactly. I shrug. It's fine. Maybe you're right, anyway. It could future-proof Alderdown if they'd move away from dairy. And I don't know what to do anymore.

It's just a conversation, Tam.

Yeah.

We don't have to talk about it now. We could do something else.

He clears his throat.

Do you want me to kiss you?

I look up, look at his lips. I can't answer. He begins to close in, and I say I don't know, have to get back, last train…

It's OK, he smiles. You've got time. Right now, you're here with me.

I frown as the room swings around us. We don't have to do this, I whisper. If you don't want to.

Shut up, Tam. I don't do things I don't want to do.

7 April, 1944

I HAD NO IDEA WHETHER MAGGIE had ultimately decided to go to the dance or not. We hadn't talked about it since that night in the kitchen, and I'd been trying not to concern myself with trivial matters, and to concentrate on work. There is plenty of it on the farm.

Herb has borrowed a handsome ruby-furred North Devon bull, imaginatively named Bully, to assist his ailing veteran bulls with breeding the cows. He asked me to help him supervise as he trialled Bully with a group of heifers, specially selected and assembled in the gated paddock behind the shed.

'Don't you give us any trouble, lad,' said Herb.

Bully was certainly up for the job. He watched the curious young cows, curling his lip, flexing and heaving with anticipation.

But that was where his virility ended. Apparently confused, he kept trying to mount the cows' heads. In fact, the heifers seemed to have better mastered the correct form for coupling, trying it out on one another as if in helpful demonstration.

'You silly sod,' said Herb.

It was easy, at first, to laugh at the problem. The poor bull was nervous, we agreed.

We entered the paddock together, tentatively approaching Bully, trying to get a hand on the chain attached to his nose ring. It's best to work in pairs when you're dealing with bulls, particularly when there are females nearby. They are just animals, after all, and the territorial instinct will take hold.

Bully didn't have a clue. Herb complained a bull will ordinarily couple with around twenty cows a day, taking just ten seconds to get the task done. But Bully had none of this efficiency. Cows are only fertile one day out of every thirty, and Herb was sure he'd picked the most amorous on the farm. They were receptive to one another's advances, at least. It was only Bully's backwards attempts that turned them off.

'Most natural thing in the world,' Herb jeered at Bully, 'and it's stumped you. You stupid bugger.'

Eventually, the young bull had his way with a couple of heifers, and both times Herb and I cheered like hooligans. Maggie, who was pruning apple trees in the orchard over the fence, looked around to see what the fuss was all about.

At the end of the day, Ronald, Herb's old friend from Sloeberry Farm, came to collect Bully.

'He doesn't know which way is up,' Herb told him, rather angrily.

'Are your cows not cycling?'

'Yes, man, they're cycling!'

Mary appeared with Lizzie at the top of the hill, calling Herb back to the house for his supper. He said goodbye to Ronald and left me alone to summon the rest of the herd back to the cowshed for the night.

They were already gathering at the gate when I came along the path, and more trotted over at the sight of me. I opened the gate and beckoned the girls out, then set off into the field to round up the stragglers. There are always a few.

It happened in the shed when I closed the gate on the last of the herd. I was moving deeper among the animals to check if they had enough to eat, when a lazy-eyed cow headbutted me, ramming me against the wall. I don't know what I'd done to anger her, but she had me trapped, and didn't want to let me go.

'Easy,' I tried to say, but there was little room to breathe.

I tried to push back. I put one hand on the top of the cow's head, and the other on the side of her neck. I shoved her with all the force I could muster, but pinned as I was against the wall, I could harness none of my own weight for leverage, and only had the ailing strength in my arms at my disposal.

I couldn't breathe. It was boiling panic.

'Hey!' shouted Maggie.

She had glimpsed me through the gate from the farmyard, and ran to my aid. I turned my head and gave her a grimace that was meant to be a smile, as if to say, *This? It's all under control.*

Maggie clapped her hands, forcing the rest of the herd back. But the cow that held me paid her no attention.

'That's enough of that,' she said, approaching slowly.

I realised she didn't want to stress the brute. If the cow wanted to, she could crush me in seconds with the heavy pestle of her skull.

'There, there.'

Facing towards her tail, Maggie stretched an arm over the cow and hugged her like a bear. Then, with her back towards me, she began to push. She clobbered my shin with her foot as she got a purchase on the wall.

Finally, the cow stopped resisting. She withdrew the pressure from my chest and allowed herself to be dragged back. She took just a few small steps, and that was enough for me to slip out of her grip.

A searing pain cut across my ribs as I gulped the air.

'Shoo,' said Maggie, shoving the disgraced cow. 'Away with you.'

'Thank you,' I breathed. My attacker tottered towards the back of the shed with an innocent mien. 'Better watch out for that one.'

'They do that sometimes. Most of the time, cows are as docile as can be. But you can never fully trust them.'

I winced as I tried to walk.

'Are you injured?' said Maggie, taking my hand and pulling my arm over her shoulders to support me.

'Just winded,' I guessed.

'You might have broken something.'

'Maybe.'

'Be black and blue come morning.'

She opened the gate and led me out into the farmyard. It was twilight now, and the trees and buildings had taken on a sombre shade.

'Maggie?' said a voice. It was a fair-haired man, coming towards us from the lane. 'Are you ready?'

'Oh, Jim,' she said, as he emerged from the shadows. 'I'm afraid something's just happened.'

So this was he. He was dressed for the dance, wearing smart shoes and a button-up shirt. Taller than me, but not too handsome from where I was standing.

'What is it?' he said.

I removed my arm from Maggie's shoulder, flinching a little as I straightened up. 'It's nothing,' I said. 'You go.'

'What's going on here?' Jim narrowed his lashless eyes. 'You're the German?'

'I'm Stefan.'

I looked away, so as not to provoke him.

'There was an incident in the shed,' Maggie explained. 'He was just given quite a major blow by one of our cows.'

'But I'm fine.'

'Well, then.' Jim cleared his throat. 'All's well that ends well. Are you ready for the dance, Maggie?'

'Sorry, Jim. I don't think I'm going to come.'

'You said you would.'

'I said I wasn't sure.'

'But I thought we could walk up to the village together.'

'That's a lovely idea. But it's been a long day, and Stefan's been injured, and…'

I couldn't help but gaze at her. Was I her excuse not to dance with Jim? I was half-grateful for this complication, but it was a complication, nonetheless.

149

'Do you mind?' Jim said, giving me a filthy look.

I tore myself away.

A complication, a trap. I have no business wondering what Maggie really means by anything – if she wants to use me to soften her rejection of an unwanted suitor. It all amounts to nothing. I would never betray Herb's trust.

As I went up to the house to collect my rations, my chest was tender, and I noticed that the Nicholsons were watching me from their window: Maggie's bedroom, which they had taken over. I looked back at them. They could spy on me all they wanted, I thought. It would not get them anywhere. I had half a mind to wave.

Father

M Y HIP HAS STARTED TO grind, shooting bolts of pain through my rattling skeleton. I walk with controlled movements.

My wife has enough on her plate already. She picked Younger Son up from the station yesterday evening. Apparently he barely spoke in the car. He's had a job interview, and perhaps it didn't go to plan. But feeling sorry for yourself won't get you anywhere in life. I tell Sandra we need to be tougher with him. He didn't get back until eight. What was he really doing, and who with? She begs me to be quiet. Says she can't hear herself think.

Neither of us wants to confront Younger Son. About his future, his place on the farm. About the name Tam. Instead, huddled together in the hallway, we argue again about my mother. My wife holds that she's hardly home enough to look after her.

She's worse in the evenings, she protests, while Ma does some washing up in the next room.

Stop, I whisper. She'll hear you.

You know I'm right, George. I can't watch her twenty-four seven.

And I'm not asking you to.

That's what's going to happen. Because I don't feel comfortable leaving her anymore.

I stamp up the stairs, take the pain in my stride. Why won't Sandra ever let things lie? My mother doesn't need a minder. She's getting older, of course, but any of us would be lucky to be half as sharp at her age. This morning she served us salty porridge, like she used to when I was a child. She talked about the hay harvest

151

and gave such a passionate critique of modern silage practices, you couldn't help but smile.

I change into my fleece and take myself off to the fields. Now that I am alone, I allow myself to hold my hip and groan. The grass shines, almost ready to be cut and pickled. Task upon task, and I still haven't fixed the old Fowler, which Mike and Pa would use to turn the land together. The shriek of the steam whistle, my father signalling to Mike at the other end of the field. My memory pulls me back three decades. It was one of the years I decided to come home and make a go of it at Alderdown. Prodigal son, my arse.

You have no respect for anything, my father scolded, dismissing me across the yard.

If you'd just give it a try, Pa, I said, trying to sell him on a state-of-the-art new tractor.

Don't talk to me about these newfangled machines. The land has a soul, George. Your brother and I know how to treat it properly.

Why can't we just have a normal conversation for once?

You don't want a conversation. You want to teach your old dad. But you've never stuck at anything for longer than five minutes. Off on your merry way whenever you feel like it, then back crying to Ma as soon as you're out of cash and you fancy some home cooking.

Blimey. Very well, then.

And while you're at it, you think you can tell me how to run a farm.

I was just trying to be helpful.

There's no alternative to hard work, you understand me? We've been doing this for generations. On my farm, when I was growing up, I thought myself lucky to have a –

That's enough now, said Ma, dressed in coal-smeared overalls, advancing to break up our endless, boring squabbling. I was grateful, always, at the sight of her. Still am.

I wait for the pain in my side to abate. The herd comes to meet me. They form a ring of recognition, led by Brenda. I reach out with my good hand to greet her. My injured arm twinges.

Mike broke so many bones that day in the fields.

Ma won't live forever, and soon I will be on my own. Alderdown needs a leader for the sake of my boys. I will yet be the man my father wanted me to be, make myself worthy of his farm. And I will not give up on Younger Son, and the fear that nests with him in that little bedroom at the top of the inner staircase. It is not too late. I will go to him and bring him out into the daylight. I will do this as often as he needs me. I will be strict. Set an example, as my parents did for me.

At lunchtime, I hobble up the hill to the house. Sandra confirms that Tom has not yet emerged. I climb his stairs. Standing in front of his door, I'm surprised to hear the unmistakable snapping voice of that snotty, vegan bastard. My fist is raised to knock on Tom's door. Instead, I listen.

Descartes viewed animals as little more than automata, says Luke, *incapable of feeling or suffering. But Darwin validated the concept of sentience from the perspective of evolutionary fitness.*

It's some sort of lecture. Tom is holed up in his room, watching videos from LivestockAid. There's a quickening inside me, the call to violence. But I won't let it carry me away. I am here to lead, not to fight.

He posited that animals are capable of…

My fist is frozen. Why can't I do it?

Gender is a consistent predictor of veterinarians' level of concern for animal welfare, with female vets and vet students showing more concern for…

The windowless landing is cold and mothballed. Deathwatch beetles click inside the beams. But when I shift my weight, the floorboards creak, and there is nothing for it then.

Due to hormonal and genetic differences between the sexes, women are more likely to empathise spontaneously, while males are more likely to systematise spontaneously…

The door wails as I enter. Tom lets out a throaty squawk.

It's midday, I say.

His bedroom is dank and perfumed, lit yellow by lamplight. There are towers of books on the floor, those Japanese cartoons he started collecting years ago. Queer stories about limp-limbed, girlish heroes. There are clothes drying on the radiator, something with sequins. Glam rock posters, peeling on the walls, Kate Bush and David Bowie with painted faces. And there in the bed: Tom, sitting up under his duvet, his pillow pinned behind his shoulders. His hair has got so long, dark ringlets around his flushed cheeks. He is wearing a full face of make-up.

Get out! he cries. Get out!

Other scholars have identified that the role of gender in animal welfare sensitivity is not as simple as male versus female…

He almost looks pretty. I am shouting something. What is. What are you. All right, all right.

Tom is screaming at me.

I shuffle back, out of the room. Fumble the door closed.

The sound of the video becomes muffled. But another voice joins Luke's.

It's someone being interviewed: *You are surrounded by death, noise, shit, and concrete. And you have to get used to it…*

Then, finally, the video cuts off. Tom and I are silent, separated by the door. All I can hear now are the beetles, eating my house from the inside out. Trembling, I make my way back down the staircase, as fast as my old bones will carry me, clinging to the handrail for dear life.

Son

I SIT ON THE FLOOR IN the corner of my spinning bedroom and crush my head against the cold wall. Is this my coming out, the culmination of years of nightmares, of running, of denial?

Somehow I doubt Dad will do the honours. How would it benefit him? He has always thought that I am his, that his kids are avatars made to cast his reflection. Once again, I have let him down, so together we will go on playing pretend. He's never been one to look at problems head on, and I have always been his biggest problem.

The problem. My mascara has run and my eyes are black holes. My make-up smears as I wipe it away, drop the dark, used rags on the floor for anybody to see. I must catch my breath. The decision is still mine, and there is only one way forward for me now. I have to talk to them eventually.

So I will make myself known. They will know me.

And then I will run. To him.

Message pending, three dots. I don't know what to think since Luke and I had sex. I am waiting for him to notice that everything has changed, to acknowledge it in words.

Do you ever watch documentaries as a family? he writes. **Just thinking of ways to plant the seed. I've got some great recommendations up my sleeve.**

Are we going to talk about what happened? My fingers hover over the keys. My jaw aches, my eyes stream.

We used to watch films on Fridays, I reply.

I wipe the tears from my face as he sends me a watchlist about the future of farming, stories to capture the imaginations of my parents, to help them see differently what's been under their noses this whole time.

I don't even skim it. There is a growing stack of poison pen letters on the kitchen counter downstairs, mostly unopened, and in the fridge there are greasy morsels of flesh, packets of processed ham, disembodied chicken breasts in bloodless pairs. We have achieved nothing.

Are you there? Luke types.

I'm not sure I can do this. I know I sound like a broken record.

He takes a second to answer me. **What were we saying about respect, Tam? Self-belief?**

He thinks I hate myself because I told him about the abuse I seek out online. It's a form of self-harm, he suggested, and must be holding me back.

It is the height of dysfunction to court the vitriol of strangers on the internet, but I have my reasons. They call me clockable, a freak, a weirdo, and every word strengthens my shield. I've been preparing for the day that my family is confronted with the real me, training myself to be immune to their response. There's nothing they can say, nothing they can throw at me. I've heard it all before and smiled and clicked away. Bring it on.

It's not me that I hate, I explained to Luke, but the version of myself I see through other people's eyes. The imposter I've always hidden behind.

But when Dad walked in on me, there was nowhere to hide, and nothing could have prepared me for the way it made me feel. I have never hated myself more.

I'll ring you when I get home, writes Luke. **Maybe we can talk more about the plan.**

Bare-faced and exhausted, I lie on my back on the wooden floor and crave the muscle of him reaching into me, pulling me through. I am in love with Luke, I tell myself. I am in love, and the room floats out of the house like a puff of smoke, and I am carried on its cloud into a future I had hardly dared dream possible.

The plan. To get away from all of this, the look on Dad's face when he crashed into my room, saw me there in the bed. The look on his face. The moment I saw myself from his perspective. I am humiliated. He is humiliated and projecting onto me. We are both projecting onto each other.

When I think of my childhood, I think of Dad and his rules. He was too much of a man to carry an umbrella. He'd splash my grazed knee with rubbing alcohol and send me on my way: plasters are for girls. Not to mention ice skating, salad, phone calls and baths. It was hard to keep track, but he made me a toy sword out of a piece of wood and I carried it everywhere like a crutch. Prince Tom. Only that was wrong too. I was meant to hit things with it, not playact some fairy story.

It wasn't just Dad who did it. I couldn't suck on a lollipop without getting comments from my peers. Little boys are supposed to be made of snips, snails and puppy-dogs' tails. That wrongness goes right back to nursery rhymes and ice cream flavours, and it doesn't let up. The lads at sixth form forced down their cups of black coffee, and talked about whisky, beer, red wine. They laughed when they saw the bottle of rosé – too sweet, too softly pink – I'd stashed in my bag to drink in the park.

Tom's so flaccid, must be gay.

I wasn't sure about that. I was too busy worrying my maleness, outrunning my hands and feet as my stature stretched on like a bad dream. I was terrified that maturing into a man would mean becoming my father.

But I must stop thinking of him. I am riding a cloud to freedom.

A shrill ringing reaches me through the floorboards, a crash landing. My mouth is full of leaves, the taste of bonfire. The floor is scorched with sooty rags, face wipes streaked black with make-up. I rub my burning eyes, scowling. The stress of that racket is unmistakeable: the cremated dinners, the rush to slam the door and flap tea towels. It's the smoke alarm. Someone, stop it?

I don't hurry. I go to my door, open it.

Rising smoke billows into my face. Real smoke. Coughing, waving a hand in the air, I descend, two steps at a time. I call out.

Mum? Gran? Hello?

Gran is sitting in her chair by the inglenook. She glares at me, beginning to cough, rubbing at her eyes. I don't know how chimney fires start, but cooling smoke could be falling from the flue. I help Gran to her feet and take her arm.

We better get outside, I say.

The sound of the alarm has panicked her, and she struggles against me to clamp her hands over her ears.

Come on, Gran.

The smoke thickens as I hustle her towards the kitchen. Then I see the source of the fire. There's something burning on the Aga, a mass of flames and fabric on the stovetop. My eyes are stinging.

Shit! I yell, letting go of Gran's arm and rushing to the sink.

Fire! says Gran. There's a fire!

I turn both taps on and fling handfuls of water at the stove. Then I fill a mug and douse the flames. They're lower now, struggling.

That's your coat, Gran. What were you thinking, leaving it there?

I didn't, she barks. What are you talking about?

I fill the plastic washing-up basin, swearing under my breath. The room is grey with smoke now, and Gran is coughing hard, so I take her by the arm again and drag her out onto the doorstep.

We're under attack! she says.

Hold on, Gran.

She takes my hands as I try to go back inside.

Don't leave me.

The faint rumble of an engine travels up from the road past the farmyard, and Mum's red Volvo appears at the bottom of the hill.

If I hadn't been home, I think – but there's no time to finish the thought. I leave Gran safely outside and rush to snuff out the fire for good.

14 May, 1944

I AM PUTTING THIS DOWN IN writing in case I ever need to explain myself. Recent events have confirmed the need for vigilance. I am not at home, and must not allow myself to feel as such, no matter how long I remain a farmhand at Alderdown and come to love this place: its lush, sweeping land and watery blue skies, and its people who live a life cloistered from the callous indifference of the city. While the war rages, I must not forget the matter of survival.

This week, a fox got into the chicken coop, slaughtering seven birds. Herb and Mary greeted the news with a ghastly familiarity; they had been outwitted again by a longstanding foe. Only, this time, they sought to even the score.

I ventured into the bloodbath to retrieve the corpses and wash away the gore. I had never seen anything like it. The fox had ripped the hens' heads clean off their bodies. Every surface was sprayed scarlet, and the congealed blood and straw stuck to the soles of my boots.

The fox took only one chicken. That was all it needed.

I wonder if it found pleasure in the slaughter of the others, or if the violence was mindless, an instinct triggered by the terrified fluttering of its prey. Perhaps there were simply too many bodies for the fox to carry, and it meant to return for the spoils at a later date.

We humans are very different creatures. We are capable of such atrocities, but we are not killing machines. For all our sins, we remain more than our primal urges.

I was washing my hands at the pump in the farmyard, admiring a circling sparrowhawk in the sky, when Maggie approached me with a shotgun, asking for help.

'Are you a hunter?'

'No, but I can shoot. I had some training.'

'Today you are a hunter.'

I have decided there is something of the boy about her: her unmade face and cropped bob, tucked behind her ears, the trousers and wellington boots. My old friend, Heinrich, had a sister like that. Her name was Claudia. As a child, she would throw herself into the fray, battling with the lads, grazing her knees and elbows. Her mother was forever scolding her for her ripped, filthy dresses and knotty hair. She said that no man would ever choose her for a wife. But men began to follow Claudia, as she grew older, all the same.

I followed Maggie as she cleared a path through the woods with the barrel of her gun. I am happy to be led.

She has told me before that her father once wanted a son.

'But he doesn't need one. Pop and I are made of the same stuff.'

The bluebells are over. We left our tracks on a carpet of wilting green, muffling the sound of our footsteps. Occasionally we would crack a twig or crush the deadfall into dust, and I was sure that the animals knew we were coming, and that the fox was watching us.

Maggie chose our route according to the wind, the direction of which she checked by licking the back of her hand, then holding it up and turning it in the air.

'It cools in the breeze,' she said.

We walked into it, so that our scent would not be carried ahead of us, into the dark of the woods.

'Have you done this before?' I asked.

'Once, with Pop. But we'd prefer to leave it to the village hunt. They ride out with the dogs in front, and the foxes have a quicker death than we can give them with the shotgun.'

I was queasy at the thought of teeth tearing fur and flesh. 'The village hunt?'

'They sometimes take our deadstock, too. Feed it to the dogs.'

'Ah. That makes sense.'

'But I'm afraid we can't wait. Hunting season starts in November, and the vicious brute will keep coming back until there's nothing left.'

It was strange, being on the frontline. I thought I would find the idea of culling a fox distasteful. I am a pacifist at heart. But I had seen what the enemy was capable of: the decapitated bodies of the chickens, strewn all over the run.

We spotted a couple of holes that might have been fox earths, dug between tree roots and under shelves of ground. But there were no fresh tracks, no pungent smells, so we moved on, again and again, until my feet were tired and my mind was drifting.

By the time we finally had some luck, the light was beginning to fail. We were mindlessly following a trail of pink knapweed, on the cusp of turning back, when Maggie put her finger to her lips.

I stepped up beside her, and she pointed between the trunks of two beech trees. I looked down into the wooded valley. Fallen boughs made mossy footbridges over a trickling red stream. The wind rustled our hair and clothes.

There were more than one. Half-covered by a wall of ferns, I counted four tiny foxes, play-fighting beside the stream.

'I see them,' I mouthed at Maggie.

We were standing very close, our arms pressed together. She nodded, and pointed again, this time to the left, further upstream. There was the mother, an animal of fire: flame-furred, dressed in a smoky scarf and charred gloves. She was paddling in the water, washing away her kill.

'Vixen,' said Maggie, pressing the gun into my hands. 'Here.'

I panicked, shaking my head. 'But the cubs?'

Maggie was matter-of-fact. 'We'll have to cull them too. It would be wrong to leave them.'

I looked down at the vixen. She was bathing her paws, unconcerned. I glimpsed her fierce expression, the yellow of her beady eyes. She had done what was necessary.

I pointed the gun. My hands were trembling.

This was just part of being a farmer, I told myself. We needed to protect our stock.

I held my breath. The vixen climbed the bank. She didn't walk; she prowled. But she was returning to her offspring. I felt paralysed. This was not something I could do. It was not in my nature.

I turned to Maggie, and she must have seen the look on my face, for she said, 'I didn't know you were soft,' and then she leaned in. And kissed me.

I was not expecting it. Her lips were tender, her hair stroking my cheek, and I did not pull away as I should have done. But I need to be clear: I did not kiss her back. I did not encourage her.

Her hands closed around mine, around the gunstock.

Then she broke the kiss, pulling the gun from my grip.

Her shot echoed in the trees, crackling through my bones. I recoiled, my hands jerking to cover my ears. The vixen collapsed.

Maggie was already walking. She climbed down into the valley. She was unhesitating, pitiless. Her job was not yet done.

I could not follow. How could she do this, having such a deep affinity with the natural world? I waited, reeling, as she dispatched the cubs.

'There's no place for sentimentality on a farm, Stefan,' she told me, afterwards. 'These are wild animals. If we'd left that vixen, she would have come back. She might have attacked the herd. Even taken a calf.'

'She had hungry mouths to feed.'

'So do we. We're feeding the people, aren't we?'

I nodded. She was probably right, though a sick wrongness ached in my throat.

'Anyway,' I said, as we left the woods, crossing the bridge to the fields where the buttercups were bruised dark by the failing light. 'You shouldn't have done what you did back there.'

'When?'

'You know what I mean. You kissed me.'

'I thought you wanted me to.'

'You shouldn't have done it.'

'Because of Jim?'

'No.' I was angry with her, and my tone was unkind. 'There are lots of reasons.'

'Well, he hasn't talked to me since the night of the dance. Licking his wounds, I think. I'm fond of him, but he wants more than I'm able to give him. I don't want to hold his hand and reassure him. Like a mother.' She rested her eyes on me. 'I think what I mean is I like men, not boys.'

'It doesn't matter, Maggie. I can't kiss you. You know that.'

She didn't reply. Just kept on walking.

'Do you understand me?' I pressed.

And then she looked back with a strange half-smile, and I felt exposed, and more than a little powerless.

I wondered if I should tell her father. Don't I owe Herb that much?

But I am afraid that telling the truth would only hurt me, as he would likely turn against me sooner than acknowledge the unlikely passions of his own daughter, and I do not want to be sent away from Alderdown Farm.

I may have been blown in on the winds of chance, but – like a sapling, growing unawares – I find that I have put down roots.

Father

THE LODGE IS A MONSTROSITY. A care home on the soulless edge of suburbia. A towering stack of minuscule balconied flats, overlooking a sparse front yard, pocked with barren flowerbeds. Sandra leads the way, makes conversation with the guide. She asks questions about storage and bedding, like she's already decided Ma will be moving in. I spy on the residents as they go about their business. Most of them are nothing like my mother. Helpless in their chairs, eyes bulging behind jam-jar glasses. It can't be good for them, excluded from the world like this. Every room here has the same queer, vinegary smell. Everywhere the same carpet tiles.

We could get a carer to come to the house, I suggest, as soon as we're back in the car.

Sandra sighs. You have to accept the diagnosis, darling. She'll get worse. She'll keep forgetting.

I don't think it's advanced. Not yet.

They said aggressive, not advanced. She needs constant support, and we can't afford to give her that at home.

Sandra is driving fast. Takes a turn too abruptly. I tut, and there's a challenge in the glance she gives me.

Sorry, I mumble. It's just... She belongs with us.

It's not Sandra's fault. I'm not angry with her; I'm angry with Tom. I shouted at him this morning. My mother's papery arms are badly bruised where he grabbed her. The doctor even commented. And I can't look at him without seeing his made-up face, screeching in the dark. I told his mother he was sulking in his bedroom, being his usual self. I don't know what else to say.

We collect Ma and Lauren from Elder Son's cottage. Lauren has had her first enquiry about the wedding venue. She's full of beans, already winding me up, though it was good of her to look after Ma. Sandra drives us all up the hill to the house, while I watch Ma in the rearview mirror. She eyes the others with something like suspicion. I sigh. Guide Sandra as she parks the car.

Elder Son has been tending to the cows. He comes to join us when he hears our arrival.

Sandra makes tea. I take it through to the sitting room, where Harry and Lauren are talking kindly to my mother. Sandra appears in the doorway to the kitchen.

Has anybody called Tom? she says, anxiously.

I did, says Harry. He didn't want to know.

Sandra appeals to me, drying her hands on a tea towel. Will you fetch him? It's not right to leave him out when we're all together.

Yes, I say, putting a hand on my twinging hip. I'll talk to him. I should apologise for having a go.

Oh, yes. Good.

Sandra kisses me on the cheek and I brave the inner staircase. I knock on the door, and this time wait for permission to enter.

Son, are you... err... decent?

There's no response. A shuffling from the other side of the door. Tom. Can I come in or not?

Then he speaks. He's short with me, irritable. Yes. Yes. Come in.

The alcohol fumes hit me at once. Tom is sitting on the floor beneath the window with a bottle under his arm. He lifts his chin, struggling to focus on me.

What? he says.

For goodness' sake. You're drinking alone now?

Yes.

Why? Is this about Gran? Look, I'm sorry. I shouldn't have shouted at you. I know you were just looking out for her. It must have been... I don't know. But you knew we were all going to have lunch together today. Your mother's making you your very own version, with… vegetables.

Tom swallows, nauseously. Looks away. I'm not hungry.

Then I think you're being very ungrateful.

Why?

Because she's trying. I'm trying. To include you.

I've tried to be a part of this family, haven't I?

There are footsteps on the stairs. Sandra appears behind me.

Come on, she says. What's happening?

The more you see of me, the more you don't want to know me, Tom slurs.

That's not true, I snap. You're drunk.

He's drunk? says Sandra, in a quiet voice. Tom, this has to stop.

I turn to Sandra. We should leave him up here, I tell her. No use spoiling it for the rest of us.

No, George, she says. Not when he's talking like this. We need to sort this out.

Why? I say, my anger flaring. We don't need to do anything; *he* does. He's too sensitive as it is. Crying over bloody dairy. Siding with those *people*.

So it's 'too sensitive' to care about animals now, is it? splutters Tom.

I raise my voice; I can't stop myself.

It's not about the animals! You don't think we care about animals here? These are people who pretend to value all living things while sending out death threats to innocent farmers. You don't see the irony in that?

You can't judge a whole group by the actions of the few…

This isn't helping, says Sandra, holding my arm. Let's go downstairs and –

You can't just tell me what to think, Tom goes on. All you care about is stereotypes. But some of them… they're good people. They're more accepting than you lot – my own family!

Accepting of what? I shout. Come on! Say it!

Tom stares back at me.

What are you talking about? says Sandra. Please...

Are you going to tell her? Is that what this is about? It's not for me to say, son. Come on. Be a man.

I'm not a man.

There it is. I turn my face up to the ceiling. A silent scream in my throat.

Of course you are, says Sandra, in a thin voice. Don't listen to him, Tom.

I'm not Tom. I'm not.

And he spills a little leather bag of cosmetics onto the floorboards. They clatter and roll. Lipsticks, powders. He owns more wands and gels than his own mother. It's ridiculous. I look to Sandra. Surely she agrees with me. Her eyes are wide and bloodshot.

Tam? she says, stunned.

It's who I am. I'm different from other people.

You're not different.

Sandra, I growl, he's saying he's like a... a transvestite.

No, says Tom. It's more than that.

I smile at him, my heart tearing. A woman, then? A woman trapped in the wrong body.

My wife's voice is cold. Being a woman isn't dressing up, Tom. It's not a costume.

This has nothing to do with costumes, he says, and I never said I was a woman. I don't know how to explain it. But I feel... I feel...

I've had just about enough of your feelings, I say. I've got bigger things to worry about than your feelings. Your grandma has Alzheimer's. We're going to have to send her away, and this is the day you've chosen to tell us all about *your feelings*.

No! says Tom. I didn't choose for you to come in here like this. You've made your mother cry.

I'm not crying, says Sandra, wiping her face.

If you hate us so much, you can get out. You can leave. I'm done. You hear me? I'm done.

I'm out of there so fast that Harry and Lauren don't have time to dart away from the bottom of the stairs. Eavesdropping, faces grave. I don't care. I've done my best for my sons. This is all I am, all I have to give them. I have done my best for my family. For Alderdown Farm.

Part II
Tam

Tam

SIMON'S PLACE IS RIGHT AROUND the corner from the tube, with better transport links to the festival. I buzz the doorbell, standing on the cracked front steps, sweating. Stupid to be nervous meeting a mate, new setting or not. I pick at my sleeves. I shouldn't have worn this coat; it's going to be a hot day, the morning air hugging me a little too close, a balmy breeze twiddling my curls. The laughter of children and the steady barking of a neighbourhood dog lift the drone of the traffic, and then a muffled footfall announces Simon on the other side of the door. He all but slams into the frosted glass.

Good timing, he grins. Veronica's just gone out.

He stands back to let me in, and we give each other a clumsy, one-armed hug. We still don't know each other very well. It's been little more than a fortnight, but sometimes it feels like a lifetime. The first days of a new life.

Would've been fine if not, I smile, though really I'm glad we're alone. Simon lives with his sister, and she's probably lovely, but I don't fancy dressing up and putting on my face with someone I've never met looking on, filling my head with imagined judgements.

I follow Simon up the stairs. He's dressed in baggy shorts and a black T-shirt, and he's towelling his damp sandy-coloured hair, coaxing it into its characteristic curtain. We enter the flat, which has recently been refurbished, sanitised by the chemical scent of fresh paint. A blank canvas, everything clean and white and new. But then I open my bag on the kitchen table, and the colours burst free. All the most flamboyant items from my wardrobe, assembled for his perusal. Simon has the happy, startled look of someone who's stumbled across a jackpot of banknotes, strewn all over a pavement.

You weren't kidding.

Take your pick. Borrow anything you like.

He makes little noises of appreciation as he looks through my things, the costume jewellery and shimmery shirts and pink jackets. He's adorable, but he doesn't know it: freckly and ruddy with a shy smile, and nerdy specs that make his eyes beseechingly large. No matter what he wears – and that's usually thrifted grandpa jumpers and hoodies with faded prints of nineties cartoon characters – he gets lost in the folds. That first day interning at Snowballed, where we fundraise, petition, and lobby for a better world, I thought he resembled a fluffy chick, squeaking as it tested its legs. But Simon watches and listens intently, and remembers everything, and I have come to rely on him and his big generous brain at work.

It doesn't take me long to get dressed. I swap my coat for golden epaulettes with a spangly fringe, which I wear on my shoulders over a lilac tank top and white leggings. My make-up is more involved. I contour, and paint elaborate flowers on my temples. Concentrating on my reflection in a compact as I glue tiny jewels in the corners of my eyes, it takes me a moment to clock that he's watching *me* now.

How d'you always know what's going to look good? he says.

I don't know how to answer, so I laugh. I'm not used to compliments, but he's counting on me to help him look the part today; where we're going, we'll be surrounded by folk who delight in expressing the bolder colours of their personalities. That's why he was so adamant we get ready together – my appearance has looked to him like confidence – and I tingle with an unfamiliar warmth as I turn to help him.

This feeling: I'm used to being split in halves, one part of me always ripped from my body and watching myself, policing my behaviour, keeping myself safe. Like a judge. But now I am hanging out with Simon, and it's uncomplicated. Here we are, just being. I put on St. Vincent, then Simon plays Basia Bulat. We chatter about our favourite podcasts, *Millennial* and *Serial*, and welcome each other's recommendations with curiosity and enthusiasm. The judge doesn't know what to do with itself.

As I hold clothes up to Simon, he asks after my housemates. I'm living with Varsha in a grand, slightly neglected townhouse in the heart of Bloomsbury, which belongs to her parents, and which she shares with four other housemates. Most of them can't make it today.

Except Heath, I say. He'll be there.

I hand Simon a metallic-silver T-shirt, which he takes gingerly, but doesn't question.

And he's coming with Jack, I add. His fiancé.

That's cool, says Simon, pulling the shirt over his head and dislodging his glasses in the process.

Hopefully we'll all meet up. Although they'll probably have a hundred friends there…

Simon is almost ready. He's wearing the sheer silver tee with denim cut-offs, and a baggy, short-sleeved yellow shirt worn over the top like a jacket. He's admiring himself in the mirror.

I stand back to take a good look at him. Almost perfect.

Almost?

I unclasp the chain I'm wearing around my neck and give it to him to put on. There you go. Finishing touch.

Awesome, he says. But then he turns to me and asks, sheepishly, What about rainbows, painted on my cheeks? Or will that look shite?

I smile. Let's do it.

I pin his flappy hair back, and when the brush tickles him and he laughs, I tell him off. I want to do a good job for him. So he controls his face, mock-serious, and then I'm the one trying not to laugh, and suddenly it's undeniable that we are more than colleagues now, more than a couple of clueless interns thrown together in the corner of a second-floor office.

The train is empty at first, quiet besides the dim subterranean thrum I've always found soothing. But as we close in on our destination, we are joined by other glittered partygoers, pink cowboy hats and false eyelashes and smiling voices, and we all know without speaking that we are friends as the carriage fills with the promise of a good day. We emerge into the sunlight like butterflies, stretching our wings, and queue up together outside the walls of the park, gathering under the mighty, multicoloured banner adorning the main gates. There are hoots and shrieks of excitement, people gathering to wait for their friends, just inside. Music pulsates from the heart of the festival.

As we edge ever closer, my phone buzzes with a text from Mum. I tap straightaway to see her message. My surroundings become background noise.

Hello darling. Silage sorted yesterday, that's one job done. Dad and Harry meeting vets today & I'm babysitting for Caroline. How are you?

Distant voices. That's how we've been talking the past few weeks, keeping things light, both afraid to discuss what happened. I don't hesitate to reply. I tell her I'm with a friend and all is well. It's not much of a connection, reporting the everyday, but I cling to it all the same. I have heard nothing whatsoever from Dad.

Simon is trying to talk to me, and I have to ask him to repeat himself. We follow the crowd into the park. There are paths lacing the yellowing turf, leading to the woods, the pond, the hall. But today's visitors spill in every direction, forming little gangs, pressing together towards some common destinations.

Drinks? says Simon, towing me towards the nearest van, where we join a queue.

While we wait, I message Heath, telling him that we've arrived. Then, holding our drinks, we set off, trying to get our bearings, the pleasant fizz of G&Ts beginning to warm our blood.

Look at all this, says Simon.

We soak up the atmosphere. The earth is radiating sunshine, with the scents of dirt and grass churned up by a thousand feet. Hot dogs and sweet pastries, beer and cheap cocktails. Boys in leafy ensembles, like colourful Peter Pans who grew up in spite of themselves but didn't let it break their spirits. Drag queens and rock chicks and muscle men looking damn proud with a twink on each arm. The whump-whump of bass, the roar of distant revellers. And, closer, the titter of small groups, talking and laughing, sweet as birdsong.

Where to? says Simon. Main stage?

There are temporary pastel-coloured signposts, pointing cartoonishly to the different attractions.

I nod, giddily, and follow him into the fray. We pass flower-power pantsuits, sequins, fairy wings and daisy chains. Friends holding hands and leaping in the air for photos in front of an expansive Progress Pride flag. Love, empowerment, celebration. Everywhere I look, good vibes. Over the moon. Even the trees are dancing.

But not us. We drink and chew the fat, and stand on the edge of things.

What are *they* on, d'you think? laughs Simon, pointing at a group of women, revolving in a ring, heads tipped back to the sun.

I laugh, but wouldn't it be nice to be like that, doing whatever the hell you feel like? Perhaps the more we watch, the less unsure of ourselves we will become.

Then Heath rings me, summoning us to an enormous tent, in which the crowd is singing along to 'Eternal Flame'. He and Jack are loitering near the entrance, so we find them easily, singing and waving, beckoning us in. Heath, who is lanky with a shaved head, earrings, and a wicked grin, is wearing a striped T-shirt, an unlit rollie in the breast pocket, and skinny jeans. He kisses me and Simon on each cheek. Jack, handsome in a boyish sort of way, is wearing oversized sunglasses with yellow rims. He waves at us, but doesn't stop singing.

Suddenly we're in the thick of it, and we know the words – of course we do – so there's nothing for it but to join in. All asking if we feel the same, if we're only dreaming. Like one congregation, worshipping at the altar of nostalgia. I watch as Simon's walls come down and he puts his arms around Heath and Jack's shoulders.

Why can't I stop twisting my face as I sing? I'm acting just as Dan, my ex, would be if he were here: defensive, singing along ironically, if that's even possible. Above nothing, really – but in denial of that fact.

So I sing louder, as if the volume of my voice will make me unselfconscious. Drowning out the judge.

Luke appears and kisses me on the mouth. Not quite a romantic kiss, but intrusive, and I let out a strange chuckle. The crowd recedes around us.

Oh, hello…

He grins. All right, Tam?

We've moved from the pop tent to one of the smaller stages, and he's ambushed me just as I'm breaking away from the others to find the portaloos. I blink at him and the music rattles, pitchy, like my ears need to pop. His hand is on my shoulder. I want to shake it off.

Yeah, I say. Yeah.

You having fun, Tam? Look at you!

He can only rear his head with that shameless smile because he has left me holding all the guilt.

I'm here with my friends, I say, pointing in their direction, practically reaching for them.

Same! he laughs. Actually I'm here with Allsopp & the Oven Mitts. They're on shortly.

This means nothing to me – my head is full – so I just raise my eyebrows at him. His smile barely flickers, but I am alert: I have given him the wrong response.

He doubles down. We're in for a treat, we are.

You'll want to get nearer the front then.

He narrows his eyes; I'm being unfriendly. But that awful afternoon, a month ago, he drew his line in the sand.

It's over, I wrote, sitting on the train, my heels on the seat, my knees tucked up against my chest. Now Dad's asked me to leave.

Fuck him.

A slight response, almost glib. I waited, but there was nothing more. I bit my cheek, mustering up courage. I can't keep helping LivestockAid.

No answer.

I don't know what to do, I persisted. I'm on my way over. Is that OK?

I pictured his furrowed brow as he considered his reply. I took some deep, gulping breaths.

Are you there? I wrote, after a minute.

Finally, he said: Yes, if you're coming now, I'll be in.

And he was, but we never moved beyond the kitchen. He didn't even put the kettle on.

You don't need them, he told me, stroking my hair, seizing me like a puppet. We're going to make them pay, all right?

I shook him off. No, I said. No, I can't. Please, Luke.

What?

I have to stop. I can't keep fighting.

He moved back, then, and we stood on either side of the room, leaning against the counters. But you've just started, he said.

No… It's our lives.

He frowned, then softened again, and took my hands. Come on, Tam. Don't let it be for nothing.

It's already for nothing. I'm sorry. All of this… What was I thinking?

He folded his arms, his face freezing over. Disappointing him felt brutal, tumbling into an icy lake. Then why are you here? he said. I'm sorry, but what do you want from me?

The weight of his questions. I looked down at my feet. Luke and LivestockAid were never the way out.

I just… I guess I need somewhere to stay.

He nodded. Have you tried Varsha?

I shook my head, a frost blossoming on my skin. He was dismissing me; we were done. He wanted nothing more to do with me.

I left his flat. He sent me Varsha's number as promised, and when I tried to reply, he responded painfully slowly, or not at all. A couple of words at a time, gagging me. Take the hint.

So, why are we doing this? Why are we exchanging pleasantries like the weeks of silence never happened?

I will him to disappear. We're nothing to each other now but a mutual record of past mistakes. I can only be so free while you are in my world, Luke. The truth about how I have hurt my family lives in you, and the threat of its revelation hangs over me like the Sword of Damocles. When you speak to me, I can feel its blade against my neck.

Please, I think. Let's never have met. Let's leave Alderdown Farm alone, and then we'll have nothing more to do with each other.

But all I say is that my friends are waiting. I've got to get back.

I get a drink, down it. Another. Then I throw myself into the crowd, moving to the music, letting my body sway with groups of strangers. One of them – curvy and bearded – steps into my orbit, twirls me in towards them. They smell like citrus and spring blossom. A drumming in my chest, too tight for pleasure. But I'm doing this. It loosens into a flutter as they kiss me, and I let them, even when one of their mates snaps a photo. Then Heath is cheering, and claps me on the back as I return to my friends, dazed.

Getting into the spirit, I see, says Simon, rolling his eyes and laughing.

We dance together as drag queens strut their stuff on stage, and we are all spilling our drinks from our plastic cups. Bacchanalia. Baptism. It's really like that, a novel feeling. Because I blend in for once. Androgyny is not my differentiator here; it is only a foundation, on which my full character can be built. And I feel sad for Dan, realising all this, and for my past self – that we protested so much, that we poured scorn on others, that we were never just ourselves.

Heath spots a celeb – a handsome man I don't recognise – and goes to ask for a selfie. Jack pulls him back, but Heath won't be stopped, and anyway the celeb seems to like the attention. So then Heath tells Jack to lighten up, and that gives him an idea.

Suddenly Jack is offering me and Simon little green smiley faces, nestled in the palm of his hand. Simon takes one straightaway, like he's done this before. And I don't know what I'm doing, but I want to trust, to be out of control, to be held.

And then I'm dancing and I'm bubbling up and it feels so good. I've never heard this before – is this new? – this music that is getting inside me. And now I'm part of it and we are all one body, like the whole of humanity is surging in the park. An energy source, a rhythm, a core. And I am just one perfect part. I am turning over in the hands of the world. I am smiling so widely that I might be laughing, and nobody is looking at me. They are just. Happy, free, every one of us. And I am watching myself watch them, and thinking the delirious thought: Man, this is me, and I know I am an idiot right now, but I don't care.

George

WE GET THE FIVE-MINUTE CALL. The producers duck in and out of the green room, where guests are left to stew. There is no natural light in here. I finish my grey cup of tea, stand up and brush the creases out of my old suit trousers. There's a chance Tom will be watching. Elder Son clears his throat. Takes a shining apple from the large golden bowl on the sideboard.

Course they're all made of wax, he says.

Comments like this are what his moral support is made of, and I am grateful. We have been watching this morning's show together on a large television, mounted on the wall. Apparently it's very popular. I've never seen it before in my life. One of the presenters is a woman called Mala Finnegan, young and beautiful, her accent old-school BBC. The other presenter, Clive Peters, is an Essex man dressed in a starch-crisped shirt. He is middle-aged, but still has a full head of thick brown hair. The two of them are perched, ludicrously, in the centre of a great cream cake of a sofa, bolstered into position by a froth of patterned cushions. In front of them is a nest of jade coffee tables, scattered with homey clutter: cacti, papers and colour-shifting candles. The domestic fantasy is spoilt by the fake window on the wall behind, with its unconvincing London scene.

I check myself in the mirror, straighten my collar. My arm has healed, and I would have had the plaster cast removed already if Sandra hadn't insisted it might serve me today to look a tad pathetic. There is a tiny microphone, clipped to the lapel of my blazer. Ready to receive my testimony.

182

Stay cool, says Harry.

Yes, I say.

But I am thinking of a memory, another time I had to bear the scrutiny of an audience. When I was a boy, I was asked to do a Christmas reading in church. I was nervous, wanted to get it right. So I stayed up the night before, rehearsing by the fire with Ma. My lone listener. She set down her knitting to applaud when I made it through the text without a single mistake.

Just wait, she said, until your father hears you.

I had to stand on a box to see over the lectern.

And there were shepherds, I recited – I still remember the passage – *living out in the fields nearby, keeping watch over their flocks at night. An angel of the Lord appeared to them, and the glory of the Lord shone around them, and they were terrified.*

It was here that I paused for breath. Took my chance to glance up, and into the congregation. I spotted my parents in the crowd. Mother nodded to me and smiled, urged me on. But Pa was not listening. He was sitting with his arms folded. Leaning to his left to talk to his own father, my strict, cold-shouldering grandfather, Ronald Calvert.

But the angel said to them: Do not be afraid. I bring you good news...

I tried to carry on. But they still weren't listening. And now I too was tuning out, lost in a rising static. There was a long silence. All the faces gaping up at me were shadowy and red in the candlelight and the gloaming. As if I had stumbled into Hell. I stammered and fought to resurface. My voice shook as I limped to the end of the reading. The whole church fidgeted and coughed and rustled.

The studio lights are dazzling as I take my seat in an oversized egg cup. I am not sitting comfortably. The presenters introduce me as Dairy Farmer, George Calvert. They allow me to say a few words about Alderdown before Luke is trotted out for balance. Did he ask to be prepped in a separate room, or is that up to the producers? Maybe they don't trust us to be civil towards one another. Or they want to save all the drama for the cameras. Has this been a terrible mistake? They play a clip of LivestockAid's infamous video.

Let's start with you, George, says Clive. Why don't you tell us what's been happening at your farm since this video went viral?

The cameras bore into me as I mumble something. About the trespassers and the keyboard warriors, about how the online abuse quickly spilt over into handwritten death threats. I explain about the graffiti and the damage done to the family, to our livelihood. Then the break-in that led to the fight in the snow, cows running riot, and – look here – my broken arm.

That must have been very scary, says Mala, head tilted to one side.

Well… I say, bridling at the suggestion of my frailty.

They stage Luke on the other side of the coffee tables, propped up tall on what looks like a spotted toadstool. They introduce him as a former model and media personality, with a portfolio of luxury properties he owns and manages in London. A slick, silver-spooned narcissist. He is dressed in platform shoes, tight black trousers, and what looks like an artist's smock – though its loose weave would hardly keep the paint off him, judging by the view we've got of his nipples. I haven't seen him in person since the winter morning he first invaded the farm like a canker. I wasn't prepared for this. The fizz of my blood, the sirens in my skull.

He says hello, flashes me a cursory smile.

His nails are painted white. A painful tug for Younger Son.

Luke, says Clive, what do you have to say to those who think this is just another example of militant veganism, gone too far?

Thanks, Clive, says Luke, stacking his hands on his right knee. First off, I have to say that I don't condone any of the abuse the Calvert family has received. I know when feelings are running high, things can get a little heated…

A little heated? I say, at once. What do you call *this*?

I lift my not-so-broken arm for the cameras.

Surely it's one thing to disagree, prompts Mala, looking between us pleasantly, and quite another to express that disagreement illegally – not to mention violently?

I condemn all threatening behaviour on both sides, says Luke, coolly, and I will do anything I can to prevent such abuse from continuing. My only enemy is the practice of enslaving and killing innocent animals, and that's what our original video was designed to target.

I've prepared for this, studied lists of statistics and facts on the train ride over. But now my memory deserts me. I fumble for words.

Most people, I declare, have no problem with dairy. Most people have no problem with eating meat, for that matter. And if you're going to consume animal products, wouldn't you prefer to consume those that come from an ethical farm?

An *ethical* farm? So, it's ethical to take babies away from their mothers, just so that we can drink the milk meant for them?

Well, obviously it's –

And it's ethical to murder baby boys?

Mothers? Baby boys? I look to the presenters, the cameras, for back-up. Cows! Cows. Those are words we use for people, not animals.

Why not? We're animals too, aren't we?

Human animals? I let out a little bark of laughter. Fine. Perhaps we are, and you can say what you like. Call them individuals. Call them lovers, for all I care. Your choice of words doesn't mean you have more respect for animals than I do. You're only a farmer because you love animals, all right? You want to work with them, to be near them. I treat my herd with respect. And then if someone wants to consume dairy, that's their choice.

Should it be down to choice? When someone is killed?

Mala holds up a hand, trying to interject.

Someone? I snap. When *someone* is killed? You're implying I'm a sort of maniac.

I didn't say that.

I don't even run a slaughterhouse.

Would it be different if you ran a slaughterhouse? You send cows there, don't you?

So what if I do? They are slaughtered humanely.

I think it might be worth explaining what you mean by that, says Mala.

I turn away from Luke, addressing my answer to her. Of course, I say. Our cows are brought just a couple of miles to the abattoir. Their final journey is carried out by highly specialised people, and they use the very best equipment to get the job done.

The 'job', Luke echoes, mordantly.

We have nothing to hide, I insist. Absolutely nothing. What LivestockAid caught on camera, that little calf, was just an accident. It could have happened anywhere. It certainly could have happened in the wild.

They hang them up by the legs and bleed them, says Luke. Why can't you just say it?

Yes, adds Clive. I'll admit I'm a carnivore myself, but when I think of working in an abattoir, I really don't want to know.

They stun them first, I say, bluntly. They don't know what's happening.

Cows jammed into death trucks, says Luke. Trembling, filthy and scared. Living enclosed, standing on their sick friends. If slaughterhouses had glass walls...

What do you think happens in the wild? No humane slaughters there, I'm telling you.

So, you think there can be such a thing as humane murder?

I almost call him Tom; I pull my voice back under control.

Animals are not people! I say. Has the world gone mad? Vigils outside abattoirs, last rites for cows. People from your organisation don't know the first thing about livestock. You're scaring them with your crowds and cameras.

Luke just listens, and I feel like I'm raving, like I've become my father.

I sigh. They're cows, for goodness' sake.

I think that's all we've got time for, says Mala. But coming up next: will 2016 be the hottest year on record? Join us after the break to find out.

We wait to be released, the cameras still on us. I stare at Luke, but he refuses to meet my eye. The coward. We don't deserve this. Living and working with animals requires knowledge and respect. My father could tell his cows apart in the dark. Mike was wedded to his herd. They would have followed him if he'd led them off a cliff. As for my cows, I'm up with the lark to tend to them. Seven days a week, three hundred and sixty-five days a year. I look at Luke's hands, the insolence of those painted nails. He hasn't done a day of hard work in his whole life.

10 June, 1944

Herb INVITED ME UP TO the farmhouse to have a tankard of his homemade apple cider. He had not made such an offer before.

We sat down together at the wrought-iron table to the chorus of grasshoppers, chaffinches hunting for insects, bees buzzing in the honeysuckle and flicking the flag irises. It was a hot day – there was a blackbird panting on the feeder – and the cider was cold and crisp.

Herb is a man of few words, and he was characteristically quiet as he sipped his drink and gazed out over the lawn. I wondered if I should speak, racking my brain for reasons that he might have wanted to talk to me, man to man. Maggie would not have said anything. I have not said anything to anyone.

Yesterday, the military police came to the farm for a spot inspection, and as far as I knew, there had been no problems. Of course there had been no problems, because I've been nothing but an asset at Alderdown.

As for you, little book, I keep you tucked inside my mattress, away from any prying eyes that might come to search the hayloft.

Herb cleared his throat. 'Stefan, I never talked to you after your bad news.'

'Bad news?'

'Your letters from home. I should have checked to see how you're getting on.'

'Oh.' This was the last topic I had expected him to raise. 'I am quite all right. You needn't worry about me.'

Herb took a long swig of his cider and stared at me. 'Your sweetheart. What was she called?'

'Emilia.'

'And how long were you courting before the war?'

'A year, but we knew each other longer than that.'

'A year? And you didn't marry her?'

'We were engaged,' I said, wondering where this was going. Herb scratched his chin with a muddy hand.

'That's a long time, he said. 'Perhaps she wasn't the right girl for you. Although you were quite heartbroken, I think.'

'Not heartbroken.'

'All the same, it can't be easy, being in another country, all alone. And then, to receive a letter like that...'

'I am all right.'

Herb frowned. 'You're not lonely, then?'

It was not an innocent question. Herb's line of enquiry had taken on a certain urgency, which I felt acutely.

I started to worry that word might have got out about the kiss Maggie gave me in the woods – the kiss I had not solicited, yet had failed to rebuff.

Over the last couple of weeks, I've seen Jim come to the farmyard with his father on a number of occasions to talk with Herb. Every time, his eyes have followed me as I have gone about my business. I had suspected he hadn't forgiven me for the night Maggie chose to stay with me instead of going to the dance with him. But what if there were more to it than that?

'You are too kind, Herb,' I said. 'I promise I am in fine spirits.'

He registered this with a shallow nod. Then he took a long, loud breath, and sat back in his chair. I hardly moved, determined to give nothing away.

'Yesterday afternoon, Mary invited the officers into the house for a cup of tea. While they were drinking it and talking, they had a word with Lizzie, who was there playing with the cat you carved for her.'

'Oh, yes?'

'Yes. She explained to them that it was a gift – that you had made it for her.'

He was accusing me of something; that much was clear. I fought to remain calm. 'If you didn't want her to have it, you could have said something…'

'I have no problem with the gift, Stefan. But we should both be aware that this might look suspicious, particularly when the Home Guard is already keeping an eye on you, and the penalties for fraternisation can be quite considerable indeed.'

'But this is ludicrous.' I folded my arms. 'They can't think I'm fraternising with a little girl.'

'Of course not. Lizzie said that you like Maggie best. She came right out and said it.'

I swallowed. 'Why? Why would she say that?'

'Probably a tad jealous. Why else? She is a quiet girl, our Lizzie, but she's hiding a whole world in that pretty head. Things you've said or done might have taken on a different meaning for her. You'll have to be more aloof in the future, towards both her and Maggie.'

'I couldn't be unkind to Lizzie. She's just a child.'

'No, but there should certainly be no more gifts. At the very least, it's evidence for the military police, something they can build their enquiries around if there are further complaints.' He looked in the direction of the upstairs windows. 'As far as they're aware, you could be gathering intelligence, the careless talk of my daughters…'

'Whatever for? I'm a prisoner, not a spy!'

Herb nodded, slowly.

'You have been spending rather a lot of time with Maggie, though. Wouldn't you say?'

'We work together. And you're there, watching us. And I would never…'

'I am not always watching. I can't watch you all the time, nor do

I want to.' He drained the last of his cider. 'I keep wondering about that night when I found you both talking in the kitchen. You were thick as thieves. And I wasn't born yesterday. You're close in age, and you see each other every day. You are young. I wouldn't blame you if you found feelings were developing...'

'I like her, but...'

'But you cannot indulge your feelings. If I have the slightest impression that I can't trust you, Stefan, I will not hesitate to have you sent back to the camp.'

'I understand.'

'And if you lead my daughter astray, if you betray me like that, I... I don't know what I'd do.'

I nodded, stricken. His daughter is the one with designs. It was on the tip of my tongue.

But he softened, then, at my troubled expression. 'I'm sorry I have to talk to you like this. These are not normal circumstances. It's not right that you young people have to put your lives on hold, or that you are so far away from home. And I understand that you are just a man like me, caught up in circumstances beyond your control. And I want to help you, and you are welcome here. You really are. But if I am truthful, I have been worrying, Stefan, and I need to make myself very clear.'

'Of course. Then... I will stay away from Maggie.'

'All I ask is that you don't allow yourself to be alone with her.'

'That's fine. It's fine.'

We were interrupted by a creaking sound, and turned to see the door to the house opening, revealing Mr Nicholson, that slimy old worm. He was watching us with a countenance of bureaucratic pomposity. I wanted to take my tankard and hurl it at him, but I am perfectly able to restrain myself, in spite of the accusations being levelled against me.

'How would the Home Guard feel about you two drinking together?' he said.

'Mr Nicholson,' said Herb, 'we're only talking about the farm. But why don't you come out and join me for a cider? It's a wonderful afternoon.'

Then he smiled at me and reached out for my tankard: my signal to leave. Our conversation was over.

Tam

W ALKING SOUTH DOWN MONTAGUE STREET in the direction of Waterloo Bridge, I'm snapped back to the here and now when I accidentally kick an empty Lilt can off the pavement. It clatters into the sunlight, where students are rushing past on their bikes, and I stop picturing the hot mess of Dad and Luke's TV debate for a second, and return to my neighbourhood and its soothing, familiar sights. Here is the restaurant Varsha loves, where we always go together for brunch. Right down the road and the best vegan eggs in London! Or so she claims. This is the shopping centre, where I ventured into the women's section: just a little experiment, to see if I could, to see how it would feel. The sales assistant didn't bat an eyelid when she rang up the blouse.

As I walk, I visualise my destination, that quiet café near the South Bank – out of sight, beyond the layers of buildings and across the river. I huff the diesel, the bitter tang of traffic. I am just meeting my big brother for coffee, so why can't I take a full breath?

But it will be OK with Harry. We've found a way to stay in touch that barely counts as communication. Different from Mum, and different in another way from Lauren, who is so direct – How are you feeling, can I do anything? – that I don't know how to answer, and resort to weakly aping her usual sunniness. Really good, thanks! How are you?

No, my brother and I have a kind of code. We send each other viral videos, maybe captioned with a string of emojis, but often without any introduction at all. A wax museum in Poland that's

193

crash-landed in the uncanny valley. The rude awakening of a man with a mirror propped in front of his face, scaring him with his own sleepy reflection. Even hiding behind other people's content, I was cautious at first; I fretted that Harry wouldn't find the same things interesting or funny. It was touch and go with that video of black holes, which he left on read for two days before finally responding – inexplicably – with the alien emoji. But it's been good, this willingness to send and receive, this growing openness between us.

I follow the broad avenues of Holborn, heading for the river, trudging past a million Prets and flags and shop window displays. This is the spot – between two pubs, a Princess and a Duke – where Snowballed rang, offering me the internship, proper paid work at a company I actually believe in. There are bikes parked here, slowing the flow of the crowd. A woman knocks a wheel with her foot, and the bike falls and blocks my path.

Standing still for a moment, the images catch up with me: Dad on my phone screen, his arm in plaster, looking so beaten. His rising panic at the onslaught of questions he couldn't quite answer. And while it is easy these days to avoid him, or simply switch him off, you can't deny who you are. Dad is in my nature, my nurture. I am not just Tam; I am a Calvert, and always will be.

I get moving again, in the thick of pedestrians, weaving around the bike as the woman who knocked it over hoists it back into position. We are all of us used to there being things in our way, and many of these we can just ignore – none of our business. But Dad can't keep doing that. He must realise, stammering his defensive half-answers, that a reckoning is coming. Just because something has been a certain way for a long time, doesn't mean it's right. He would rail against historical wrongs – the slave trade, the disenfranchisement of women – that once were accepted as the norm, yet he can't bring himself to look at his own role in today's injustices. And this bloody-mindedness only looked like frailty on TV, where he acted so well the part of the proud cis man, disappointed in the world and his changing place in it.

I'd never thought this before, but perhaps I am better suited than him to whatever lies ahead. Here, in this cosmopolitan, urban society – where the reconstructed rule, where we are allowed a kind of divinity in shaping our own images – I am not the outlier I was back at Alderdown. Maybe it's Dad who is maladapted to this brave new world, in danger of falling with the farm. In the city, rural life and its outdated customs are the butt of the joke. Hard to imagine the old ways persist in all their muddiness when everything here is sanitised or synthetic.

My phone buzzes as I step onto Waterloo Bridge: another tap from a nearby admirer, who I'll probably never meet. I have received enough of these now that I seldom look at them. It only took a few days of living in the city, plugged into my new social networks, to challenge all the old beliefs that Dan instilled in me: that nobody else would ever want me, that love and attention are rationed and I should take what I can get. This app has helped me a lot. Plus, sometimes it's nice to remind myself that Luke – *the* Luke Underwood – wanted me. And he doesn't do things he doesn't want to do; I'm well aware of that now.

I stop to look out over the city. The river still feels filmic to me, too recognisable the world over to be the background for my little life. Yet here we are, our family drama unfolding beside the great grey Thames and the towering skyline. I always thought London an inhospitable place. Transient, anonymous. A desperate hub of ambition, with no coherent culture to accommodate its visitors. But that was before I looked closer, and saw that it was a kind of patchwork, reassuringly repetitive, and held together in communities of countless combinations with neat little threads. Anyone can stitch themselves in here, if only they realise their pattern.

My phone vibrates again in my hand. The tap has escalated into an invitation to drinks with a handsome man. I say yes, let's do it. If nothing else, to reassure myself that this morning's intrusion will cause no lasting damage to my new life.

Harry, too, has messaged. I know you weren't sure, but can dad come? He really wants to see you.

Oh, god. It's only Dad, and we are on my turf. And won't it be fine, especially now that I can so easily walk away if I have to protect myself? Perhaps this is the next step: I must reconcile my family and my past with my present situation. After all, I am getting used to the collision of different worlds. LivestockAid and Alderdown. Dad and Harry on the streets of London, with its salad bars and vegan options. Maybe that, at heart, is what this city is about. The coarticulation of antithetical values. Paradox.

Now I am walking along the South Bank, and there are school trips and tourists, and little kids running rings around their parents. Dad rarely took us out at that age. Mum had to tell him to hold our hands when we were crossing the road, and then he hauled us along like he was taking out the rubbish. Maybe his mind was on more precious cargo than his children.

I regret my reply to Harry even as I type it.

And then I am at the café. I'm not ready for this.

George

WE'RE ESCORTED TO A LOBBY and handed complimentary gift bags. Branded stress balls and stationery. A woman with bad posture and a furrowed brow clops out of a side door as Elder Son and I step into the lift. She is clutching her phone, white-knuckled.

More than inconvenient, she bleats, as the lift doors hum closed. We are in deep shit.

A glimpse of someone else's hell. Then Elder Son and I are descending.

Luke's long, bony face floats in my vision. The afterimage of a harsh light. This can't be personal. I've never done anything to him. Yet I have felt enough wrath in my time to recognise the rage in that boy. He hates me. Or hates what I stand for. The hostility of a world that refuses to agree with him. I am Luke's enemy, but I could be anybody.

For me, it's very personal. How could it not be? He has besmirched our vocation. Cast us as the villains of the piece. Attacked our business and our home, our heritage and hearts. He has made us unsafe. Mobilised an army around the world. An army that has conscripted my own son.

The lift whirs.

Job's a good'un, grins Harry. Don't you think? Anybody watching would see that nutter for what he is.

I am not so sure. Everywhere I look, unfamiliar knots of machinery confront me with our changing world. I am not quite here as we drop to ground level. I focus on the numbered buttons, the lit symbols.

What will this have done, saying my piece on national television? We can't carry on with the threat of more visits from LivestockAid, more attempts to harm our business. Sandra is afraid to go out and leave the farm when we're in the fields. People need to see that we are just like them. We don't deserve this. And we are not the problem.

The lift chimes our arrival. We proceed along a shining corridor, past a blockade of turnstiles, which convey us back outside onto the crowded street.

We'll have to wait and see what good we've done, if any. The hate mail will be our gauge. When the letters stop, we'll be in the clear. Then we can rest easy, sleep through the night. Sandra and Lauren can have their lives back, can start to make new strides with the wedding business. They've been getting interest since the rebrand. Lauren is hopeful that bookings won't be far behind.

As for the farm, this week, I will get my cast off. I'll be a better help to Elder Son.

You all right? he says.

I respond curtly, like it's a silly question. Yes.

He places a fatherly hand on my arm, and I pull it out of his reach. I'll talk to him, he says. OK?

He means Tom. Has he replied? I ask.

Yes, he has.

Well?

He won't budge, Dad. He doesn't want to see you.

For god's sake. What did he say?

It doesn't matter. Let me handle it.

Like his mother, keeping me at arm's length. I can't be trusted with such fragile things, with holding the baby. And that's what Younger Son will always be, as Mike was. Given every opportunity, his hand held through all of it.

When I came home for Mike's fifteenth birthday, bearing gifts from the city, I was double his age. But he was already a farmer. Being our father's favourite, he'd been mentored. Gathering in the sitting room, my parents and I watched him unwrap the vinyl I'd carefully selected as his present. He thanked me with a blank smile, set it aside, and threw my parents a quizzical glance. That was when I first suspected my little brother thought he was better than me.

It's been about six weeks since Tom moved out. I thought he'd be back sharpish, having run off in the heat of things. And we'd have the chance to try that terrible conversation again. The evening he left, Sandra and I went into the sitting room together and put the telly on. An old James Bond.

Man talk, said Sean Connery, dismissing a little blonde woman with a smack on the bottom – a bit much, even for me.

Sandra sighed.

Don't worry, I told her. He'll phone any minute.

But he didn't. The next day, she sent him a text, told him we were worried. He replied just to say that he was all right, and to let him be.

He has to learn there are consequences, I said, when Sandra told me. He needs to take responsibility for himself!

Sandra walked away. That night, she moved into the spare bedroom. I went in, my tail between my legs. I sat on the edge of the single bed, where I used to sleep as a boy. She was facing away from me, hair piled in a messy bun. I wanted to touch her, but there was a warning in her silence. I smoothed the linen, a faded blue-and-yellow print I didn't recognise, and gazed at a framed still life on the wall that she had once done as part of an art class.

Shall we talk about it? I said.

I can't. Not now.

When?

Please, George.

199

So I got up and left the room. She wants to blame me, but communicates only through a furious busyness, interrupted by bouts of quiet tears. If I knew how to fix it, I would. If Tom would just talk to me, then I could confront him with the truth. I am not the one poisoning this family, bending it to his whims.

Fine, I tell Elder Son. So be it. But you tell him from me…

As I talk, I'm aware of the traffic. A grumbling taxi, a passing cleaner who meets my eye. A sudden paranoia that everyone is listening and judging forces me to lower my voice.

You tell him that we need to sort this out, for the sake of the family. I'm willing to do that. All right? You tell him that.

Harry squints. Like the sun is in his face – no chance in this smog. For the first time, I notice the lines around his eyes. There are silver threads on his young head.

How about I tell him sorry, Dad? I think that's where I might start.

I mutter and shrug as he walks away. They're meeting at some café nearby. Apparently Tom's now working, doing an internship. Harry didn't know any more about it, said they've only been texting for a few days. I wonder what the job entails. That's the thing about Tom. He pretends he can't do anything so that we all run around, making allowances for him. But I've always wanted him to step up. I've always believed in our Tom.

With a few hours to kill before we have to meet for the train, I had an idea that I might visit some old haunts. Back from the times when I was the worry. I pictured myself, young again, smoking a spliff. Wandering along Hackney Canal beside the slow, calm water. Full of the future, in the days when I could still make a run for it, or else just cover things up. Like the bright pop-art murals we used to spray on crackling paint jobs. The big end-terrace we squatted in, 17 Blakemore Road, got sold up and renovated. Maybe it's an elegant home nowadays, or a couple of rental flats for yuppies to blast through. Or even an office full of self-satisfied, moralising millennials. As much as I wish I could go back, I have lost the lightness of youth.

I'm directed by the urban sprawl. I walk past towering shop displays of fruit and veg that pay no mind to season or provenance. The London summer smells of beer and fumes, of drains and rubbish cooking in the sun. So unlike the sweetness of the countryside. My legs ache when I stop by the Thames, looking south. Old, washed up, past it. Cast away by my own family. A couple of scrawny pigeons scrap over a cigarette butt. Beyond them, the unstoppable surge of time flows between the banks of buildings, and we are all tiny and insignificant. Dragged along in the current.

It takes me a second to realise my mobile phone is ringing. Its tone is tinny and false, and I struggle to answer. Tap the green phone icon. No, no. Hold and drag. A timer appears on the screen and a faint voice begins to chirp. I am flustered as I lift it up to my ear.

Harry?

Dad, you can come and meet us after all.

Oh?

It's OK.

All right, I mumble, my eyes blurring. All right then.

I find the café, a no-frills sort of place with a scuffed wooden sign, painted messily in rainbow stripes. There are tables and chairs outside that look like they might have been salvaged from an old school. The boys could have sat in the sunshine, but indoors it is. They're past the counter at the back of a long room.

When I first see Tom, I refuse to look at him. My face might give something away. I don't know. His curly dark hair glows with red streaks. Little studs flash on his earlobes. There's a jewelled ring in his nose, as far from bull-like as I've ever seen one. His complexion is soft and unblemished. On a woman, these touches might have been fitting, even beautiful.

He wants a reaction, I tell myself. He's always been like this.

I remind myself of what's important and approach the counter. I have to ride this out, or we'll never get him back. Pa's tough love never did me any good. I was always running, a stranger in my own home. By the time I settled down with Sandra, it was too late for me and him. He died of a heart attack, carrying kitchenware from the memorial hall to the stall Ma was running at the summer fête. They tried to revive him, surrounded by shards of smashed china. What would he have thought of me, there at his funeral, dry-eyed and full of heartache? I only cried once, down in the farmyard where the drama of our lives had played out. I only did what he expected of me. He wanted me to fail him, so that's what I did.

This café is dairy-free. I take my coffee black. The man behind the counter is a real state. His dark-grey mop is tied in a frizzy bun. His skin is greasy, sunless. His teeth are stained. He hasn't made a bit of effort, neither is he friendly. Looking around, this whole establishment stinks of apathy. There are old crates nailed to the bare plaster, and these are stacked with fake plants and mason jars stuffed with fairy lights. I know what they're going for: unfussy, unpretentious. Like it's immoral to strive, to have standards. But they're in dire need of one of Lauren's total makeovers.

I pull over a chair, set my coffee on the table, which is made from a stack of pallets. Then I lean over Tom and reach around his shoulders. I pat him awkwardly on the top of the arm.

It's good to see you, son.

He squirms. Well, he says, Harry thought we should try to talk.

Yeah. Elder Son nods. Dad wanted to say some things. Didn't you?

I am sweating, here in the cool shadows. I want to tell Younger Son that we are family, that this has all been a load of nonsense and I'm ready to put it behind us. But it's got worse. Glitter on his cheeks. What does he think he looks like? People won't accept this. This isn't how to behave if he wants to be taken seriously.

I'm sorry, I say. My mouth is sandy. You know, the things I said last time… That was no help to anybody.

Tom nods, a small smile on his lips. He sits up a bit. OK. Thank you.

I half-expect an apology from him in return. But what would he apologise for, if not for appearing before me like this, right now? I'm embarrassed to be sitting with him.

Your mother's very worried about you.

Where is she?

She was afraid you wouldn't want to see her, I say, pointedly. And she didn't want to get hurt.

Right, he says, narrowing his eyes.

Harry shifts suddenly. His chair legs yowl. Tell Dad about the internship, he says. Sounds pretty cool, and there's likely a job at the end of it.

Oh? I say.

Yeah, I love it, says Tom. I'm working for this non-profit, Snowballed. We campaign for progressive politics. It's a great place to work.

I bridle at the thought of him joining a band of woke, meat-free revolutionaries. Right, I say, flatly. What did you study maths for, then?

It's actually very useful. Finance, data analysis.

It's all about data these days, says Elder Son, approvingly. That's what they say, isn't it? It's what all the big companies are doing, selling data.

We're not selling it. We use it for campaign strategy, to get insight into the people we target with our comms.

My coffee is too bitter without milk. I make a face. *The people we target.* I imagine a sniper inputting a set of coordinates. Lining up his victim.

Sounds interesting, I say. You're enjoying it?

I am, says Tom, beginning to smile. His hands are shaking on the tabletop. What's he nervous for? Not on my account. Bloody tragic.

Where are you living?

Tom takes a sip of his plant juice. It's great, actually. I've got a room in a big house belonging to a friend of mine, Varsha. Well, it belongs to her parents. They must be loaded.

I am smiling too rigidly.

Tom continues. It's four storeys, right in the heart of Bloomsbury. They bought it so she could live cheaply with her mates. She's a food writer. And London is so expensive.

Clearly not if you know the right people, sniffs Harry, rapping his knuckles on the side of his chair. How do you know this girl?

Just… Through people.

I gesture at all his gear. Is she into all this too, then?

Tom darkens. She's cis, Dad, if that's what you mean.

Siss?

Like, her gender identity matches up with the sex she was assigned at birth.

Right, I say, not getting it.

Yeah, we do live with a trans woman, though. Vicky. She's been so welcoming. Works at the Tate Modern.

Of course.

And Heath is bi. I like him a lot.

Elder Son sits back in his chair, lifting his coffee. Trying hard to get it right. That's cool, he says. So, are you and him… a thing?

Tom blinks at him, then lets out a humourless laugh. What? No! Why would you think that? He's got a fiancé. Jack.

Sorry. Harry reddens, poor chap. I just assumed… The way you said it, I thought maybe something was going on.

What are you on about? Because he's bi?

All right! You don't have to bite my head off.

Tom sighs. Must be hard, I think, having cavemen like us for relations. He takes a stud earring between thumb and forefinger, twirls it delicately. I'm not, he says. Look, all you need to know is that I'm good. I'm finally being myself, and I've found a f… a community…

He was going to say family.

…that accepts me, and that's something I've never felt before. It didn't seem possible that I could feel like this. You know, like I'm not just treading water. Surviving. And it makes me think that maybe I can get on with it and live my life; I don't have to control everything. I don't know. I'm probably not making any sense.

Elder Son is nodding frantically. I am at a loss.

Of course he's not making sense. Were we that terrible to him? Then why do I remember it so differently? His screams of laughter when I carried him on my back. The rope swing I hung for him and his brother from the old oak tree at the edge of the orchard. The sandcastle extravaganzas we used to build in Cornwall, Tom delivering bucketful after bucketful of seawater for the moat, lugging it across the beach with an ecstatic devotion. I gave my boys the childhood I never had.

Tom, I say, what's this all about?

It's Tam, he corrects me. Rejects me, the name we gifted him twenty-two years ago. It's Tam now.

But you realise you're just the same? Under all of that, you're the same person. You can't change who you are, Tom.

I know that, he says, defiantly. I am the same person. But maybe I seem different to you because I'm openly expressing myself, and all the things I've had to hide.

For a moment, I'm taken in. Who is this, and where is Younger Son? This person holds himself differently. This familiar stranger, who treads the tightrope line between man and woman in such a way that my eyes can't help but drift from one vision to another, rabbit to duck. As if I never raised him, haven't known him his whole life. Younger Son. My boy.

He knows I am lost for words.

How's Gran? he asks.

She's getting used to everything, says Harry. The Lodge. It's really not so bad from the looks of things. The staff are nice.

That's good.

She's asked after you a couple of times.

Oh, I really want to visit.

She can't see you like this, I blurt, my head throbbing, the pressure building.

Tom looks at me, coolly. Why not?

You'd confuse her. Upset her.

I don't think she'd mind.

You're being selfish, Tom.

Dad, says Elder Son.

Tom stands up. I've told you what to call me, he says. I'm going to try to be understanding and give you more time. But I'm not about to stay here and be dead-named.

What are you talking about? I say.

He turns away.

Don't go! My voice cracks with panic. I'm sorry, Tom. I'm just trying to… I don't understand why you would do this.

I look down, can't be seen this way. I take a deep breath, remembering my own father. His large hand cracking down, turning my red face. *Stop it. Stop crying or you'll get another.* I wipe my eyes with my thumbs, press hard. I look up again at Younger Son, if that is who this person is.

Please. I'm sorry. Whatever you're going through, your mum and I want to understand it. We're family. All right? We need to stick together.

There are other customers in the café. A couple of young women sit on a threadbare sofa against the wall behind the counter. They keep their mugs to their lips, poised. Pretending not to watch us.

Tom looks down at me, impassive.

I get it, he says. I see you. And I'm sorry, for what it's worth. I'm sorry for a lot of things. But this isn't one of them.

Then he hugs his brother goodbye and takes his leave without another word.

3 July, 1944

For the past three weeks or so, I have kept my promise, and my distance from Maggie. Whenever she and I have found ourselves alone together, I have made my excuses. There was usually some manner of escape route to hand. Our summer working days are often as long as the sunlight allows, with evenings spent out in the fields, watering, trimming and shearing, taking our meals al fresco. I stowed away in manual labour.

But I could not avoid Maggie entirely. I saw her under Herb's watchful eyes, and I felt we were being watched too by Gerald and Billy, and Nora the Land Girl. I wondered if they had heard rumours about us.

There was a harsh edge in Maggie's voice whenever she spoke to me.

'You can get more hay in that wheelbarrow,' she told me, when I was too eager to roll a load away across the fields.

I stopped to glance at her.

'Don't just stand there,' she said, so I forked another pile of hay into the wheelbarrow. 'For goodness' sake. Pat it down.'

'Maggie,' said Herb, looking mystified.

I said nothing as she turned back to her own barrow.

I hoped her father had spoken to her, explaining the need for discretion. All I could do now was demonstrate my goodwill to indicate that my distance was nothing personal. And yet my efforts to assist her with farm jobs were met with cool resistance. If Herb and I joined her in the cowshed to help with the mucking or bedding, or I approached when Herb was netting the cherry tree and she was holding the ladder, she would give me one look and then disappear, as if in retaliation for all the times I'd done the same to her – but that was only to ensure we were not left alone together.

Yesterday morning, I entered the milking parlour and was surprised to find myself face to face with Jim Calvert. He had come early to the farm to collect some fertiliser, and Maggie had invited him to keep her company while she got on with the milking. She peered out from behind Bertha's udder to see my reaction.

'Jim, Stefan. You've met, haven't you?'

'Briefly,' I said.

Jim spoke to me with scorn. 'Yes. But I know all about you.'

'Is that so?'

He had blocked my path, his hands on his hips. 'Careless,' he leered, as if he were cracking a joke, 'winding up as a prisoner. Got yourself caught, did you?'

'I was shot down, actually. Have you ever flown a plane?'

His features are strangely ill-defined, his lips thin, and eyelashes and eyebrows faint. His smirk ran like water, turning to a scowl.

'I would have if my family didn't need me on our farm. We're providing for the people – you understand? – and our mission seems to be going rather better than yours.'

I found myself uneasy, all my muscles tensing as if I might need to spring into action at any second.

Then Herb interrupted us, arriving from the farmhouse, and the moment was over. I took a stool and set to milking, grateful to have something to do with my hands, something to look at. The hot milk hit the bottom of the tin pail like a bullet.

We were almost set up, Maggie and I. Herb and Mary left the farm just before midday, carting three of their finest pedigree cows to a busy livestock market in the Midlands. For people who rarely left the county, this was quite a journey, and they were anxious, though quietly so.

'That's where you get the best prices,' Herb explained, distractedly.

I helped him lead the mature cows, udders unmilked and full to bursting, across the yard. They had been shampooed, and were primped and shining. Even their collars had been freshly polished. Mary stood back to admire them, clapping her hands in satisfaction; they were ready to enter the ring. Herb was wearing a bright, white smock, and had combed and oiled his hair with a careful side parting.

'You look smart, Pop,' said Maggie, her hands on Lizzie's wriggling shoulders. 'Good luck with the auction.'

'Thank you, darling. I'll set a good reserve.' Herb kissed her on the cheek. 'Will you be all right here?'

'Of course we will. Don't worry about anything.'

'Keep an eye on this one,' said Mary, kissing Maggie, then crouching to embrace Lizzie.

'We'll see you tomorrow, Stefan,' said Herb, turning away with barely a nod in my direction.

There were no instructions for me, no strict warnings. I was an afterthought, but I suppose I have proven myself, and if it weren't for the bleak circumstances of my being here, I would by now have become a friend, if not a part of the family.

Besides, Maggie and I would not have spent our evening together if it weren't for the storm clouds that were already beginning to gather on the horizon, like an army pressing in to do us harm.

The rain began to fall at lunchtime. It had rained on and off for the past week, and the river was swollen, but we had no idea of what was to come. We let the cows stay in the meadows, for one thing. They were lying in groups, chewing happily under the shelter of the trees at the edge of the wood. We thought the clouds would pass over, and then the herd would be able to enjoy another burst of sunshine before it was time to come in. We continued our routine work in the farmyard until the volunteers decided it was too wet to stay, and they headed for home.

The rain got heavier and heavier, forcing Maggie, Lizzie and me into a barn, where we waited for it to pass.

'It's like nighttime,' said Lizzie, her mouth hanging open as she peered out at the darkening farmyard.

The rain started to run into the barn. Outside, the whole yard was covered in an inch of swirling water. I was starting to worry.

'My hayloft was leaking again last night.'

'The ground is waterlogged already,' said Maggie, looking uneasy. 'There's nowhere for the rain to go.'

'Let's hope it stops soon.'

But it didn't. The sun was blotted out, a month's worth of rain falling in a matter of minutes. Water gushed down the hill and into the yard.

Finally, after what felt like hours, Maggie decided we could wait no longer. We had to bring the cows in before the fields were all swamped.

We sloshed our way along the muddy paths, passing through slippery wet gates, the rain in our eyes. When we reached the open pasture, Lizzie let out a yell of fright.

Half of the meadow had vanished. The lowland was completely underwater, with the occasional rising peak only just visible. The fence followed the curve of the ground where it appeared to dive deep into the river, and then the woods began, floating on a tarry lake.

'Over there,' Maggie was shouting. 'Over there.'

On the other side of the flood, a good sixty cows had become trapped on a lone island, and they were steadily losing ground.

'We have to save them,' cried Lizzie.

'Lizzie, no,' said Maggie. 'You have to go back.'

'I don't want to.'

'The water is deep. It's too dangerous for you here.'

'But the cows!'

'No, you have to get back inside. Get inside and stay there. Do you understand me?'

'I understand.'

'Then go,' Maggie cried. 'Ask Mr Nicholson to come. Tell him we need his help.'

The girl bolted, splashing through the swamp.

'What are we going to do?' said Maggie, turning to me. 'It's too deep to reach them. I could swim...'

'You can't,' I told her. 'Look at the water. The currents.'

There were branches swirling on the surface. The cows grouped closer together, moaning. I felt their fear in my gut.

Maggie was resolute. 'But maybe if...'

'No,' I insisted. 'Nobody is swimming in that.'

Together, we devised a plan. I ran back to the farmyard, and while Maggie called out to her beloved herd, I took a length of thick rope and donned a pair of gloves.

'Here,' I said, handing Maggie one end of the rope meant for tying halters, which she looped through a peg in the ground, then knotted around her fingers.

I tied the other end around my waist. Then I went down to the wooden fence, just before it dipped beneath the surface of the water, and climbed up onto the first rail. My hands were clammy in the gloves. I shimmied along as far as I could, right out, over the surging river. The cold air filled my head, almost stunning me as I remembered the night I fell from the sky. The fence moved with me, swaying.

Maggie's voice was carried by the wind.

'You'd better not bloody fall in!'

I focused, reached up for a low branch, then used it to step up onto the top railing of the fence. From there, I climbed into the tree. The branches were less rigid than expected, and I felt that they could crack at any moment, and send me hurtling into the floodwater. But I kept climbing, moving between the arms of the tree, then to the next tree and the next until, finally, I was able to drop down beside the cornered cows. They scarcely reacted, unable to move.

It took tying them, Maggie pulling on the rope, and me standing behind them and pushing, for them to remember their limbs. Dragged into the current, in the deepest of the floodwater, their backs were still visible. But the water was ever rising.

Maggie and I screamed and coaxed and bullied to get those cows to move.

When the first climbed up the hill on the other side of the water, I could have wept. But I was too busy trying to get a hold of the rope again. Maggie had tied it to a stick in an attempt to lend it some heft, so that she could throw it out to me – to tie to the next cow.

One by one, we forced them down into the water, then urged them up to safety.

'Where is Mr Nicholson?' Maggie shouted. 'Where is he?'

They didn't all make it. In sum, fourteen cows were swept away. Either they couldn't fight and panicked, or they slipped and fell. The water got underneath them, lifting their hooves. Each time, Maggie held on to the rope and shrieked, and eventually the rope would come up empty.

'I have to go after them,' she said.

'No, we have to carry on…'

Only when the last cow had crossed to safety did I start my climb back through the trees. As I lowered myself onto the fence rail, which by now was immersed in the rising water, my foot slipped.

I plunged into the freezing river. I saw a flash of teeth behind a blond moustache and I was tumbling through the sky, away from the burning wreckage of my plane. Groping madly in the currents, still looking for my safe landing. Somehow, I got a hold of the fence post.

Maggie was wrenching at the rope around my waist.

I surfaced, and pulled my way along the fence to safety, choking up the ice in my lungs.

'You stupid man,' said Maggie, holding my face, her nose against mine, her fingers in my hair. 'You stupid, stupid man.'

I only wanted to return to my hayloft and rest. While undressing, I covered my numb body in scratches.

Tam

*G*RAN CAN'T SEE YOU LIKE *this. You're being selfish.*

Got to keep moving, follow the steps down to the tube. The platform is packed, the train's delayed, but my legs won't let me stop, so on I go through the warm, muttering bodies. I'm past them before they can look at me.

At the far end of the platform, I take another exit and follow the signs to a different line. Just walk, put some distance between us. Don't stop to think. The train pulls in at the top of the stairs, and the doors are bleating, closing. I hop on, walk right down the carriage, as far as I can go. There's a *Metro* newspaper on the floor, Trump and Hillary emblazoned across the cover, orange and blue. The train begins to rattle and rock. And there, finally, I stop.

I take a seat, a breath. Inhale deeply, slowly, through my nose. Release, lips parted. Steady.

There's a man sitting across from me, a few seats to my left. His eyes are on me. There is thick, dark hair sprouting from his shirt cuffs. He blinks, slowly, coughs the air from his lungs. Why is he staring at me like that?

I look away, child's logic: he can't see me if I can't see him. But my skin still tingles with danger.

I sit up straighter, shield my pink lips with my hand, and cast a subtle glance back up the carriage, where a few passengers are talking amongst themselves. There are two pairs of parents, with kids and suitcases. If I needed help…

His eyes press into me, searching, until I start to see what he is seeing: an androgynous, alien thing. Cornered, rigid. And there it is, the old feeling I used to have. A cold, sick disgust at myself.

Gran can't see you like this.

The man shifts his weight and I lean away from him. But he just smiles as the train creaks to a stop at a station, gets up and heads on his way. The doors hang open a moment longer, extending the false threat. My pulse taps at my throat. Then we are rumbling away again, though the danger stays with me.

Gran can't see. You like this.

I turn to my phone for distraction, reading any old words – without comprehension. Varsha and Lara and Heath. Simon and my work emails, and all the latest messages from Friedrich. We've got a plan now to meet up, but should I? Maybe it's right to maintain my distance from all things family. For a while longer.

You're being selfish.

Am I? He's had weeks to process this, yet Dad was looking at me like I'm mad. It lurched me back to my bedroom at home, the moment he walked in, the look in his eyes when he saw my true face. But I'd told him to get out, been able to cut things short before he'd had the chance to say anything.

What happened in the café just now was somehow more exposing, more intimate, more painful for its veneer of civility. For the way I still wanted his approval. Desperately. For the suggestion that Gran needed protection against me. For the quiet sting of that old name and everything it represents. Tom, Tom, Tom.

I leave the tube and the brightness of the day is like a dream. I am trying to unpick it. Why do I long for their love? How can I stop? And how can I want to honour them, yet feel this anger – this rage – that inspired me to betray them in the first place?

I cross the road, enter an alleyway, then step into a courtyard in the ruins of an old church. It's quiet here. I brush a tombstone with my fingertips. It's overgrown with creepers, wildness bursting at the wrought-iron bounds of the cemetery, testaments to lives lost already to time, to history nestled in among these modern buildings.

I need to see Gran. I won't let Dad keep us apart. She is on her last descent and will soon return to the earth. This is no cause for concern; she was never afraid to muck in. A memory flashes through my mind: how she freed the neighbour's cat when it got stuck behind the grate at the edge of the cattle shed, and how she barely seemed to notice the ungrateful scratches it left up her arms. I remember how she would watch without comment when, as a child, I dressed up and danced in the living room, clapped when I pirouetted to a stop. How she picked me and Harry up from school, and when I was quiet and wouldn't say what was wrong, she took a bag of fruit gums from the glove compartment and shook a handful onto my palm.

And I suppose it wasn't normal that she grew up working on the farm rather than helping her mother in the kitchen, so how did all of that start? And how much or little did Gran care about convention as she pursued her own passions? How much of a fight was put up?

When I was little, she had no past, born with grey hair and loose skin. But underneath all that, she was solid as a tree trunk. Always confidently herself. Gran, the matriarch, dispensing moral guidance with the wisdom and serenity of having seen it all before. Her quiet stewardship of the farm and the family. This too shall pass.

I will always need this, her voice in my head. Dad can't tell me to stay away. How am I supposed to feel about myself if I'm not even allowed contact with my own grandmother? She wouldn't want that, and it's between us, isn't it? At the very least, we can still talk to each other. I refuse to let her go. So I find the number for the Lodge online, call it, and ask for Maggie Calvert. I wait a few minutes, settling back into myself as the receptionist deals with my request.

Suddenly I hear her voice, unchanged. Hello?

A rush of warmth. Gran.

Yes?

She sounds distant; my fingers tighten on my phone. Gran, it's me.

Darling. How are you?

She knows; she doesn't need to see my face, and I have always felt most comfortable disembodied like this. For the first time since leaving Harry and Dad, I smile.

I'm good, Gran. It's really nice to hear your voice.

Why? What's happening?

Nothing's happening.

No? Well, you know I love to hear your voice too. But you can pick up the phone anytime.

How are you doing, Gran? Are they looking after you?

Who? I'm quite all right, darling. I'm just… I think… I just stopped for a coffee, actually.

She's trying to make sense of her surroundings, of the cup she holds in her hands, of my familiar voice in her ear. The individual pieces make sense, but not together. I almost know what that's like.

I was just with Dad, I tell her. And Harry.

Good, good. How are the girls?

Now it's my turn to hesitate, to get my bearings. She means the herd, doesn't she? I answer honestly. I don't know, Gran. I'm not home anymore. I'm in London.

Are you?

Yeah, but I miss them.

I frown at this strange thought; I *do* miss them, in a way.

What are you doing in London? she says.

I've moved here to start a new job.

You've moved? I didn't know…

I'm sorry, Gran. I thought you did.

But that's wonderful news. You should have told me. When we were having breakfast.

I swallow. She's losing me; I'm losing her. But I will continue to be here with her. There will always be a quiet understanding between us. It's getting stronger all the time, the pull of family; whenever I take a corner, there is a turning for home. And I can't deny what I've done to Alderdown by inviting LivestockAid in. I have hurt them all. I have endangered this place that means everything to Gran.

I'm really, really sorry, I say. I just want you to know...

You're a funny bugger, George.

I flinch.

I'll be better at keeping in touch, I promise.

You worry too much, she says, breezily, and I can hear a smile in her voice. You can fill me in on the details when you get home, all right? Now, I'd better go. I've got an appointment. They'll call me in, any second. OK?

OK.

Good luck!

And she hangs up.

George

SANDRA'S TALKING AGAIN. NO SOONER have I shut the front door behind me than she appears at the foot of the stairs, anxious to hear about London. Her hair is wrapped in a towel, her eyes puffy. Dusty twists and rolls around my feet. I try to bend down to stroke her, but a jolt of pain straightens me out again.

I saw you on the telly. You did it.

That's all she says about the interview before asking after Younger Son.

He's got to get it out of his system, I say, taking the copper kettle from the stove and pouring us cups of tea. Better he does it there, out of the way.

Sandra sits down at the kitchen table. She shakes her head.

I should have been there, she says. Who has he got if not his mother?

I stay standing. I've been sitting too long today, and the action of lowering myself into a chair causes my hip to lock.

He knows we're here for him, I say. We've always been here, and we'll be here if and when he wants us. There is nothing else we can do.

Do you remember when he was little? He was such a sweet little boy, always running around outside, playing his boisterous little games.

Mm.

Do you remember those horrible little potions he used to make with water from the stream? Lord knows what he put in them, petals and lichen and bird crap all floating on the top. I always thought it was such a 'boy thing' to do.

I look at her over the rim of my cup.

And he used to love dressing up, she says. He had that wooden sword. He used to say he was Prince Charming. That's why I just don't see it, you know. This… change. You don't just wake up one day…

Exactly, I say – but I have started thinking. When I was a child, playing make-believe of any kind always irritated my father, whatever the scenario. So I never thought of it as the right sort of behaviour for a boy. But then, there's no denying that I was one, that I am now a man. And I apply the same logic to Younger Son. He is what he is, regardless of the kinds of games he liked to play. Likes to play still.

All the same, my wife is lying to herself. Her lips are pulled tight and thin, and I half-suspect we are sharing our thoughts. It's not like we caught him raiding his mother's wardrobe. But he saw things differently, an impulse we tried hard to suppress. When he wore his prince costume, he twirled the plastic sword like a dancer's baton. His muddy mixtures were love potions. Throwing himself into the action-packed adventures that left him with grazed knees and mud on his coat, he was always the heroine, Princess Leia or Lara Croft. We were forever correcting that slinky, pigeon-toed gait of his.

But these were merely bad habits he needed to shake, as we've all had to do at some time or another. The quirks Tom picked up were never the real him, which we just needed to dig down to excavate. Just dig a little deeper.

Sandra drives me to the hospital the next day to have my plaster cast removed. The doctor slices it into two shells with a circular saw, makes cuts along the length of my arm. The saw whirs like a power tool, and I have to remind myself that I am in safe hands. Normally I am the one administering procedures, only my patients are the cows. The tension melts from my shoulders when I am finally free to go.

It's good to be behind the wheel again. After work, I take a trip to the Lodge. Ma sits by the window, frets her fingers in the knit of her old jumper. The home diminishes her. Stripped of her tough farmers' mettle, she is like a winter tree. I have Auntie Lizzie on video call, but Ma seems not to know her. It's morning in New Zealand, and Lizzie has things to do. Hikers arriving at the guesthouse. Ma doesn't return her farewell.

Outside, the summer evening is suffocated by a blanket of cloud. Warm rain has begun to fall. It trickles down the windowpane in rivulets, gathering weight and speed. Ma watches them like a child forbidden to go out and play. So, this is how it ends.

I pull a chair to her side and perch upon it. You haven't touched your tea, I say.

Her fierce response: What tea? That's not mine.

Yes, it is.

She eyes it suspiciously.

Have you been sitting there all day? I ask, hating the thought of her languishing in this room, her brain turning to mush.

Nowhere to go. It's raining.

Yes, but what about the lounge?

The lounge? she snaps, petulant and vulnerable.

I give into her resistance, won't insult her with false cheer. No, you're right. It's all a bit depressing, isn't it? I don't blame you for keeping yourself to yourself. I'm sorry, Ma.

She says nothing.

I survey her enclosure. Someone has made her bed, tucking the floral duvet under the mattress – something she hates – with hotel-like indifference. The floor is wood-printed linoleum, easy to clean. The blue-grey curtains match the lampshade on the bedside light, as does every lampshade and curtain throughout the entire place. The few possessions deemed inseparable from Ma as a person have all been tidied away into the built-in wardrobe

221

behind the door. Clothes she's given noticeable rotation the past few years, a couple of photo albums in which half the snapshots are faded, loose and muddled, and some favourite books, which she hasn't read in years. All tidied away.

How can we abandon her here when she has so little time left? The doctor predicted it wouldn't be more than a couple of years before she's so sick that she can no longer feed or dress herself. There is nothing beyond that senile infancy, just as a newborn perches on the edge of the void.

I know I can't promise anything, but I take her hand. Do it anyway.

I'm going to find a way to pay someone, I mumble, to look after you, back at home, when we're all out.

Hmm?

We treat the elderly worse than animals. I should never have let Sandra twist my arm like this. Between us, I'm sure we could all find a way to look after my mother at home, save her this misery. And when I step away from the farm work for good, I can be there all the time. I can't bear this, the sight of her pale face. Eyes that have seen so much over the years that they have begun to forget.

Harry and I went to London and saw Tom, I say, determined to connect with her. It was really weird to be back there and see how everything's changed. So busy, though I suppose it always was. Anyway, he asked after you. Sends his love.

She jerks her hands away, turns sharply to face me. His love? she says. Where is he?

London, I repeat, struck by the depth of feeling.

You can't do that.

Do what?

Send him away.

I am taken aback. I didn't send him away, I say. He wanted to go.

He didn't. You gave him no choice.

Ma, that's not fair. Who told you that? It was his decision.

222

But he didn't want to go. He wouldn't leave me.

Who's told you this, anyway? Was it Sandra?

I don't want him to go. I won't let you!

She puts her head in her hands and lets out a deep, rattling sigh.

Has Tom spoken to you? I continue. There are two sides to every story, you know. We may see things differently; we may have even fallen out. But I would never dream of sending him away. You know that. And actually he seems to have landed on his feet. He's found himself a job and a decent place to live, so you really don't need to worry about him. All right? Please don't get yourself worked up over this. It's not necessary.

She whispers something. A name.

I lean in. What was that?

She lifts her face from her hands and blinks, as if burned by a shocking light. Her eyes bulge, pale and grey. Where are we? she says.

Ma...

What is this place?

I can't believe she is this confused. It is too much, too quick. You're just staying here for a while, I say.

Please. I don't want to...

She seizes me by the arms. Her grip is desperately tight, just as a toddler, torn from her parents, might surprise you with her strength.

I know, I stammer. I know.

I'm sorry. We shouldn't have... But I'll do anything, Pop. Just don't do this.

It's me: it's George. Ma, it's your Georgie!

She is weeping now, and out of reach. She repeats, over and over: I want to go home... I want to go home...

My hip throbs as I drive in the pouring rain.

Sundowning, that's what the nurse called it, coming to my aid as Ma began to wail. Behavioural changes at dusk. Yes, it's quite common to feel like you're in the wrong place, she explained.

Somehow I have strayed too far. Crossed into a nightmare world, where cows can speak. No such things as men and women. Family is no more, and we no longer know who we are as we all waste away. Because there is nothing to eat if we refuse to consume any other living thing.

Thunder chimes with the engine of the Land Rover. Music for the end times.

19 August, 1944

SINCE I GOT TO ALDERDOWN, I have learnt to recognise the trees, the wild animals, the birds and the flowers and the names of the clouds. I have learnt a new vocabulary that pertains to the non-human, yet has somehow brought me closer to myself. The stars in the night sky form a musical score, and in the early mornings, when the birds first start to sing, I try to mimic them, to capture the otherworldly melodies that wriggle and burble in my throat like a living being. I think sometimes the birds are listening. Sometimes they even answer back.

I have told Maggie not to come and see me, but still she comes. Sometimes she knocks on my door at night, and it will not do to turn her away. She is determined, her eyes steely. I brew the tea on the glowing embers of my fire, and we sit and talk by lamplight. She is haunted by the night of the flood, and my company is all that offers her any relief. I cannot deny her. I have been stalked by my own ghosts, and it is only in finding kinship and security here that I have been able to outrun them. Consequently, we understand each other, Maggie and I.

For days, we have been summoned to fetch the beaten, bloated corpses of drowned cows, some of which were carried miles down the spilled river before the water dumped them – in reeds, ditches, even gardens. The Edwards family will not talk to Mr Nicholson. The cost of his failure to come to Maggie's aid has proven too high.

The meadow is a trampled battlefield. There is no grass on the slope down to the river, nor in the trenches around the hills.

There are no flowers. The plants have all been buried by silt and an avalanche of slippery topsoil. At first, hungry crows flocked to peck at the surfacing worms. But the sun soon dried and cracked the mud, and that part of the field is now as still and quiet as a cemetery.

Only the waving green of the trees beyond – the ash and elm branches that helped us save some of the trapped herd – attests to the late summer, rising serenely above the wasteland.

This afternoon, Herb borrowed a ferret from the Calverts. Named Aesop, it is a vicious thing, white with a dark muzzle, and an awful snarl. Our task is to flush out all the rabbits, moving meticulously through Alderdown's many acres. This will take several days.

We started in the small field behind the orchard, where the air was thick with pollen, and catching in my throat. Maggie is a champion rabbit-hunter, and she was excited to be doing something about the pests. Fruits were ripening in the hedge behind her as she carried Aesop, struggling in his wicker basket.

I am not used to predators, but Maggie's joy was a great diversion. I find all of her emotions irresistible.

'He has a terrific bite,' said Herb, and I was not sure if he was serious or trying to tease me.

'I'll protect you,' said Maggie, laughing at me, a honeybee swooning about her dark, pinned locks. 'You just concentrate on netting the rabbit holes.'

The cows were unconcerned about Aesop. They paid us no attention. I knelt down to peg the corners of a net over a burrow. Herb covered another. The aim was to block all the visible exits to the run.

While we worked, I spotted some field mice, darting freely between their snug holes in the dried earth. Here in the chaos of the countryside, it sometimes occurs to me that the world is all at play, something we humans tend to neglect, or at the very least forget. We are afraid of the wild, over which our control remains intolerably poor.

Maggie took the end of a piece of string which was hanging over the lip of the basket. Aesop was thumping his head against the lid, trying to prise it open. She held it firm, slipping the basket under the net, keeping hold of the string.

'Patience, you little fiend.'

Then she lifted the lid, and Aesop was free. He scurried close to the ground like a lizard. Maggie's string was attached to a collar around his neck, tying him to her so that he wouldn't get lost down the rabbit hole. I was a little alarmed, and took a step back, but Aesop knew what to do. He sniffed for a moment at the entrance to the warren, before diving straight in.

The last time Maggie had an animal tethered to her, we were trying to save lives, not take them. Over our heads, crying lapwings inked the sky.

'Poor things,' I said. 'They don't stand a chance.'

Herb looked surprised. 'Have you never heard the expression, *breeding like rabbits*?'

'They won't go to waste,' added Maggie. 'We'll eat them, and before you know it, we'll be doing this again. Let me tell you. They'll always come back.'

The first rabbit emerged, chased out into the open air. It was a silky chestnut thing, fired straight into the net. Maggie lunged to dispatch it, and the rabbit froze at the sight of trouble. Easy prey. A solid blow to the back of the neck put it out of its misery.

Lizzie, just back from school in the village, came running towards us through the orchard. All week she had been excited for the summer fête, and I wondered if she might be coming to me for more help, as I had already provided puppet show props, whittled from pieces of wood on the farm, which she had then painted with her mother.

But when she arrived, we saw immediately that she had been crying.

'Dry your eyes,' said Maggie. 'We're catching rabbits here.'

'Whatever's the matter, darling?' said Herb.

'It's Mrs Nicholson,' she said. 'I heard her talking in the back garden. There were women from the village.'

'What women?' said Maggie.

'Only Susan and Judith,' said Herb. 'Your mother invited them to discuss the kitchen stall at the fair.'

I had a hunch the women themselves were not the problem.

'What was Mrs Nicholson saying?' I asked, and Lizzie turned away from me, running past Maggie, straight into the arms of her father.

'Lizzie?' said Maggie. 'What are you talking about? Mrs Nicholson talks a lot of nonsense. You know that, don't you?'

By this point, there were rabbits surfacing all around, with nothing to catch them but the bulging nets, for all three of us were attending to Lizzie. A rabbit squeezed under a gap and fled towards the hedgerow.

'Stop that now,' said Herb, taking Lizzie's hand. 'I'm sure we can sort it out, whatever it is. Why don't we take a little walk together? What do you think?'

He turned and smiled at us, me and Maggie, as he led the girl away. Just then, Aesop emerged from the warren, sated, a dead animal in his jaws.

Herb and Lizzie did not return, and soon Maggie decided it was time she too was included in the gossip. We parted in the farmyard, though the sun was still high. She sent me home to my hayloft and made her way up the hill to the farmhouse, carrying Aesop in his little basket under one arm, and a sack of limp rabbits in the other. I am waiting, now, for her to come to me, but it is late, and my lamp is burning low.

Tam

IT'S THE NEXT EVENING, AND my housemates are all assembled in the front room. There is cumbia clapping and shimmying from the sound system. Antonia is burning incense on the bookshelf again, Lara making a point of grimacing and waving a hand whenever the scent wafts her way. Vicky is sitting on the kitchen island next to a stack of junk mail, eating peanut butter from the jar with a teaspoon, and Varsha and Heath are both stretched out on the corner sofa, tucking into a bag of vegetable crisps.

Varsha looks up as I enter. Tam, I didn't see you yesterday.

Oh, yeah. I went to bed early.

How's your family?

Everyone staring, listening. I'm bad at this, at being the centre of attention, at broadcasting to a group when the situation is sensitive and you really should be tailoring the story differently to each individual.

I dunno, I shrug, pouring myself a glass of water, buying time. Maybe I need to be more patient.

What does that mean? says Vicky.

I hesitate. She thinks Dad's a total monster. They all do. And I don't need to go down that route, so I say I've got to run; I'm meant to be meeting an amorous stranger for a drink. Then I turn to go, even though it's the last thing I want to be doing, leaving the consolation of my friends and the warmth of a house that's full of life, and venturing out on my own.

Soon, I find myself taking a seat at a booth in the corner of the diner-style bar Rohan has chosen, listening carefully as he tells me why his car's at the garage, about an altercation he had with another driver, and all the reasons he was technically right and the other driver was technically wrong. He has a broad, endearing smile, but he doesn't look much like his pictures, which I suspect were taken a good while ago. Maybe I just want Luke. I order sauvignon blanc, gulp it back too fast, then request the rest of the bottle. Rohan has a pint, but he's talking so much that he's barely touched it. His cologne is strong – not a bad scent, but it's changing the way my wine tastes.

You're a cutie, he says suddenly, brushing my hand with his.

I can feel my face growing warm, and I genuinely don't know if I'm hot for him or just get off on flattery. Thanks…

I love guys like you. Small. Bit girly. You sub?

Like we're on a call with bad signal, it takes me a moment to react, and then all I manage is a thin laugh. I excuse myself to powder my nose. Once I'm alone, I stand in front of the mirror under the off-colour lights and try to connect with myself. I don't know what I'm feeling, but it's not fair on Rohan, the way I can't stop longing for Luke, the validation of his beauty. My mouth is turned down, and I look drawn and tired. I touch up my make-up and force myself to smile, widely, like a fool. Then I drop the act when the door swings open, startling me, and a man comes in and enters a cubicle. I return my lip gloss to my bag and busy myself with my phone.

Varsha's checking up on me, so I confess that Rohan's not what I expected. From behind me comes the sound of a bolt of piss striking toilet water.

Send me his photos, she says. Sounds like he's used a filter.

He's nice enough, I protest, though I obediently forward his pics. I should give him a chance.

Leave, she says. Look at those photos! He's a fucking android.

I can't just leave, I reply, confounded. How could anyone survive the awkwardness of cutting short a date? Impossible.

Noo, you amateur! :P Don't make me come down there.

There's a flush, and then the man re-emerges from the cubicle. He shoots me a quick, almost curious look, still standing there with my phone, but then he starts washing his hands and keeps his eyes on his own business. I realise I'm hardly breathing; it's never comfortable being in the Gents with a painted face.

Varsha follows up with a longer message. **Seriously, I was heading out anyway, d'you want me to come and save you? Ffs, if you don't fancy him it's worse to string him along. Just sneak out.**

The man exits and I'm alone again, though beginning to worry that I've been in here a tad too long.

I reread Varsha's suggestion. I shouldn't sneak out, should I? I can't blame him for wanting to hide his reality when society is so punishingly judgemental. But then, I suppose some people would condemn him for not taking responsibility, for not accepting himself and his lot in life. Isn't he just out for what he can get? Hoping he can manipulate people into meeting him, and then relying on their suggestibility to get what he wants?

I return to our booth, where he's sipping his pint and looking a bit lost. He really isn't much like his pictures at all. He's looser, lined, and dark around the eyes. But he smiles when he sees me, and I sure as hell don't look my best today, and anyway it's not his fault we're all image-obsessed. Maybe I need to take a little longer to see if our personalities are a match.

Sorry, I say.

It's fine.

I sit down, and he launches himself back into the conversation, and only then do I realise how difficult it would be to get away from a man this garrulous, even if I had Varsha's confidence. And he did say he liked me because I'm small and girly, and ask me if I'm a sub… Am I just a pushover?

He fills up my glass, winking. So, what do you think a financial consultant does, then?

What's behind this, the way he frames everything as a question?

Whatever I reply, he tries to put himself above me, taking control of my answer.

If you could go anywhere in the world, he asks, where would you want to go?

I don't know, actually. Maybe Paris… for Fashion Week.

Nah. Not Fashion Week: it's busy enough as it is. But I could show you a good time in Paris. I'd take you off the beaten track, I can promise you that.

I stifle a yawn, beginning to flag. If nothing else, he cares what I think of him. He's trying to impress me, and he draws attention to the things he's self-conscious about, like he's anticipating criticism and trying to neutralise it before it comes.

I had to take some time off the gym, he explains, because I've taken on more responsibility at work. So I'm actually bulking right now.

I frown and sip my wine. That's cool.

I could puff up and refuse to grant him any power, but he's practically vibrating with insecurity – some other version of me. So I find myself rolling over. I try to show him the kindness I would want to receive, even as the date goes from bad to worse.

Embarrassingly I've never set foot in a gym, I say.

It'll be another story when I cut. Trust me. I could wreck you.

I don't reply. I'm wondering about people like this, who seem highly defended to the point of being aggressive. What traumas are they nursing? I am preoccupied with the growing realisation that I need to let Rohan down – if I'm right that he wants me – without causing more hurt, and without provoking him to take his pain out on me.

We get up, and he touches my arm and thinks aloud about our next move, seemingly keen to keep things going.

I'm really tired, I say. I think I need to go home and go to bed, to be honest.

The subtext cuts through. He starts to flinch, but then pulls his face under control. He clears his throat, momentarily stuttering and inarticulate. No, I-I-I actually said I'd meet my mate, anyway, and they just texted to say they're out. I didn't want to let you down though.

Not at all.

We step out onto the pavement, and there's a faint, fine rain falling on the warm ground. Petrichor rises pleasantly around us as I initiate a hug, to which Rohan responds stiffly. There's a scream of laughter from the karaoke bar across the road, and I'm always paranoid that I've done something wrong, that I'm the object of derision. Rohan is already off, barely saying goodbye, and immediately I regret the friendly hug, just in case I've wounded him with my magnanimity. He disappears into the streams of people crossing between the slow-moving traffic – the Ubers and the towering red buses – and just like that it's as if our meeting never happened, and I'm anonymous once again.

It's humid on the bus, and I am already sticky as I take the seat nearest the driver. I do this for protection, too uncomfortable to brave the top deck alone. I flick through social media on my phone, feeling strangely like a shoe I've worn my whole life is suddenly on the other foot. From the back of the bus comes a loud gabble of Spanish. It's an older woman, and something about her tone – proprietary and direct – suggests she's talking to someone she knows intimately, probably a family member. She has a jagged manner, unlikely something that she chose, rather the shape she eroded into over time.

I open the app. Rohan is online too. Maybe he's searching for his next match, or maybe he's lusting after me, or maybe he's just killing time. And then he's gone.

Must have blocked me.

I begin to type Luke's name. His profile picture appears, a tiny window into the past. I wilfully put my phone away.

The modern mating ritual is a digital exchange of words and images, empty promises whispered through the screen, nudes designed to make your body react even after your mind has started to lose interest. This is a marketplace, transactional and goal-orientated. Totting up scores: acquisitions, rejections. And it's even harder for us enbies, easy targets for other angry queer people, who are looking to negotiate their pain by defining themselves against their own kind. They are more acceptable than we are – they fit in better – and it's the most powerful they've ever felt, talking down to us.

But you don't need to empower yourself by oppressing others, by subjecting them to the same censure you suffered. Just as parents don't need to be their kids' first bullies, their children – all grown up – don't have to pass that pain on.

I enter the kitchen, rubbing my eyes. Vicky is sitting with her girlfriend, Pippa, on the sofa, eating crème caramels from little ramekins. They're half-watching a cheap true-crime documentary about women who kill, the screen casting its ghostly light across their faces as they turn to me.

Home so soon?

And suddenly my voice is gone, trapped somewhere in my chest. My throat is burning. It's embarrassing, overflowing like this, catching myself by surprise.

Tam?

Vicky has jumped up to comfort me, Pippa right behind her. And I am trying to laugh it off like I'm not about to cry for no reason in the middle of the kitchen in front of friends I'm still in the process of making.

Hey, say the women, as their outstretched arms encircle me. Hey, it's OK!

No, no, I sniff, earnestly. I feel good, really. I feel fine.

I know, says Vicky, tutting, patting me on my shoulders. I know.

George

IT RAINS ALL WEEK, BUT the work goes on. As the mud climbs our boots, we all grumble over the summer weather. The safest problem to discuss. One morning, I'm greeted by Sandra tramping across the garden, swearing. A fox has got into the chicken coop and killed one of her prized Orpingtons. It has left the severed head, its favourite calling card. Black feathers have floated through the little gaps in the chicken wire. How many times have we been here? A farmer's déjà vu.

I discover how the bastard got inside. The fence is well-fortified, buried a good ten inches. The wire curls outwards at the base to provide an additional barrier. But one of the wooden posts at the back of the coop, nestled into an overgrown cherry laurel and ensnared by Irish ivy, has become rotten and soft. Loosened the edge of the wire mesh. All the fox needed to do was peel it back, like stepping behind a curtain. I find myself apologising to the chickens out loud. Custodianship is in large part a matter of protection. I have failed in my duty.

Elder Son and I are at each other's throats today. He follows me into the farm office. I turn my back on him, wipe oil off my hands with a dirt rag. I have been trying to fix Mike's old Fowler again.

We don't need the Fowler, he says. It's a waste of time.

It's a good, honest machine, Harry.

It's just old-fashioned.

He keeps pushing me. I try to keep the anger off my face. I realise Elder Son had to step up while my arm was bound, and in fact had wanted this for a long time. But the authority has gone to his head.

We should get rid of it, he is saying. You know we should. If you're lucky, there'll be a collector who's interested. Or maybe a museum.

We have decided to go to the livestock market and sell two of our cows. This is supposed to take the pressure off, but it has done nothing for our moods. We select Daisy and Cowlick, who are grateful for the attention. As we soap and pamper and prepare them for a grand presentation, we prepare ourselves to say goodbye.

The market, a hangar-like warehouse, is bustling, full of cool, muted farm smells. Here, we are among our own kind. A sea of fleeces, flat caps and shirtsleeves, greying hair and ageing faces. Overworked, dragging ourselves through the day because there's really no other option now, is there?

We exhibit Daisy and Cowlick in a pen near the entrance. I am relieved when the bids start coming in. We fetch a good price for the pair.

We are on our way out, cowless, but with some newfound breathing space, when we come across Poppy Simons. A straw-haired woman with a toothy smile and a swollen red nose, she used to own the Grange Farm on the other side of the village. We fell out of touch when she moved away about ten years ago. Just far enough that we stopped seeing each other around, trying to pass on little country lanes.

George! And this isn't your Harry?

She hasn't heard about our recent troubles, so I don't go into them. Her finger has never been on the pulse, she admits, but word of a new initiative by LivestockAid has been spreading through the market all day, and it's our turn to hear about it.

They are planning to share an interactive map, publicising the locations of every dairy farm in the country, in the hopes that their followers nationwide will help expose the so-called animal rights violations happening in their local areas.

They're calling it *Take Stock*. Have you ever heard anything so ridiculous?

I'm not as alarmed as she's expecting. Alderdown's been on the map, so to speak, for a while now. There is no panic left in me. Besides, where were my colleagues when the video went viral? Probably avoiding us. I am almost reassured that none of this was ever truly about Alderdown. Dairy is the enemy, full stop.

I wouldn't worry, I say. That can't be legal. I'm sure it will get shut down.

No, no, she says, and she beckons over another woman, whose short hair and shoulders are damp; it must be raining again. Hel, says Poppy, what were you just telling me about LivestockAid and the FSA?

Oh, just that the data is all publicly available, yeah, through Food Standards.

Poppy turns back to me, aghast. So, you see, it's all technically legal!

Afraid so, Hel continues. The site is really just a spreadsheet overlaid onto Google Maps.

That's not good, I concede. But breaking and entering is still a crime, at least as far as I'm aware!

I try to make my getaway. Point towards Harry, who's gone to greet another farmer. It's Joe, the older brother of one of his friends from sixth-form college, who runs the flourishing Cedar Dairy and Creamery over the river, on the town-side.

Better be off, I mouth, as Hel and Poppy chew the fat.

Sadly, I don't think people like this care much about the law, says Poppy.

Yeah, says Hel. And I think they want to replicate their stunt at Alderdown.

Poppy glances at me, recognising the name of my farm. I don't stop to indulge her. I grasp my hip as I approach the lads, trying not to limp.

Listen to this, Dad, says Harry, excitedly.

Joe, dressed in an expensive tracksuit, his teeth all veneered and pearly white, starts telling me about his latest venture. Last year, he sold one of his historic buildings to a woman who's converting it into a bed and breakfast. Then he used the capital to invest in some new technology, a state-of-the-art milking robot, which doesn't need farmer supervision to run. I've never heard of such a thing.

How's that work then? I ask, irritably.

He tells me that the robot operates in a booth at the end of the cowshed. The cows are coaxed in with food, but they soon start to associate the booth with the pleasant relief of an empty udder. They begin to take themselves in willingly, as needed. The milker, available twenty-four seven, stretches out its long, mechanical arm and attaches itself. Then it stores data in the cows' collars, which the robot can recognise, and the farmer can access from his computer.

Bloody brilliant, says Elder Son. What did I tell you, Dad? It's all about data these days.

I am quiet for a second. We need to nip this hare-brained idea in the bud. Farming with robots seems like a sort of race-to-the-bottom scenario. The animals can only lose out. I am suddenly uneasy to be here, at this market, where it is undeniable that our cattle is chattel. Mere possessions, exchanged for their economic worth. I know I am a hypocrite. We are numb to it, all of us. But there are limits we must respect. I step up to defend the old ways.

That's all very well, I say, loftily. But I don't think cows should be confined to the shed all year round.

They're not, though, says Joe, grinning. They get access to the fields as long as they've been milked recently. That's what the collars are for. Tracking.

Man, we've got to look into this, says Harry.

I wait until we're back in the truck before trying to talk him down. He is driving.

238

What do you think, Dad? he says, not watching the road enough for my liking. That robot could solve a lot of our problems.

I scoff. How is a bloody robot milker going to solve our problems, Harry, when we're under scrutiny for the way we treat our animals?

Well…

For god's sake, I say, thinking of Mike, of my father. You have to be realistic: these new-fangled methods, they're inhuman. They're taking things in completely the wrong direction. It's not natural. People want their dairy farms to be natural!

What do you mean? We already milk with a machine. This one would put the cows in control of the process, and we would get so much more time for other things. You wouldn't need to work so much…

Personally *I* don't mind hard work.

Harry glares, but wilfully ignores the implication. And the cows would be more relaxed, he says. They're less stressed, apparently. Live longer. And if we can't turn this business around, Dad – I don't know if you've noticed – that will be it! Done. There's only so much more we can do.

And you think this robot is the answer? Then by all means….

A relaxed herd is a profitable herd…

Even if we could afford it…

…and we need to find a way to make more money, before…

Harry. I slam the dashboard with my hand. That's it. End of discussion.

You can't do that. You can't just tell us what to think.

I reel at that 'us', which definitely includes his brother.

As long as I'm here, I say, I'm still the boss. This is my farm, my parents' farm, and it's my job to keep us on the right path. All right?

I instantly regret this outburst. I am channelling my father, but it's not just my farm. It belongs to all of us. It's ours. And I am the boss only because I am afraid Elder Son continues to need the wisdom and support of a mentor. Except that is not what I am giving him. I am crumbling at the hip, just barely hanging on. We trundle home in anxious silence.

24 September, 1944

IF ANYBODY IS READING THIS, if it is to become evidence, I will state the truth in no uncertain terms.

The Nicholsons' accusation that Margaret Edwards and I have conducted an illegal affair and should be prosecuted for fraternisation is baseless. Their claims that we have wilfully broken the law, meeting for anything other than farm work and the occasional harmless conversation, are all false.

While we have spent time together, as this book will show, our relationship is one of friendly colleagues. Our connection is what one would expect of any two people who have worked side by side for over a year. If we cannot work together without our relationship being wilfully and pruriently corrupted, then I am pessimistic about the future of the modern world.

I appreciate both my debts and my privileges, living and working as a prisoner of war in this country, and will continue to serve my sentence with honour and integrity for as long as my destiny remains out of my own hands, and hanging in the balance.

As a final remark, I should say that Maggie has recently become engaged to Jim Calvert of Sloeberry Farm. I wish the happy couple nothing but the best.

Tam

THE ATRIUM AT SNOWBALLED IS cavernous, with its shopfront windows and sun-bleached floorboards. But somehow it feels homely too; there's always someone making use of the drinks machine, and the air is sweet with coffee beans and chattering voices. The vast ground-level space is open plan, housing the reception desk, a comfortable seating area for visitors with some reading material that's mostly for show, a pool table, and two long tables with benches for meetings, breakfast, and Friday lunch – one of our many perks.

We take our seats and the food is brought to us, table service. Today the menu is lentil and sweet potato cottage pie, stodgy and comforting, and a chocolate tart for pudding. There are ice buckets filled with wine and lager. We pass them down the tables with wet hands. Normally all the teams have to mix, and I was nervous about this at first. But it's a special occasion today, and we sit wherever we like.

Simon and I are being made permanent Ballers. Reece, the Head of Planning, gifts us bottles of champagne and cards of congratulations. *Every snowball starts with a single snowflake...* There's a round of applause. I've worked with him recently on a campaign about reducing plastic packaging, an initiative of which the public is overwhelmingly supportive, and he is singing my praises, says he can't speak highly enough of the appendices I put together for the master deck. I lower my eyes and blush. Another round of applause.

We stay downstairs after lunch, and keep drinking. Only a few take the lift back up to their desks – deadlines – the rest of us helping ourselves to the remaining booze. I can't believe we're doing this on company time, but the bosses are all here, raising their glasses with the rest of us. Reece is fetching more wine from the back.

I'm listening to Simon recount all the myriad ways he's fallen off his bike when Fraser, a Campaign Director in his mid-thirties, asks me to chuck him a beer. I look at him, blankly. He terrifies me, the kind of guy who treated me like shit growing up, because he is so perfect and normal. Not that Snowballed, where the food is vegan and we all have our pronouns in our email signatures, is the natural habitat for someone like him: a tall, loud, deep-voiced rah with a rugby build. Bit of a dad bod, but you can tell he took it all seriously back in the day. We haven't had to spend much time together yet, and I already get the feeling he thinks I'm an idiot.

Tam? he says.

I still haven't got him that beer. I hurry over to the ice bucket like a pet playing fetch, then bring him a dripping bottle with intense concentration, trying hard not to trip over my own feet.

Where was I? says Simon.

I think you were on your arse, says Reece, in the middle of the road outside Pizza Hut.

Then we're getting ready to go out, and when I stand up I find the room is softly spinning. I suppose we've been drinking for a few hours, and I can see my reflection in a purple screen that partitions the seating area from reception, my work make-up that's all about contouring and subtle refinements, the necklace and cream blouse and smart black jacket. And it looks like I'm moving in slow motion – out of time with the world, but in time with myself – and there's a silent shout of joy in my chest.

Tam, you're so fucking drunk, says Simon, taking my hand.

We go to the Sass, a gay bar just up the road, where we're greeted by bubble-gum pop and campy theatrics. I've never been in before; it looks like any other London pub from the street. But it's grotto-like inside, with fake foliage sprouting from the walls, a spangle of fairy lights, and velvet curtains draped where they have no utility. Simon strikes a pose in front of a series of poster-sized, black-and-white prints of muscular men in the nude, holding power tools, wearing helmets, wielding truncheons. Then we notice an incredible replica of Miss Piggy, standing in full diva ensemble back at the entrance, and rush to get selfies with her.

Fraser is at the bar with his lawyer wife, who's just arrived. He beckons us over and buys us drinks as a circle of laughing, pink-cheeked Ballers forms around us. I've always been cynical about work families, corporate mumbo-jumbo designed to distort a transaction in which you're simply meant to be selling your labour. But I am really feeling that famed sense of belonging, and I'm not gonna lie: it's actually quite nice.

More drinks, Aperol spritzes. My phone is wriggling in my pocket, and I have a feeling that a man sitting by the window is trying to get my attention with that fiery, insistent glare of his. But we're in the middle of a heated discussion on journalists. Whenever a press release goes out, they have to talk to the papers. There are evidently the favourites, those who will give stories the time and attention they deserve. And then there are the other ones.

No, she's not listening, says one manager. What's the point in a call when she's not listening to a word you say?

Another adds: Well, I get her to put the quote down in writing and send it back to me so I can rewrite it. You know, what I *actually* said.

My head is swimming, but there was that one journalist I met a few weeks back – that editor we sat with at the long tables over coffee. We went over our campaign line-up for the year, and it was my job to take notes. At the bottom of the page, I remember I wrote 'hates wind energy – property values'.

So I pipe up: We met with Horace Trotwell the other morning and decided he's a total no-go for our wind energy campaign. Said it's ugly, bad for house prices.

Of course, Fraser mutters.

And some weird stuff about wind farms causing cancer.

Oh, what a fucking dickhead.

I nod, swirling my drink and slurring. Yeah, but you can't blame him hating the wind. With that toupee.

There's a pause. Then Fraser roars with laughter and clinks his glass against mine. Amazing, mate. You're all right.

Soon, we are all dancing, and life just gets better and better. Tonight is about more than the job offer; this is the best I have felt, the most relaxed in my whole life. Fraser cheers and lifts me up, into the air, and then I am crowd-surfing, and his wife is telling him off because it's dangerous. But I am already being lowered safely to my feet, light and laughing. Simon helps steady me. And I look up. And the night is still young.

George

A COUPLE OF EVENINGS LATER, SANDRA has arranged a video call with Tom. She says she doesn't know what we're supposed to do, but we've a better chance of moving forward if we actually talk to each other. I am quietly grateful to Younger Son for agreeing to these little opportunities to reach him. I am quietly furious, too.

The cows know that autumn is on its way. They begin to crowd at the east of the meadow, where the ground rises towards the orchard, and our mature Bramley apple trees are fruiting. They wait expectantly for falling treats, watch them swell and ripen on the branches. Swallows gather on the powerlines criss-crossing the fields, ready for their long flight south. I am unsettled by these reminders of the turning seasons. Not enough progress this year.

I wave goodbye to Elder Son. So like Mike, standing there, static as a scarecrow by the main gate. He's been keeping his distance ever since we argued. I head back towards the farmhouse, Dusty at my heel, and chide myself for driving him away. He is the future of Alderdown, this place that's in our blood. If he decided to give it up – as I once did, after one too many quarrels with Pa – then I will have failed.

Sandra has made beef bourguignon. We sit and eat together at the kitchen table. The sunlight is bright like it's the middle of the day. We keep the windows and the back door open to let some fresh air in. Sandra scarcely touches her food, pushes it around her plate with a trembling hand. I struggle to comfort her – I am nervous too – but I find her foot with mine under the table.

Your sock's damp, she says.

We revert to form, talk of the comfortable nothings we share. Trivial accidents like broken crockery, encounters with friends in the village shop. We are calmed by each other's voices, the familiar faces we pull. I am pleased when Sandra starts to eat. For the first time in months, I feel like her husband again.

I wash up, then we sit side by side on the sofa. Dusty between us, both of us comforting our fingers in her fur. The screen is propped up on a pile of books in the middle of the coffee table. Sandra takes a deep breath.

Are we ready to listen? she says.

I nod, dutifully.

He has to listen to us too, she continues. If he wants us to understand him, he has to try and understand us. It has to go both ways.

Let's just see how this goes, I say.

I realise we never once discussed what our approach to parenting would be, a pattern set in the early days of our family. When Sandra was first pregnant, with Elder Son, she'd put her feet in my lap and talk in excitable bursts. About all the things we would need to buy, the colours she wanted to paint the baby's room: blue for a boy, and yellow, rather than pink, for a girl. I massaged her feet, small and soft, and thought through my calculations. I enjoyed knowing that I could afford to keep us, back then, when Mike was running things, and the family farm symbolised a financial security I'd never been able to sustain on my own.

Tom is calling us. Sandra leans forward to answer. And then he's there, sitting on a bed, leaning against a blank white wall. He's taken the nose ring out. His long hair is pulled back into a ponytail. The camera obscures much of the detail of his make-up.

Hello, darling, says Sandra, tightly composed. I'm sorry it's been so long. It's so good to see you. How are you, darling? Are you keeping well? You look well.

I'm good. How are you guys?

Oh, you know. Sandra smiles and nods at me, as if we are sharing some private joke.

Plodding on, I add, stiffly.

How are Harry and Lauren? asks Tom.

Not bad. Harry and I have been doing silage for the winter. Just keeping on top of things.

And Gran?

I hesitate, trying to put my feelings about my mother and the Lodge into words. Sandra swoops in.

We've been popping in to see her most days, she says, and we like to have her here at the weekends, at least while we can.

That's good.

Yes, she's definitely seeming more settled. Wouldn't you say, George?

I wouldn't, so I keep quiet.

Maybe you'll come *home* soon – Sandra places undue emphasis on the word – and spend some time with her? I'm sure it would do her good to see you. You were always her favourite.

Tom narrows his eyes. Oh, so you wouldn't mind me seeing her, then?

What've you been up to? I interject. How's the new job?

Actually, he announces, there is something I wanted to tell you.

I nod, steeling myself. I try to be like my endlessly patient mother.

Do you remember Friedrich Becker, that German guy who was emailing a few months back?

Sandra and I exchange a look: where is this going?

Oh, she says, yes.

He wanted a tour of the farm, I remember.

Yeah, says Tom. Well, we met up the other day, and what he told me was just… Totally unbelievable, honestly. His grandfather wasn't just a prisoner of war here. There's so much more to it than that.

What do you mean?

248

He was... I don't know how much to...

He looks like he's searching for words.

It's a lot, Dad, he says. He was... a part of the family.

I think that often happened with prisoners of war, says Sandra. Especially once they were put to work.

He said he's tried to reach you, but you haven't responded to his emails.

That's my fault, says Sandra. I just haven't had the headspace recently.

Well, I really think you should meet him. He's only in the UK for the summer. I think... You should hear it all from him.

So I say we'll get in touch. I'm interested if he can tell me more about the farm and its history.

Maybe your gran can get involved, I add. See if we can stir up some memories.

That would be something, he says.

And... *Tam* – I force the name out. Younger Son can't stop himself from smiling – It's nice to hear you're taking an interest in Alderdown, and the family history.

Tom looks up at the sound of his bedroom door opening. A woman's voice says, Babe, you eating with us?

Then she jolts into frame, dropping down beside him.

Oh, hey, she grins. Are these your folks?

Yeah. George and Sandra. And this is Varsha.

We greet her shyly. The slight delay on the call is amplified by our uncertainty, but Varsha seems to be a sunny, energetic character.

Thank you for taking care of him, says Sandra.

Nah, laughs Varsha. *They* take care of us. Literally, Tam does all the bills and everything.

She pokes him with her elbow.

You even cleaned the other day.

Oi! he protests. You make it sound like it was the first and only time.

I'm kidding, she says, smiling into the camera. We all love Tam. You raised them well.

I chuckle. That's very kind of you.

We're quite fond of him too, mumbles Sandra.

Hey, says Varsha. We were actually just talking about Take Stock. Are you guys OK?

We're fine, says Sandra, waving a hand. Thanks so much for asking.

It's a big statement, isn't it? says Varsha. People really want things to change, and they're determined for you to hear them.

Tom is studying his fingernails. I want to demonstrate to him that we can be fair and clear-headed about the whole thing.

Definitely, I say. But I think I just feel sorry for them, to be quite honest with you. They're fighting a losing battle. These stunts just undermine their message. All they're going to have achieved if people start trespassing all over farms is a lot of spooked cows. They'll traumatise the animals they claim to love so much.

Anyway, says Tom.

What upsets me the most, Sandra shares, is the fact that these are home addresses. They're not just businesses, or places of work. Children live there. It's wrong.

Do you think children are more vulnerable than animals, then? asks Varsha.

Sandra laughs, shocked. Varsha glares at us, almost unblinking. We had both assumed we were talking to a sympathetic ear. But Varsha is one of them. Of course.

I clear my throat.

Let me tell you a story, I say, trying to keep my anger under control. My younger brother, Mike, loved animals more than anything. He could win the heart of the most stubborn bull. He'd have the damn things eating out of his hands. He lived and worked here his whole life, hardly took a day off. He was married to the herd, never had a wife – or even a girlfriend. He knew everything there was to know, more knowledgeable than any vet, and when he went to bed every night he'd be reading books about animal behaviour, cramming his head with even more information. He loved his cows that much. We used to joke and say he was the cow-whisperer.

Tom shifts awkwardly. Varsha just listens, her eyebrows raised.

A few days after his fiftieth birthday, I continue, he went out as usual, and opened a gate to let the cows cross from one field into the next one over. He knew what he was doing, my brother, and the cows knew him. Mutual trust, that's what they had. Only I found him later, and not in the gap between the fields. No, he was lying in a heap at the foot of the stone wall, a few metres to the side of the gate. He was covered in mud, not moving. He had been crushed against that wall and trampled to death. All but four of his ribs were broken, and part of his spine was shattered. The internal injuries he'd suffered were so horrific, they couldn't pinpoint exactly what had killed him.

I'm really sorry, says Varsha. But I don't see how that changes anything.

You don't?

Varsha just stares at me.

Life isn't some fairytale, I say, where things are all good or all bad.

I turn to Sandra. She is looking away, her face wan and twisted. She is humiliated. I take her hand.

I think we're going to go, says Tom, quietly. I think we should go.

27 September, 1944

I WAS TOLD TO KEEP TO myself, to stay in the hayloft. I hoped we were just biding our time, waiting for the crisis to ease. But a part of me knew it had become too serious for that.

In absolute darkness, I felt my way down the ladder to the dusty, straw-covered ground, and turned myself upside down. There, on my head, I did standing push-ups against the wall. My temples pulsed with blood, warding off my nightmares, until I collapsed. The barn filled with the sound of bombers, and I awoke with streaming eyes.

Nobody brought me my rations. On a normal day, I would go up to the farmhouse to collect them, and sometimes Mary would stand in the doorway of the kitchen and chat to me, while Lizzie sang and shouted behind her, trying to get my attention. I could not consider such things without a sinking feeling of emptiness and dread.

As the time passed, and hours turned to days – three in total – I was even afraid to venture up to the privy, so instead crept deep into the tangled prickles behind the shed to do my business.

My hayloft has never before felt like a cell, but everything has changed, and all too fast.

I ought to burn you, little book.

Early this morning, when I was half-awake and lying in a daze, there was a knock on the barn door. As it opened, a mouse scuttled over my legs, across the ground and into the hay bales.

I scrambled to my feet, my limbs stiff and painful, to see Herb enter. He looked pale and tired, but spoke to me with his usual gentleness.

'I'm sorry we've left you to yourself for so long.'

'Don't apologise. It's fine.'

'The past few days have not been easy.'

'If there's anything I can do…'

He shook his head, and I fell silent.

'I did worry, for a time,' he admitted, not meeting my eyes. 'But I never thought it would come to this. In a way, I blame myself. I'm the farmer, the man of the house. I'm supposed to guide and protect.'

Then he told me the news that had sealed my fate.

Maggie is expecting. She has seen the doctor, who has confirmed her condition.

I could not grasp this.

'Can I speak to her?'

I don't know what I would have said.

'What good could that do?' Herb said, somehow faraway. 'What possible good could that do now?'

In my anger and desperation, I wanted to plough past him. I wanted to tell Maggie it was a mistake, this arrangement with Jim. It was madness.

'They will be married before Christmas,' said Herb.

A rush to dignity. Maggie, I am sorry.

I cannot imagine her without her country wear, walking down the aisle in a pretty white dress. Lifting it up over the wellington boots she has worn so often that they have made permanent marks in the skin below her knees.

I will not say what happened when I was left alone again to ponder the future, except that I had another visitor, who came to do me harm.

I'm afraid I was the mightier adversary – my nocturnal compulsion to exercise standing me in good stead – and, looking down upon my humiliated assailant, lying there in the dust, I wondered if I had just landed myself in ever greater danger.

Afterwards, I awaited the consequences. I sat, contemplating the barn doors, creaking in the breeze, a fearsome blade of light opening and closing between them. I was guilty only of defending myself in the heat of the moment, of simply reacting. But I doubted that defence would be enough, all things considered.

In the end, he did not come for me again. I believe his pride hides a craven heart, and perhaps admitting to this defeat might sully the victory of my expulsion. I am grateful, for I suffer the same keen shame. Let there be no witnesses.

Tam

VARSHA'S NOT HERSELF. SHE'S BEEN out all day, and when she gets home, she's reluctant to join us. It's gone ten, and we're assembled in front of some TV show about mountaineering, and trying a new takeaway pizza with vegan cheese. She doesn't want any – the poison you lot put in your bodies! – but after a bit of badgering she takes a seat on the ratty deckchair next to the corner sofa. We're all watching the screen, but our bodies are angled in towards each other so that we can chat too. Varsha, though, is on the edge, turned to face the kitchen, sipping a pint of water through pursed lips, and tapping distractedly at her phone.

I scoot forwards and try to catch her eye. Is this because of the other day? After the video call with my parents, she called Dad a *fucking carnist*, and I guess I got a bit defensive. Because it's more complicated than we might realise, untangling centuries of culture and market forces, and it's easy for outsiders to criticise, but this has been my family's livelihood for generations. So she said I was being pretty patronising, to which I replied that I was sorry but it just seemed like she didn't want to see the nuance. She really laughed at that, and said, Anyway, Tam, if it's just a philosophical discussion, why are you getting so damn emotional about it? And then I told her she was being a dick.

I apologised straightaway, and she said it was fine, and we're OK. But maybe we're not.

There's a weight in the pit of my stomach. Varsha has been so good to me, and it's not her fault she doesn't care about my family like I do. I watch, wondering if the others, busy laughing, can feel

255

the broken link in our web of connectedness. Or maybe I'm being overly sensitive again, and whatever's happening with Varsha isn't a big deal, and absolutely nothing to do with me, in any case. But I'd know for sure if she'd just look at me.

And suddenly she does. Our eyes meet, and then she cuts me off with a jerk – like she's got a shock, or a crush has returned her lingering gaze. Her cheeks darken, and I have the sinking feeling that there's another difficult conversation ahead.

It's only when Heath and Jack go to bed, and Lara to the bathroom, that I get my chance to speak to her. She has already started tidying the room, stacking the pizza boxes. She refuses to look at me, and I have no doubt now that we have a real problem.

I mirror her, taking a blanket off the floor and folding it into a neat square. You OK?

Course, she says, keeping her eyes down. What's up?

I put the blanket in the crate we use as a coffee table, observing her anxious energy as she fidgets about the room.

Not much, I shrug. Did you have a good day?

She stops behind the kitchen island, where she's just turned on the taps. Leaving them running, she turns to look at me properly for the first time since getting home. Crosses and uncrosses her arms. Look, I don't know how to tell you this…

You can talk to me.

She sighs, and turns off the taps. I saw Luke earlier. I know you guys grew apart.

That's OK, I say, hesitantly. You and he are friends.

Tam, listen. He told me something, and it's none of my business. Like, I don't know why it would bother me, but I'm feeling super uncomfortable about it. So I'd rather just get it out in the open and then I can wash my hands of it.

I perch at the end of the sofa, cold fear stirring my gut. OK. What's going on?

LivestockAid is on the move again. They've got a new plan. At Alderdown.

I sit up straight, my hands on my knees. Fists clenching, unclenching. What kind of plan?

I wasn't going to say anything. But I can't be in this house and see you every day and keep it to myself. Not after the other night, everything you said.

Oh god.

Are you going to tell them? Your family?

Tell them what, Varsha?

No, I want to know now. Before I do this.

There's an echoing gulf between us, like the room has grown huge and alienating, and I am alone with my choice. It would be easy to lose this newfound equilibrium, so hard-won. And obviously I respect LivestockAid and its mission, but I am also afraid for my family. Plus, there's the matter of making amends, and the terrible secret of what I did to them. If there's more danger coming to Alderdown Farm, aren't I making that betrayal worse if I don't tell them everything I can?

I don't know what I'm going to do, I say.

You might get me into trouble.

I understand.

But it's fine; do what you must.

I am starting to imagine a time when my parents really accept me. They're willing to do Zoom calls. They've invited me home. And Friedrich has made me see it all so differently, like Dad is just a man who was once a child. I don't know why I ever thought he could be anything else.

Look, I think I have to tell them. I don't have any other choice.

Varsha nods. I knew you were going to say that. Shit.

I'm sorry.

No, I'd do the same if it were my parents. For fuck's sake.

She comes and sits down beside me on the sofa, puts her hand on mine. And suddenly I realise we're not so far apart. She, too, is having to choose between her principles and protecting someone she cares about. She's looking at me now, into my eyes, and –

really seeing her – I smile, softly. Not with happiness, but with gratitude. She squeezes my hand and takes a deep breath, ready to begin.

George

PENNY, ONE OF OUR RADIANT reds, gives birth in the night. Harry and I find her first thing in the morning. She's standing with her calf in the middle of the cowshed, chewing lazily while her little one suckles. Gives us a look that seems to say, *What, this?* She's done it on her own time, days before we would have started to prod and hurry her.

Look at you, says Harry, like a proud parent. Clever girl.

She turns, leisurely. Strolls away, dragging her baby, who isn't done drinking, by the mouth.

Maybe we'll have an easy day, says Harry. I think we're due.

But my hip says otherwise. I have been standing for under an hour, and there are already beads of sweat on my brow. I struggle through milking as usual, sharing the task with Elder Son. But when it's time to release the herd into the fields, I run out of steam. Lean on a fence post for a second.

You coming? says Harry.

Just a minute.

What is it?

He leaves the cows to clump at the next gate, and walks over.

Dad?

I've just got a bit of pain.

Pain? Where?

In my hip.

You need to get that checked out. Might be serious.

It's fine. I'll be all right.

Don't be a martyr. I've seen you hobbling about. You're getting on, old man. There's no shame in it.

Cheeky sod.

I make it back to the farmhouse with the help of a stick from the last batch Tom gathered for us in the winter. I might be tearing something with every step that I take. The September sun is warm, but the cold wind is penetrating. I am two temperatures at once, utterly out of sorts.

It's not like you to complain, says Sandra, pulling out a chair for me in the kitchen. Does it really hurt that much?

I grit my teeth, suppressing a whine as I lower myself onto it. Sandra sits down beside me, puts a gentle hand on my knee.

You've gone grey, George. You need to see a doctor.

I've just recovered from my broken arm, I protest. I'm sure if I take it easy for a week or so, I'll be right as rain.

You're going to the doctor. It sounds like arthritis or something.

There's none of that in my family.

Sandra rolls her eyes. Trust you to be different. I'll get you an appointment.

As she makes the call, the light from the windows dims. Bars of shadow pass over the land, filling the kitchen with gloom. I am afraid for Harry. He has stepped up in the face of all our challenges. But there is too much work for him to take on alone, and we still aren't in a position to hire. I cannot afford to be out of action.

I am referred for an X-ray, which confirms that I need a hip replacement. Doctor Ibrahim scolds me. Soldiering on will have only accelerated the damage. I potter about, preferring to stand than sit or lie down. I hanker after fresh air and a pretence of normality. Somehow, hearing words like *inflammation* and *osteoarthritis* has made the pain even worse. This morning Sandra had to step in when I couldn't put my boots on. Tying my laces while I cursed in frustration.

Now it is evening. I stand by the gate and look out over the meadows. They have been grazed clean over the past few months. Penny joins me there, pushing her head out. She cries over her lost calf, already separated. Poor girl. It is a cruel world, but the hours become days become years. They distance us from our pain. She allows me to stroke her, her eyes wide and shining with questions.

It is what it is, I whisper. What more can I say?

Then I wonder what's got into me, philosophising with a cow. Drag myself back to the house with the shuffling walk of a dying man.

A car pulls into the yard, a black Volkswagen I haven't seen before. My stomach knots. Leaning on my stick, I wish Elder Son was here. This is a version of myself I don't recognise. The wind picks up the dust, swirls it around the car as it edges to a stop next to the barn. There's a young man in the driver's seat. He unbuckles, starts to get out.

I release a long breath. Friedrich Becker said he would arrive around six o'clock.

George? he says, coming over to me with a tan rucksack slung over his shoulder.

Hello! I say, coming to my senses. You made it. Nice to meet you.

We shake hands. There is something familiar in his smile. The way he purses his lips, as if beginning to form words. He's shorter than me, his hairstyle buzzed, his face untidy, with a scratchy, tawny beard. He is a little twitchy. I am overly cheerful to put him at ease.

I point to the farmhouse. Let's go up. You'll have to bear with me.

He looks at my stick, exaggerating his concern. What's happened?

I wish I had an interesting story. My hip has just gone. My age is catching up with me.

I'm sorry. I thought it might have been to do with the problems you've been having. Tam was saying you'd been injured.

We enter the garden, my hip rubbing as we go. It is strange how easily others can say the name Tam. I glance at Friedrich, checking for signs of mockery. But there are none. He breezes over the fact of Younger Son's identity crisis as if he's hardly noticed it.

My arm's all mended, I say.

Still, it sounds like it's been a bad time for all of you. I'm grateful that you've invited me here in spite of all of that.

It's no bother, I lie. Keeps us on our toes.

Well, all the same...

I'm looking forward to showing you around the farm and hearing your grandfather's stories. Fantastic to think that Alderdown made such an impact on him.

Oh yes, quite an impact. And Maggie lives here too?

Afraid not. Recent development.

When he doesn't reply, I glance at him. He's crestfallen, his mouth hanging open. Desolate, even – like someone has just died.

No, no, I say, quickly. She's at a care home down the road. The Lodge. You can meet her – I don't see why not – if you really want to.

I usher him into the house, through the utility room and into the kitchen. Sandra is already cooking.

Ah, hello! she says.

She wipes her hands on her apron and approaches our guest, greets him with a kiss on the cheek. We haven't entertained in a while, and there is a slight tension in the room. Sandra is a heightened version of herself.

Just *wonderful* to meet you, she says. Tom was so excited to talk to you.

Oh, yes?

Come through, come through.

Sandra leads us through the messy kitchen and into the sitting room. A plastic carton of olives, still sealed, and a bowl containing an opened family bag of crisps wait on the coffee table.

I didn't know what time you were getting here, she says. How was the drive down?

Oh, the country roads are so narrow and winding... But it is beautiful here.

I point to the sofa. Sit down, I say, gruffly, and Friedrich obliges. What can I get you to drink?

George, says my wife, crossly. You'd better get cleaned up.

I'm fine.

You're filthy.

Well. I roll my eyes at Friedrich, who isn't quite sitting back in his seat, looking between me and Sandra like he's struggling to follow an obscure bit of theatre. Best not to argue now, eh?

I leave Sandra to see to our guest and make my way up to our bathroom. I stand in the shower, allow the water to rinse me clean of the day. In its warmth, I forget the pain in my hip. I am energised by the thought of the evening ahead. A fascinating guest, some good conversation, a few glasses of wine.

I dress and head downstairs, fast as my body will allow. The phone is ringing in the kitchen. I pick it up, comfortable and fuzzy-headed.

Hello?

A choked voice says, Dad?

Younger Son.

What's happened? I say, immediately convinced that he's in trouble. I see him in an ambulance, or losing his job. Standing on a bridge somewhere above a breakneck drop.

Dad, this is going to sound crazy, but LivestockAid are coming.

What?

I heard through a friend, and I had to warn you. I'm so sorry, and...

Sandra and Friedrich enter from the sitting room, holding glasses of wine. Sandra is glowing, like she's just been laughing. The look fades as she listens to the conversation.

Slow down, I say. What do you mean LivestockAid is coming?

LivestockAid? Sandra mouths. I hold up a hand, signalling for her to wait.

They'll be there at nightfall to free all the animals, says Tom.

Nightfall. Are you sure?

They want to set an example to inspire their followers up and down the country to do the same thing. They'll be ready. It won't be a small group. They'll have equipment.

They can come here with bloody tanks, as far as I'm concerned. They're not getting near my animals.

I told you as soon as I was sure.

Yes, well done.

This isn't the way.

And you're one hundred per cent certain? How did you find out?

Friend of a friend. They're on their way. Dad, should I come down?

No, don't worry. I don't want you to be in harm's way.

I'm really sorry, Dad.

Why are you sorry? You've saved us, Tom. It's going to be all right.

I hang up, then explain the situation to my wife and our guest. I am tingling with anticipation. The enemy is coming, but we have the advantage. Sandra takes the phone from me and calls the police. Friedrich and I head back into the sitting room. I insist we not let this ruin our evening.

I had no idea it was still so serious, says Friedrich. Would you like me to leave?

What? I say, as if invasion is garden-variety fare for a dairy farm. Don't be daft, Friedrich. Not after you've come all this way.

Well, all right then.

He glances at the door, perhaps about to make a run for it. This is probably not the visit he had hoped for.

Why don't you go and get settled? Can you entertain yourself while we deal with this?

Of course.

We're having shepherd's pie for supper.

I shoot him a blank, sociable smile. Time is strange, I think. Here is the grandson of an old enemy turned friend. This is not the only war our farm has seen, nor the worst by far. I'm encouraged by the thought.

Sandra appears in the doorway.

A police officer is coming, she announces. Shouldn't be long.

Good, good.

Friedrich swings his bag onto his back, waiting to be seen to the guest room.

Please tell me at any point if you'd like me to leave, he presses.

Whatever for? I say – a stupefied cow, happily strung up for slaughter.

When I was a boy, my father made it clear that I was to fight my own battles. *Don't come crying to me.* So I would take a beating to get my ball back. Or better yet, dole one out and come home with bruised knuckles and my head held high.

But he wouldn't recognise the world we're living in now, where you can be prosecuted for trying to defend your own property. It is time to accept outside help.

I call Elder Son. He arrives with his wife, and he and I decide to go down to the farmyard together to wait for the police, keep watch for anything suspicious. Sandra wants to come too. But I persuade her that we need someone to hold the fort, and Harry promises to ring her with updates. So she and Lauren stay at the farmhouse, entertaining our German friend. They put on music and ask him about his life and work in Berlin, and we shut the door behind us on a disappointed Dusty, who always wants to follow us outside.

The cows are quiet, happily exhausted from a long day in the fields. There is an occasional rumble from the shed. But when I poke my head in, the girls are so settled that they hardly seem to notice me.

The yard is struck through with shadows by the time the police arrive. The low sun makes the concrete sparkle, the corrugated iron shining gold. It is dark earlier and earlier.

The cavalry approaches, a group of officers kitted out in riot gear, plus a pretty young woman, and a couple of smart policemen who wouldn't look out of place doing an office job. I have seen so much of the police this year, I am almost reassured by the sight of them. Things have changed since my youth, when I used to scoff at the *pigs*, chasing us out of our London digs in the middle of the night. Bunch of conformists, blanching at a whiff of ganja smoke. Booking petty criminals to reassure themselves of their questionable power.

The woman shakes my hand. Inspector Robson. I had been looking to one of her tall male colleagues as the senior officer, a mistake I try to cover by keenly deferring to her expertise.

Whatever you suggest. You're the expert, I inform her.

I suppose she is not so young, and I am just old. Harry treats her with immediate respect, the kind he never showed to his schoolteachers.

They'll probably come through the woods, then cross the fields to get here, he says. Rather than coming through the main gates.

Best we wait for them here by the cowshed, says Inspector Robson. No point hunting for them up and down all these little roads. They'll just give us excuses.

Are you going to arrest them?

We'll play it by ear.

Harry nods, looking disappointed.

Our main aim is to contain the problem, says the inspector. See that nobody gets hurt, and there's no damage to your property.

The riot gear? I say.

Just in case.

I leave Harry with the police. There are nine officers. It seems like overkill, but apparently it is proportionate to the expected number of intruders. We told them there were a good twenty when LivestockAid first showed up – and that was just to get a video.

I am hopping with nerves, hardly using my stick. I keep watch from the gate, look down the footpath into the fields. The intruders could easily climb the wall at the back of the cowshed. I don't want them to get that far before we head them off.

They appear in the dark like mould, black spots at the edge of the woods. My vision is grainy. But soon enough, they are an unmistakable line, jostling ever closer. I limp back to the yard.

They're here, I say, in a loud whisper. They're crossing the fields.

The officers decide to stay unseen until the intruders enter the yard through the gate. This is so the encounter happens with decent light and with the main entrance drive of the farm just to our right. That way the crowd can be controlled, dispersed onto the road rather than back into our fields.

It takes them a long time to arrive. I want to go back to the gate to check I wasn't just seeing things, but Inspector Robson stops me.

Eventually, we hear the faint wail of hinges.

The police form a line and close in, Harry and I following behind.

We pass just beyond the border of the floodlight, into black shadow, round the corner of our office off the milk storage unit. It is quiet but for the whirring of electrics. The trudging of feet. My breathing is shallow and misty.

Then there's a startled shout, and we are face to face with LivestockAid. It's a smaller group than I was expecting, around a dozen people. Luke is at the front, dressed in a magenta hoodie, a tool bag dangling lightly from his forearm.

Can I ask you what you're doing here? says the inspector.

Fuck, says a voice from the back of the group.

How did you...? says Luke.

You know this is private property. Please leave now, and go home.

All this for us? one of the activists says. They're all in on it, see.

The government too. They'll do anything to keep those animals enslaved.

No, Harry pipes up, you're just breaking the law.

A woman erupts from the crowd. Storms past Luke, right into the line of officers. It's the beanie-wearing vegan who first interrogated me at last year's open day.

Have you even looked, she says, at the conditions on this farm?

A constable seizes her, pulls her hands behind her back.

Don't you want to see what you're fighting for? she cries.

Easy, easy now, says the inspector.

Everyone stay calm, adds Luke, but his voice is shaking, and I want to laugh. We've finally got him.

I step forward. I can't stop myself.

Nice try, Mr Underwood, I gloat, one hand on my bad hip.

He blinks at me, moonlit and elegant and absurd. Someone told you?

Someone did. Because what you're doing is wrong, and most people are not on your side.

You're wrong! a woman shouts.

I ignore her, high on the thrill of winning. You're going to have to face the facts eventually.

Inspector Robson steps between us. But Luke moves to the side so that he can still see me. We've really got him. He is shaking with rage.

So, you gonna leave then, or what? says Harry.

There's a scuffle between another activist and the police. They are restraining two of them now. The rest of the flock are beginning to stray from their leader. Edging past him, sloping off in the direction of the road.

That's it, Harry rallies. Go. We've got the law on our side.

Thank you, says Inspector Robson, turning to the stream of retreating LivestockAiders, ushering them out. Please just go home. Nothing good will come of staying here tonight.

Off you go with the rest of them, I say to Luke. You've lost.

I've lost nothing, you old fool, he says, holding his ground, eyeing my stick. Every day, more and more people are coming round.

You keep saying that, like it justifies the way you go on. I know people are questioning things, shaking things up. Trends have always come and gone. Even my younger son is giving veganism a try. Experimenting. But that doesn't mean you should go on the warpath until everyone agrees with you. You know, it was your own allies that warned us you were coming; they told my son, and he stepped in, and he's the kind of person who could have sympathised with you.

Is that right?

It is. Something to think about. Maybe you should reconsider who you can trust. Sounds like you've been lied to, Luke.

I'm flattening him, surrounded by an army of my own. For the first time, his composure crumples.

You might want to get your own house in order, old man, he says. Your Tam is the one who got us here in the first place. They reached out of their own volition, gave us the guided tour, even unlocked the shed for us. We've got Tam to thank for our Alderdown video. Pretty successful campaign, that, and all down to you and your helpful family.

I almost fall, leaning on my stick, holding off his words. My throat locks tight.

Luke's teeth flash. But no, you're right, the world is on *your* side, and you're undoubtedly on the right side of history, too. How could anybody disagree with you, you old charmer? You miserable old bastard? Maybe that's a question you need to take away with you. Could try asking Tam.

He heads for the lane, and I only watch him go. The farm throbs like an injured beast. A great roaring in my ears.

Harry comes back from the fields, where he's just shut the gates. He is smiling at a job well done.

Hey, he says, his voice slack and happy. Dad, what was all that about?

*

I tell them what Luke just told me. Sandra is washing up. She drops a glass in the sink, smashing it. Then she turns with suds up to her elbows and plopping onto the kitchen floor. Friedrich is in the sitting room with Lauren, who comes and stands in the doorway. Harry goes and whispers to her, and she lifts her hands to cover her mouth. Sandra dials Tom's number, then presses the phone between our heads. Our ears conjoin us as we suffer together – as parents, as one animal.

When Tom answers, his voice is bright but thin. Hello?

We speak over him, over each other. Tom, you... you...

How could you do this to us? says Sandra.

What's happening? he says, and I wonder how many times he's pulled this act, this bare-faced lie.

What's happening! I echo. You're the one who bloody brought them here. LivestockAid.

What were you thinking? Sandra cries. That Luke, that horrible man.

You let them in and then you lied to us. For months. Must have been a right laugh, eh?

Tom has realised. He lets out a shrill plea. It wasn't like that. I was humiliated and scared. I thought we could...

We don't want to hear it, I say, coldly, forcefully. Don't you dare play the victim. You can't manipulate your way out of this one. Making out that you're so hard done by. Nobody understands. And all the time, this is what you've been doing. You must really despise us.

Were we such bad parents? says Sandra.

Tom's voice is tiny. I'm so sorry.

Are you? I say. Sorry you got caught.

I never planned for this to happen. I just wanted you to listen...

I don't care what you wanted, I yell. This is our business, Tom. Our family business!

Our lives! says Sandra.

You can run away and turn your back on us and start again, but this is how we live, how we survive. I can't tell you how… It's like you've taken a knife to us, Tom.

Please, he says. Can I come home?

I don't want to see you.

But I need to explain…

You know, says Sandra, her voice shaking, we would have got there with everything else. I don't think there was anything we wouldn't have been able to overcome.

Mum…

I feel like you've broken my heart, Tom. I can't believe it's you, the boy I called my son.

Tom sounds different now, flat and emotionless. I knew you would never understand me, he says. I knew it was all going to come out one day, and you wouldn't want me anymore, and you would stop loving me…

So you thought you'd get us first? I say, incredulous.

I'll always love you, sobs Sandra. But you've hurt me more than I could have ever imagined. What did I do to deserve this? Listen to me, Tom. Listen. We are barely holding ourselves together. I'm just not strong enough for this…

Mum…

She passes me the phone and turns away, putting her head in her hands. Harry and Lauren wrap themselves around her, sheltering her as she cries.

Well, that's it, I say. You've made your decision. You've chosen your family, and we are happy to be left out of it. *Tam*.

Wait, he says, breathless.

But there is nothing more to say. He thought he would tear us apart one day; he has finally done it, if not in the way he predicted. I can hear him babbling, shouting into the void. The house is full of feeling, his and ours.

The end. I cut him off.

*

We gather in the kitchen, amidst the rubble. Friedrich can't possibly know how this feels. I am impatient for our hollow conversations with him to be over so my family and I can return to the falling bombs. At last, he retreats to the spare bedroom.

Oh, Tom, says Lauren, once the coast is clear. Why would he do this?

Little fucker, says Elder Son. Why did I stand up for him? What a fucking mug.

Lauren tries to stroke his arm. He shakes her off.

What actually happened? she says.

He bloody organised it. He let them onto our property.

I nod, a cold fire in my chest.

It just doesn't seem like him, says Lauren.

He won't rest until we're completely humiliated, says Sandra. None of them will.

Don't let it get to you, I tell her, uselessly.

Where did I go wrong? she weeps.

Oh, Sandra, says Lauren, gently. It's not your fault.

I bite my tongue. Tom is a grown man, adult, whatever. He is responsible for his own actions. I take Sandra's hand and squeeze.

What are we going to do? says Elder Son.

What *can* we do?

Well, someone has to talk to him, surely? says Lauren. There must be more to this. Tom loves you all. He wouldn't…

Lauren, says Harry, as if pulling a child back from a busy road.

I'm sure if you give him the chance to explain…

Explain this? How? He knows we've been struggling enough as it is.

I know. But he's obviously been going through it, you know, emotionally. And people can do terrible things when their heads aren't right. When my auntie June got made redundant, she ended up running off with an actual…

Forgive me, I snap. But I don't want to hear it. OK? This is *our* family we're talking about, so please just leave us alone, would you?

Lauren nods, then barely speaks for the rest of the evening. She and Harry leave before I can pull myself together and make it right. Sandra tells me off, says there'll be nothing left. No family, no farm. I toss and turn in bed, and battle with the ache in my faulty hip. The least of my worries.

28 September, 1944

I LEFT THAT SAME AFTERNOON. THEY had all agreed, up at the house, that it would be safest for everybody, given the potential for the scandal to grow beyond our ability to contain it, if I returned to Hayes Hall. I asked if I could say goodbye; I could not stop myself. I wonder if they really all agreed. Herb is the man of the house, as he said himself.

Hayes Hall sent a single officer in a car to come and collect me. Herb came to see me off, marching down the hill from the house, a grim expression on his face. The Nicholsons hurried after him, gussied up like they were ready for church.

'Good riddance is all I'll say,' said Mrs Nicholson.

'Yes, about time,' her husband agreed, smiling widely. 'First you lose Paris, and now this. This is your just deserts, Jerry.'

'We knew Mr Edwards would see sense eventually.'

'Do you mind?' said Herb, his back to them.

I could not bear to look up, obeying the officer who opened the door of the car and ushered me onto its backseat. I was in a high state of emotion, and I suspected my expression might give them great satisfaction, so I hoped they would not come close enough to see it.

'You can't still be defending him, Mr Edwards,' said Mr Nicholson. 'The game is up.'

'Yes,' said his wife. 'It's quite obvious why you're sending him away.'

'He is going at our agreement,' said Herb, quietly. 'There are

274

worker shortages all over the country, and other farms will benefit from his expertise.'

'Of course,' said Mr Nicholson. 'So, when is the baby due?'

Herb rounded on them. They flinched, but he was already pulling himself back.

The officer tapped on the roof of the car. 'Mr Edwards...'

Herb's voice was tight. 'My daughter is indeed expecting a baby – with Mr Jim Calvert, the man who is to become her husband. As for when it's due, I hope you will both be long gone by then.'

With that, he turned back to the car, leaning over to talk to me through the door. His instruction was clear.

'Do not write to us.'

I understand. He has to think of his business, his family, his daughter. I know he has become fond of me, and I would have continued to serve his farm, and even his country. We are all victims of this terrible war, which rages endlessly. We are prisoners of circumstance.

So, I am back at Hayes Hall, though there is no space for me, and I make a bed on the dormitory floor with the blankets Herb allowed me to take from my hayloft.

I will likely be transported to another camp, which could be anywhere. I fear I am destined for a steamship to Canada, so far away, where a great many have been sent before me.

It has been hours and hours, but morning will not come. I am falling, once more, through the dark of the night, away from everyone and everything I have grown to love.

I was not ready to leave Alderdown.

Alderdown, with its buildings from another time, gripping fast to a changing world. Its meadows and woods, streams and gates carefully closed by loyal keepers. The calves curled up in the creep like a litter, a family, and eggs warm and feather-flecked in the chicken coop. Neighbours passing on horseback, the natural music of hooves on the lane. Days dedicated to slow rhythms, ploughing, planting, harvesting. Cornflowers and shepherd's needles. The golden miracle of a loping hare.

I could have been more careful. If I had just had the strength to set aside the business of living. If I had remembered I am less than human here.

On the farm, I was a resource, much like the dogs and cows and chickens.

At the camp, I am little more than a hostage.

I have come to know my place, not just intellectually, but as a deeply felt belief about myself. I want to go home, and I whisper to my mother and father. I am afraid they would not recognise me. I am so sorry. What a fool I have become.

I do not know if I will ever see the Edwards family or Alderdown Farm again.

Little book. You are all I have. Little book.

Tam

I AM WRESTLING WITH INSOMNIA, WRITING notes to myself in bed.

Even if they can't forgive me, I can live a full life without family.

The world is ending, but the sun still rises. Its sickly light seeps through the curtains, creeps up my bed. It stains the walls yellow.

Lots of people are estranged from their relatives, and it's what I've been practising this whole time, setting out on my own.

There is a growing pain in my chest. If I don't concentrate on steadying it, my breathing is laboured. Don't you dare play the victim. I think of Gran, all alone at the Lodge. This too shall pass.

I can tolerate this feeling, I scribble. *Anyway, it's what I deserve.*

Then I scrunch my notes into a tight ball, imagine it's the feelings inside me, and throw it away as hard as I can.

Dad used my real name. *You've chosen your family, and we are happy to be left out of it. Tam.* Like he was only doing it because I'd got my wish, and the destruction of our family was the ultimate toll. A price I was always going to have to pay. Except that's not true; it wasn't inevitable.

I want to tear my hair out. It was never right for me to try to change the family, to revolutionise the farm. But I couldn't see past it. And the consequences...

This is how we live, how we survive.

I should go to them, shouldn't I? I have to go back to Alderdown, even though I've been told to stay away. If I don't do something, I can't change the way they think of me.

It's like you've taken a knife to us. We are barely holding ourselves together.

I will always be a bad, irredeemable person. I will never be able to go back.

You can't manipulate your way out of this one.

I'm going to be sick. I sit on the edge of my bed, curling my toes into the carpet. The world outside is waking up, engines and voices and distant sirens. That pocket watch hanging from the front of the chest of drawers was a graduation present from Mum and Dad.

Were we such bad parents?

I can taste the sourness of my own breath. The mess I've made. Nobody will forgive me.

I can't believe it's you, the boy I called my son.

I run to the bathroom and heave.

I call Reece and tell him I can't come into work today. Then Luke, but he doesn't pick up his phone.

I call my brother. I wait until I hear his voicemail recording – *What's up? You've reached Harry Calvert at Alderdown Farm, but I can't talk right now* – and then I hang up.

I get dressed and head to the kitchen. Heath is in there, always an early riser, so I wipe the pain from my face. He's just made a pot of coffee, and pours me a cup.

Tam? You're shaking.

I keep my eyes down and my voice low. Not feeling so good.

He leans away from me, like I might be contagious. Oh, you should rest. Go back to bed. Want me to bring you anything?

That's OK. I've got to go out.

Are you sure that's a good idea?

I'm going home, I say, and it's not quite a lie – I haven't yet made my mind up.

Heath seems relieved. They'll look after you, he says, confidently. I always wish I was a kid again when I'm sick. Being sick as an adult is the worst. I remember when I was living alone and I got the flu, and I felt like I was dying, even though I knew it was just the flu and I'd get over it in a few days. But I convinced myself that I was on my deathbed and, like, dying in the loneliest, most tragic way. Like nobody fucking cared about me. Isn't that sad?

Luke doesn't answer his door, so I wander into a nearby corner shop. I'm not hungry, but maybe some food will help plug the chasm where my heart used to be. I get some bananas and vegan yoghurt because I'm not sure what else I can swallow, and when I go to pay, the gleaming shelves of alcohol catch my eye. If I could just let go a little, feel that warmth, the loosening. But it's so early.

Minutes later, I'm sitting on the steps in the doorway to Luke's building, swigging rum neat from the bottle. Willing it to burn through me, to do its worst. I feel soothed already, like I've bought a one-way ticket somewhere, trying to outrun the shame. Or maybe I just hope Luke will come and rescue me, unable to deny any longer the damage we have done.

By the time he appears, my body is stiff and I need a piss, and it hurts when he takes me by the arm and yanks me to my feet.

What the hell do you think you're doing? For god's sake, come inside.

Sitting there, numbing myself, I'd started indulging fantasies of tenderness, where Luke would hold me and tell me everything was going to be OK. But he is pushing me roughly into his flat and demanding, in a panicked voice, Did anybody see you?

He doesn't want to be associated with someone like me – what will the neighbours think? – drowning their sorrows on his doorstep.

I am apologising profusely. It was stupid.

Then he stands in the entrance to the bathroom and watches me use the toilet, like he doesn't trust me enough to turn his back for five seconds.

What the fuck, Tam? he's saying. What are you playing at?

You told them, I cry, emptying my bladder, trying to maintain my balance. How could you do that?

OK, OK. I told them.

You wanted to hurt them. And me.

I don't want to hurt anybody. You're pissing on the floor.

I finish and turn to him. You never cared about me.

Stop being dramatic. You're wasted. We're not doing this now.

Then when? I take a step towards him, then almost fall, closing the gap between us, shoving him back out into the hall. No, I snarl, we're doing it now, you fucking arsehole.

Get out, he says, gritting his teeth, pointing at the door.

You really don't care, I say, defeated.

He has turned pale. You're being very aggressive.

I rub my eyes. You do whatever you want, I say. You screw things up, then disappear.

Listen to yourself! I know I'm a good person, Tam. I'm just doing what needs to be done.

Tell yourself whatever you like.

Then he grabs me by the scruff of the neck, wrenches my face to his. This is about *you*, he says. This is your problem, not mine.

My head is pounding. I can feel his breath, see the angry red vessels under his skin. So that's it then? I whisper. You're done.

He spits his words into my face. What the fuck is wrong with you? I don't have to do anything. I'm not your boyfriend.

Of course not, I sniff, icily. We're not even friends.

We're not? Then he throws me back into his front door, shouting, Fuck off, Tam. Just fuck off.

I stare for a moment, my reactions dull. Then I fumble with the door.

Out on the tilted landing, I turn back to Luke. My life is over, I say.

And he shuts the door in my face.

George

FRIEDRICH ENDURES HIS STAY ON Alderdown Farm, much as I imagine his grandfather did when he found himself here in trying circumstances.

I grab my stick and bury my troubles. Give Friedrich the tour I promised him, just to take my mind off things. He carries a proper camera, the bulky, old-school kind, and snaps photos of the strangest details: dried boot prints in the dirt, the rusting gate poles where the paint has peeled away, the derelict stone milking parlour, where the windows are all boarded up. I show him the wedding barn, as we take the path down to the meadows. He's convinced that his grandfather slept there in its hayloft.

So, this is the place where he spent so many hours, he says, looking out towards the woods. This is where he learnt to herd the cows, and where he saved them from the flood.

I suppose so, I say. Saved some cows, did he?

I am sceptical that he was so involved, a captured enemy at such a time. How could he have been? Anyway, my mother came of age during those long, arduous years. She and my father forced to grow up too fast, become the traumatised and severe young parents I remember from my own unhappy childhood. And she never talked about prisoners of war or helpful German labourers, or de facto enemies turned unlikely friends. What she talked about was her terrible fear, back then, of invasion.

It puts everything into perspective, thinking of those times, watching Friedrich click his camera like a tourist. As much as he tries to relive his grandfather's story, he is detached from its lived reality. I suppress a yawn, wondering when he is going to impress me with his tales about the farm, and whatever it was he said that made Tom so excited. Perhaps Stefan Becker was vegan.

He tells me he is looking forward to meeting my mother. His grandfather's journal features her heavily, he says. Of course it does. Sandra has gone to collect her from the Lodge and bring her home for lunch. I watch the clock, looking forward to the home comfort and normality her quiet presence brings. Her Saturday visits have quickly become the highlight of my weeks.

We are sitting in the front garden in the late-summer sunshine when Sandra arrives. She drives up the hill and parks in her usual spot by the gate. As she gets out of the car, the breeze makes a flag of her hair, lifts it like a storm warning. She catches my eye, but quickly looks away. Ma opens the passenger door before I can get there to do it for her.

Hello, I say, stooping to kiss her on the cheek.

She almost flinches. But there is enough that she finds familiar about me and this place. Every time she makes it home, I see a partial return to herself, as if she is awakening from a long dream. But then she must go back to the Lodge, and it takes more of her every time. The creep of an incoming tide.

We have a guest, I tell her, from Germany.

Friedrich extends a hand, addresses her with a nervous smile. Hello, I've heard so much about you. My name is Friedrich.

Ma freezes. The colour leaves her cheeks, and her eyes go very round.

Ma? I say. It is like she has seen a ghost.

Friedrich's hand drops to his side. Mother lifts her own hands to her face. Gagging her mouth, fingers clawing.

It's all right, I say, with an apologetic look at Friedrich. But then I see his eyes are shining with feeling, and I no longer know what's happening.

Sandra locks the car and comes to stand by my side.

This is the man I was telling you about, Maggie, she says. His

282

grandfather worked here during World War Two. I wonder if you can remember.

It's so nice to meet you, says Friedrich, beaming.

What is this? I say; it is as if the two have met before in some other life.

Ma's hands come down to her chest and she totters towards Friedrich, closing the small gap between them.

Stefan, she says.

Ma!

She looks like she's about to flop against his chest, but she merely touches his cheek, cupping his face. To an outsider, she might appear to be his fond grandmother.

I'm sorry, I say, cringing. Ma, you're confused.

Stefan, she says, gazing into Friedrich's flushed face.

This is too much. I step in, taking her by the arm.

You've made it back, she says, ignoring me. A tear streaks her cheek. How did you do it?

A flash of anger. I have been left out of the joke.

No, Friedrich is saying. No, I'm not Stefan, Maggie. I'm his grandson.

I'm not sure this was a good idea, I say, trying to pull my mother away from this man, who is really just a stranger at a time when I don't know who I can trust.

I'm sorry, says Friedrich.

I think we're upsetting her. Sandra, a little help?

Ma jolts. Knocks me back with surprising strength. My hip spasms and I almost fall. She lets out a shrill shout.

No! Don't!

Maggie, says Sandra. Calm down!

Let me go.

She thrashes with her free arm, tries to break away from Sandra. I snatch it out of the air. Hold her tightly. Friedrich takes a few steps back.

What should I –

Ma, I say, you're all right. Please calm down.

Let me go.

She fights and struggles.

What's the matter with you?

She's getting worse, losing herself this early in the day. The thought overwhelms me, and I squeeze her arm a touch too hard. She yelps.

You're hurting me!

Sandra and I release her, then, and I hold up my hands in surrender. Ma stumbles a few steps towards the house, then stops. Looks between us all, her eyes wild and unseeing.

It's me, I tell her. Your son.

Then it's as if reality dawns on her. A clarity filling her with still, early-morning light.

Please don't fuss, she mumbles.

It's all right, Maggie, says Sandra, reaching out, this time allowing my mother to take her hand willingly. Why don't we go inside and see about lunch?

Friedrich resolves to leave straight after the meal. I am not happy. We sit around the table and make polite conversation, killing time. Mother is quiet, but occasionally she will take a long, hard look at our guest like she wants to ask him a question. Usually I am comfortable with silence, with long tracts of time passing by without the reassurance of chatter around the table. Only now I am hosting, and there is pressure to talk, to entertain. I am too exhausted. I can't hear myself think in the din of my mind. Cutlery scrapes and clinks. We are eating lasagne and a garden salad. I chop everything on my plate into little morsels and swallow without tasting.

So, I say, looking pointedly at Friedrich. Are you ever going to tell us what you came here to tell us?

Friedrich chews. Gathering himself, finishing his mouthful. I don't want to be cynical and ungracious, but I wonder what really happened between him and Tom when they met up in London. I don't know my son, never thought he'd be capable of hurting us like he has. Now I am afraid that this is some extension of his plan to sabotage us.

I'm sorry, says Friedrich. You are already dealing with so much. The last thing I want to do is make your lives more complicated.

What do you mean by that?

Yes, says Sandra, trying to joke. Take pity on us, please.

I finished translating my grandfather's journal, says Friedrich, putting his elbows on the table. I thought he would want me to come here and tell you... Perhaps that's why he left it, why he never – I don't know – destroyed it? He carried all this with him for so long...

Carried what with him?

Friedrich scratches his chin, smiling timidly. What happened here during the war, he says, connects us. It ties us together. And maybe that's why I feel your troubles so keenly. I won't risk telling you what I told Tam.

Why? I say, irritably. Why on earth not?

It would be too abrupt. I can't do that. It's the wrong way. But I'll give you the journal, the translations. And then you can choose. And if and when you're ready, you can read it all in his words, and he'll take you through it properly, as it happened.

You're scaring us, says Sandra. What could you possibly–

She stops, and her mouth falls open. Then she turns to look at my mother before her gaze finally settles on me.

A thought begins to form in my own head. I refuse it.

Ma never talked about Stefan, I say, angrily. You never said anything, Ma. But you were always telling stories. If there's anything to know, I would know it already, wouldn't I?

She looks back at me, lost in fog.

They made her promise, says Friedrich. They were all just trying to get through, you see. They were all just trying to survive.

*

So he goes, and leaves us with the journal. A folder of printed pages, spiral-bound. I sit in the dining room with the lights on and the window open, and read through the night.

13 April, 1945

ANOTHER DAY DIGGING UP OLD roads. I don't know what it is, but presently I find I only want to work. I am not bothered by the chill in the air, nor the fumes from the factory next door. I do not mind my work being observed because I know it will meet with approval. I just want to keep busy, and tire myself out until I am too exhausted to think. I was hammering at the ground when Heinrich told me the story, which I want to set down here in full.

'So,' he said, 'this Italian bloke was talking to me about one of the German prisoners in his camp. Listen to this, Stefan. He only went and got one of the local nurses pregnant, didn't he?'

I directed all my discomfort into the muscles of my arms. 'How about that.'

'The German prisoner,' Heinrich repeated. 'Not the Italian. Are you listening?'

If I hadn't had a pickaxe in my hands and a strenuous job to do, he might have been able to read my reactions. So far, and much to my relief, I haven't had to open up about my past, and I was nervous that Heinrich was onto me.

I paused for breath and stretched. 'Of course I'm listening. So, what happened?'

'Well, it went to court, obviously. He said he meant to marry her as soon as possible.' He nudged me. 'That's what they all say, eh? Oldest trick in the book!'

I turned away again, swinging my pickaxe, hacking at the road and producing a spray of little stones. 'Maybe.'

'Apparently it's happening all over Liverpool, and probably the country too. British girls sneaking letters into camps. Hankering for a taste of forbidden fruit.' Heinrich laughed, scratching his shin through his prisoner uniform with the curve of his axe. 'Can't blame them. I haven't had so much as a smile from a lady ever since I got here.'

I like that he is always happy to hold forth and does not ask for more from me than I am able to give him.

'So,' I said, trying to be nonchalant, 'what happened to them?'

It was like he had already moved on. 'What? The German man and his bird?'

I nodded.

'He was found guilty of something or other – improper relations – and sentenced to twelve months in prison. Ridiculous, isn't it? I suppose it could have been worse. He's just swapped one prison for another.'

I wondered what the nurse thought about all this. Was it over for her, or did she still feel something for the father of her child, and want the impossible?

I beat the ground, and the splintering force dissipated across my shoulders.

'It's sad, to be honest,' I said.

'Well, yeah. What did they think was going to happen? Fencing a load of young bucks off behind barbed wire and telling the girls they're off limits. Very sensible. You can't police every single relationship. It's got to come down to the parents, hasn't it? If I had a daughter, I'd never let a man near her. Ever.' He looked at me. 'Anyway, why the long face?'

'It gets you thinking. There's a baby involved.'

'Yep. What a disaster! That's why you've got to keep an eye. Women are little fools, you see. Don't know their own power.'

I cannot sleep again. It has been almost seven months since Alderdown, and I am like a homesick schoolboy. I lie awake and listen to the pigeons and the sounds of the men, snoring, and wonder if the child has been born.

2 October, 1946

I DON'T KNOW WHAT I WAS thinking today. Perhaps I am closer to Heinrich than I like to admit. The officers assembled us in the downstairs hall to sort us into our new details, and they asked me to assist at Fallowden, a local dairy farm down by the River Mersey. I was dizzy, thinking of the sweet grass, and the curious bovine faces with their pink noses and long lashes. The men generally like working at Fallowden; the farmer is said to be a kind leader, with a good sense of humour. But I knew at once that I could not face it.

'What do you mean you won't do it?' said an officer, whose growing smile only provoked me further.

'I don't have to do what you tell me,' I said. 'The war is over.'

'Is that right?'

I know he was just doing his job. I know he probably thought I was self-important. But, in that moment, he stood for the British government, and every other person I have met during my time held hostage by this country, who just expects me and my kind to serve them, to work and work, with no regard for our humanity. There is no greater sense of entitlement than that.

And shouldn't we have a choice? Wouldn't that go some way towards restoring the freedom we have been promised for over a year, a freedom that is not high on any agenda, and does not appear to be forthcoming?

'If I'm a free man,' I said, and I can't believe I dared, 'shouldn't I get a choice about what I do?'

'I would have thought it was better to be out and about, making yourself useful, but you can waste away in here for all I care.'

Once, I fell in love with this country and its people. But the war is long over, and the facts are plain as day. We are little more than slaves. They will not let us go as long as we are useful. We labour from morning until night, and survive on the bare minimum. We still wear our uniforms with their target-practice patches and a colour code to symbolise what kind of enemy we are. They move us at will. We travel from camp to camp as the British government requires. We still don't draw our pay in sterling.

All the same, the man is right. I want to keep busy. I don't want to stay here and rot.

'What about road maintenance?' I said, quickly losing my nerve. 'That's what I've been doing for the past year, and I haven't had any complaints.'

'Calm down,' said another, equally imperious officer. 'What is this all about?'

'I can't work at Fallowden. I can't work on any farm.'

'Mr Becker?' The man examined a list on a clipboard. 'Whyever not? We thought, based on your file…'

'I won't do it.'

'Well, I'm afraid the decisions have been made. This is a complicated operation, and if we had to negotiate with every one of you, I don't think we'd get much done. Do you?'

I let the others step forward. I was seething.

It's all about power for these people. They think they are better than us. They like to read aloud the ongoing rules against fraternisation, which we prisoners now try to flout whenever possible as a matter of principle. The locals are only too happy to help us; we are not to use licenced premises, but they invite us, nonetheless. Every other week, we join them at the pub. Here and there, our friends are fined a pound for these infractions. They laugh about it – you're worth a few bob – and we try to laugh with them.

For them, the war is already becoming a memory. On the anniversary of their victory, they took to the streets for fireworks and parades, and we prisoners swept up their confetti.

Taking advantage of their good fortune, they seat us in classrooms, and lecture us about democracy. They want us to return home with our heads full of dreams, repelled by National Socialism, and sentimental about our captors. But I have fallen out of love with Great Britain, defender of human rights, which will not repatriate its own prisoners.

When he got the chance, my Italian friend, Fabrizio, came to my aid. He volunteered to swap places with me, taking the farm job, and leaving me to his role repairing roads. The officers made an allowance, just this once.

Little book, you have kept me company. You have never betrayed me.

I was afraid of confiding in you in case somebody stole you away and discovered your secrets. But the truth is that I do not matter. We do not matter. Or, at least, you matter only to me, and it has been long enough.

I have written to Alderdown, against Herb's wishes, but heard nothing back. I wonder if my letters are being intercepted, and if I should give them up.

But we are no longer at war, and some things are more important than propriety, or even shame.

I will not give myself over to despair.

It has been a month since Heinrich's death. I look at his empty bed. It was the middle of the night, and he had gone to the bathroom. I lay there for an hour, telling myself there was no need to get up, that he would be back any minute. I should not have waited as long as I did.

28 April, 1947

So, little book. Yesterday was the day. Herb Edwards came to see me, like he said he would, and we sat and talked, and he answered many of my questions, and quashed just as many of my hopes. I am only now recovering from the drink. I sat up late with a bottle, long after my friends had fallen asleep. Today, I will begin to recover.

We met at the Wheatsheaf. I tweaked my buttons and bit my nails. What was he going to say to me? After so long apart, his letter had been brief and instructive. I broke the skin on my thumb, chewing the knuckle. But Fabrizio and Konrad were well aware of my situation, and they were sitting along the side of the bar with two local girls, Grace and Sarah, whom they have been courting. From there, the four of them could keep an eye on me. Besides, I knew the pub, and its people. I know Frank, the barman, and have shared an evening with many of the flat-capped regulars, gathered around the edges of the room, playing cards and nursing their drinks. Herb was no longer my boss, and this was my home turf, not his.

I took a seat at a small table in clear view of the front door. Frank's seven-year-old son, Tommy, sitting on a bar stool with his lemonade, was getting restless. He kicked the dark-wood panels of the bar until Frank snapped at him, and then he came over to join me.

'Stefan, will you play marbles with me?' he said, taking a small bag from his pocket.

'Maybe later. I'm meeting someone, and he's about to arrive.'

Tommy sloped off, shoulders slumped, and in that moment, I thought about my child, and raising children, and I was unprepared for the awful spear of emotion that struck me and sent the room spinning.

I had just minutes to compose myself before Herb Edwards arrived, little changed. As he entered, he used his back to hold the door open for a young couple, who were on their way out. He nodded to them as he lit his pipe, then searched the room with his eyes until he spotted me, standing up at my table to greet him.

We drank cider, for old time's sake, and talked like we were mere acquaintances, with little stock in each other's affairs.

Herb told me he was on his way to source more cattle, prize-winning Ayrshires that had been recommended by a friend of the family. I told him about the work I did, mending roads, and about our camp accommodation next to the social club.

Then the small talk was over. Our smiles began to fade.

I thought I saw a glimmer of panic in Herb's eyes.

'Well, then,' he said, his hands at his face, swapping his drink for his pipe.

I swallowed. 'Yes…'

'So…'

My knee was jumping under the table as I set the question free. 'How's Maggie?'

'Very well. Very well indeed.'

'And… the baby?'

There was a cheer from the dartboard. A couple of old men were standing in a cloud of smoke, slapping each other on the back.

'Little Georgie Calvert,' said Herb. 'He's our pride and joy.'

'Calvert?'

'George Calvert.'

Jim's name. Of course.

Herb continued. 'He's just turned two years of age. They grow

294

up so fast. One minute he was only a baby. Now he's a fine little man. And a real chatterbox.'

'I'm glad,' I said, doing everything I could to hold my head up high. 'I've waited to hear. I wrote you all letters…'

Herb looked grave. 'Yes.'

'Did you get them?'

'Mary and I would open them, in the beginning. But we've stopped, Stefan.'

'Most of them were for Maggie.'

'Maggie has moved on. We had a difficult year or so, trying to make her see sense, but she has made real progress. She doesn't talk about you anymore. I know that's hard to hear, but it's the truth, Stefan. She is looking ahead, and she just wants what's best for the baby, and for the family.'

'Then she never read the letters?'

Herb sat back in his chair, stern and disapproving. 'Come on, now,' he said, through a mouthful of smoke.

'But what happened between us is not unheard of, and I am not a prisoner anymore. I am just a man. One day soon, I know I could marry her, if she wanted me…'

'Maggie is already married.'

'I know. And maybe it is too late. But if there is any chance…'

'Please, Stefan. Do the right thing. Take responsibility for your mistakes.'

'But Maggie and I were…'

'It doesn't matter. It's time to leave her be. Let her rebuild. Let her make space in her heart for Jim. He is just a young man, and he has stepped up so selflessly to be a husband and father. He has got you both out of a lot of trouble.'

'Does she love him?'

'They were childhood sweethearts.'

'That's not what I asked.'

'She has always loved him, Stefan. But love is not the only thing. Maggie has had to grow up. I think you would find she is no longer the wild girl you fell for. She understands that we have to make sacrifices sometimes, that life is full of compromise. She understands that more and more each day.'

I looked away. Underneath all the signs advertising Scotch whisky, there was a wartime plaque: *loose lips sink ships.*

Union Jack bunting, red, white and blue, stretched along the wall.

I tried to hide my tears, but they were spilling over, and I knew my friends were watching me, and I had little to defend but my dignity.

For a moment, I hated Herb Edwards. I wanted to tell him how lucky he was that he hadn't been sent away from home in the service of someone else's cause. I wanted to ask him if he knew what it was like to be alone, not to know when it would end, if ever. I wanted to tell him he hadn't the faintest idea whether or not he would have been able to resist the offer of love, or the ·embrace of family, or even the delusions of both these things, in the most alienating of circumstances.

'You have your whole life ahead of you,' he lectured me. 'When it is your turn to go home, when you get your orders, you should go.'

'I cannot give Maggie and that man my blessing,' I told him. 'I just can't.'

'So be it. But let that be the end of it.'

Tommy ambled over, his fingers tangled in the stretched, green wool of his jumper. He glared at Herb, then looked back at his father, who was polishing glasses behind the bar, as if considering calling for reinforcements.

'Who are you?'

He was never shy; growing up in a public house made one bold.

'Herbert Edwards.'

The farmer stretched out his hand, and Tommy looked at me for direction, taking in my watery eyes.

'He's *family*,' I stressed, and I'll admit it was mean of me. 'He's my guest.'

Then Tommy shook Herb's hand, though he still looked worried. He blinked up at me. 'Why are you sad?'

'I'm not sad, Tommy. Give me a minute, would you?'

He ran back to the bar. His father handed him a rag and a glass to polish.

I was done. I thanked Herb for his time and asked him if there was anything else he wanted to say to me. He said nothing. He appeared to be concentrating on his pipe, smacking his lips like a fish.

'Goodbye,' I said, and we shook hands. Then I had the last gulp of my cider and took my leave, heading for the door.

'Wait,' Herb said, behind me.

I stopped, and he beckoned me back to our table. He spoke in a low, even voice.

'You and George are of the same blood. That will always be true. Maggie has said, many times, that she would be happy for you to come and see him one day, should you feel the need.'

What game was this? To say such a thing to me, so late in our meeting… I wanted to scream at him. But he didn't give me the chance.

'To be quite frank, Stefan,' he explained, 'I considered not coming to meet you at all. I knew it was the right thing to do, but I have been very angry, and I don't think Jim would approve, especially given the way you men said goodbye. I stood outside the pub, telling myself I had to go in and see you, only I felt that I couldn't possibly face you without losing control. I thought, perhaps, I should tell you that little Georgie had died.'

I could only breathe and swallow.

'Thank you,' I said, finally. 'Thank you for telling me the truth. For not saying he was dead.'

'Stefan, I know I can't be the one to finish this. I've never had control over you lot. It's thinking I had control that got us into this mess in the first place.'

I stood there, unseeing, surrounded by the babble of cheerful voices, and I asked myself why I wanted to be with Maggie and our baby – a boy called George, who did not know me.

'He has a father,' I said.

'Yes.'

'And Maggie would prefer me not to...'

'Yes.'

I wanted them both for myself. I wanted them selfishly. I was not in a position to provide for them. I was an alien, an enemy, a shadow. Living in between. I could not be the kind of father my little boy deserved.

So I told Herb that I would do as he had asked me, and go.

George

I SIT AND READ AS THE moon makes its arc across the sky, and the room fills with moths and gnats. I read despite the demonic cackle of fighting foxes on the other side of the wall. I read until I reach the truth. And then I set the pages down, and go and wash my face and brush my teeth. Sandra appears on the landing, the floorboards creaking under her feet. The birds are chattering outside.

George, were you up all night? she asks, blearily.

I brew some coffee and sit in the front garden, sipping the bitterness. He was never my father, Jim. They lied to me, he and Ma. My father was Stefan, a German prisoner of war I had never heard of until this year, and he is dead, and reading his journal is the closest I will ever come to meeting him.

Harry is worried about me, but I tell him all is well.

We work mechanically, may as well be the robot he's been bugging me about. The cows are plugged in, eating silage. Milk is pouring through the pipes.

I think I love Alderdown Farm. But I hate it too. I spent so long running away, and I took up the mantle because I felt I owed my father something. His efforts could only be good and righteous, so I was wicked and shameless for not being like him. Not being him. Not being the apple of his eye, like my brother was.

We take the cows out to the fields as usual. Then I leave Harry to his jobs and make my way back to the house. Sandra has gone out. Stefan's journal is still on the dining room table. I will not think of him as my father.

I take the document and drive to the Lodge. I think of trips along this road when I was a little boy. Sitting in the Fowler with Pa, rocking from side to side, proud to be there with him as he went about his business.

My father. Jim.

Did he ever think of me as his son?

Ma seems to recognise me today. She embraces me and we head into the little courtyard together, where there is another old woman, sitting in a mobility scooter and sunning herself luxuriously. I sit down with Ma on a wooden bench in front of a planter full of weeds.

Stefan was my father, I say.

My mother looks at me, calmly.

And you never told me. Why?

No way back, she says.

No way back?

Harry rings me. He has a down cow, toppled and helpless. Her eyes have been pecked out by magpies, but she is still alive. He sounds flustered and upset. I tell him to call the vet, just to put her out of her misery. Another one for the knackerman.

Pa never loved me, I say to Ma. I always felt it.

He has enough on his plate, she replies.

He never even liked me. But why? I was just a baby, and he chose to step in and become my father...

Ma strains with a deep, shaky breath, then shuts her eyes.

I tried so hard to please him, I continue. I tried so hard to please him, and then I ran away because it was never good enough. I could never change his mind about me.

Ma's face is weathered like old stone. Once, she was a young woman in trouble, and her father was trying to protect her. I understand it. He must have thought he was doing the right thing. And she and Stefan were victims of their circumstances. Of their failure to be neat and tidy at a time when things needed to be simple.

Marrying Ma made Jim her saviour. The family's hero. He had always wanted her, but they weren't happy together, or at least it took them a long time to be happy. Pa used to look at me like I was standing in the way. But Mike, their second child, was a new start. A life they'd started together, a sign that my mother had finally moved on.

When it is time to leave, Ma is upset.

I'm sorry, Ma, I repeat.

She holds me by the sleeves and cries.

I drive home. I have become the man who raised me, trying to live in his image to make up for shortcomings beyond my understanding, let alone my control. I have raised my children according to his demands, hoping they would fall in line. But there was nothing I could have done to please him, to change who I was for him. And now I'm trailed by a dark shadow, the guilt in the corners of my eyes, because I've done the same to Younger Son. Set him up to fail. I've bound my love with impossible conditions.

Joining Sandra in front of the telly, I own up. It is my fault. I am the one who's driven him away, never allowing him to be himself. Themself. I will make an effort with their name, their language.

I should reach out, I say.

You do that, then, she replied, her eyes pink and tired. I don't want anything to do with it.

That's all right. But this dysfunction we've been working through, it has to come from somewhere.

Dysfunction isn't even the word, says Sandra. I don't know what to call this family.

You're right. You're right, darling. And someone has to take responsibility, and I realise I've never done that. Have I? I've just insisted things stay the same, and buried my head, and lost my temper with anyone who's dared to rock the boat.

This isn't some harmless rebellion, George.

I know. We'll have to work through it, and Tam will have to take responsibility too. But the least I can do is stick around and let him. Them.

If you say so.

I promise you. I'm not going to let them go. I'm not going to give up. Pa never gave me a chance, and that's stayed with me, and it affected my relationship with my brother, and now it's driven a wedge between us and Tom. Tam.

Your father? What did he do?

He never wanted me, Sandra.

She peers at me, lost. So I tell her what Tam already knows, what Friedrich came here to say.

When I ring Tam, the call goes straight to voicemail. I don't blame them. Who in their right mind would pick up a grenade? But how else can I tell them I come in peace, that the first step is to clear the smoke? I leave a message, promising that I mean no harm.

I'm sorry for what I said, I tell them. I'm sorry for all the years I wasn't there for you. Tam, I want to try… Please talk to me. This isn't supposed to be an ambush; we can meet on your terms. Will you call me back?

But they don't. I sit in the office with Harry. He's been managing the farm almost single-handedly. His sleeves rolled up, his face blazing with purpose.

I dunno, Dad, he says, distractedly. He probably hasn't listened to the voicemail. Might be afraid to.

They.

Really? He looks up from his writing. Are we doing that now?

I nod.

Fine. I just… I see him as my little brother, you know?

I know. But that's not all they are.

Christ.

I know. Do you want a cup of tea?

Since when do you make the tea? Harry laughs. Go on then. Two sugars.

I stand, aching, trying to make myself useful. Harry stops me at the door.

I'm going to send him a text, he says. I have something to tell him. You should try that too.

Hmm.

He rolls his eyes; he knows I struggle with text messages. He scoots over on his office chair, reaching out a hand.

Give me your phone. Now, what do you want to say?

That I'm sorry, I dictate, as his thumbs tap away. That I don't want to fight anymore. I want to work through this together. I know I haven't made it easy. But I love him… them. And I accept them.

Harry looks up. You can't put all that in a text, Dad. Save it for face to face.

He hands me my mobile.

You didn't send anything? I say, put out.

Harry has returned to his paperwork. Course I did.

I peer at the screen, struggle to decipher the little words without my reading glasses.

Hi Tam. I forgive you, and I want to apologise too. Please give me a chance.

By the evening, there's still no response. I sit with Sandra in the front garden, resting my sore hip. She is talking to her sister on the phone. She has a knack for distracting herself, for setting everything aside. I expect she has learnt this from all the years of living with me.

Harry crosses the yard, having brought his cows in for the night. He climbs up the hill to the house to say goodbye to us. The trees are rustling and watchful.

Tam replied? he asks, frowning.

Not yet, no.

No? What? He stuffs his hands in his pockets. That little bitch.

Harry!

I dunno, Dad. After what he did – *they* did – they should think themselves lucky we're being so understanding.

Maybe.

What more can you do though? I dunno.

He removes his hands from his pockets, scratches his head. Lauren appears behind him, wearing a turquoise summer dress, taking the path up from the cottage.

Everything all right on the farm? I say.

Yep, says Harry. All good.

Great.

Err… Mum, Dad?

Sandra is still on the phone, but she mimes blowing him a kiss.

Lauren reaches us, and we say hello. She takes Harry's arm, hugging it to her. Hey babe, she says, her eyes shining.

Mum, can you listen a minute? It's just… We never got a chance, and it's been twelve weeks, so…

What? I say, like I haven't heard right.

Lauren looks exasperated. Shall we all go inside?

Hold on, Kate, says Sandra, lowering the phone to her chest. She looks up at Elder Son.

We flock around the kitchen table. Sandra and I are trying our best to look impassive, but our faces are beginning to break into smiles.

Harry takes his wife's hand, pauses for dramatic effect. Lauren and me are going to have a baby, he says.

Lauren grins, raises her hands. I'm pregnant.

A breath, and then Sandra jumps up and rushes to hug them. I am not far behind.

I hug Harry before his mother has even let go. He is chatting away, but I can only half-listen. I am ecstatic, the years opening up before us. I hold my boy. At last we are strong, a tree with fathomless roots and branches. Growing tall, reaching into the unknown.

What about Tom? says Sandra. Have you told him?

I texted earlier. I thought maybe he'd have the decency to respond. Not sure exactly what we're supposed to have done – he shrugs at Lauren – but there we go.

Really? I say. No reply?

Why do you think I'm so pissed?

But we are on cloud nine, and nothing can ruin this moment. Sandra makes a celebratory pot of tea and we talk for the next hour. Then Sandra and I watch, standing side by side, as Harry and Lauren wave goodbye, and disappear around the corner. Our Harry, his own man. Striding away from the farmhouse, his childhood home, and into the life he is making with Lauren.

Tom should have been here, says Sandra. Tam.

Mmm, I say – on a high.

Then Sandra falters, her voice quavering. What if something's wrong?

Wrong?

She goes inside, and returns a minute later with her address book.

I've got the main phone number, she says, for the house he lives in.

Why? You think they're in trouble?

I'll just check he's all right.

We don't want to intrude…

She is already dialling, lifting a finger to silence me. There's a creeping unease between us. Tam may well be nursing their wounds, but it's odd that they haven't replied to Harry's news.

Hello, she says. Is Tam there?

She frowns.

No, Varsha, this is… It's Sandra. His mother. No. He's not *here*.

She mouths at me, *They thought he was home with us.*

Her voice sounds faraway. Well, when did you last see him?

Tam has been missing for two days, and all our grievances are forgotten. We blame ourselves for telling them we were finished;

there was no way back to us. Because Tam cares – about us, about what we think. I know this because I never stopped caring what my father thought, even as I railed against him.

We call the police and report Tam as a missing person. We navigate the details of their changing physical appearance and identity, lay bare the intimate details of our last conversation. I am grateful that the woman on the phone offers no comment.

Then we ring Harry, and he and Lauren come to the house.

We're going to find them, says Harry. We shouldn't jump to any conclusions.

Lauren orders a Chinese, but nobody eats.

He called in sick, says Sandra, the morning after our big blow-up. Why do you think he did that?

Harry shows me Luke's social media page on his phone. We could ask him, he suggests. Maybe they're together.

He types while the rest of us gather round.

They came by, Luke replies, and gave me an earful for telling you the truth. That was the day after I visited your farm. But I haven't seen them since then.

What time was it?

Sometime in the early afternoon.

And how were they?

I don't know. Angry, upset.

You might be the last person to have seen them.

I'm really sorry. I hope they're OK. I'm worried too.

Then please let us know if you have any information.

I will. And I'll notify my followers, and ask them to spread the word.

We don't thank him. Tam was his pawn. He has as much cause to feel guilty as the rest of us.

Now, we don't know what else to do. We've called Tam's friends. We've given the police all the information we have. All that's left is for us to worry.

I remember the rush of love when I held my baby on

my shoulders, and they directed my gaze with a tug of my ears.

I visualise Tam the boy, our Tom. The familiar sight of the back of their head each day when they got in from school and parked themself on the sofa in front of the television.

It's gonna be all right, says Harry, grey-faced, and not even convincing himself.

Sandra scrolls the internet. Refreshing and refreshing.

Someone take this away from me, she says, sounding strangled.

They've probably just run off somewhere, says Harry. It was a big argument at the end of a really rough time.

Exactly, says Lauren. I'd probably want to be alone too.

Tam is gonna be fine.

I just nod, my thoughts stampeding.

It's just after we go to bed that the phone rings with news. They've located Tam in a London hospital, with no wallet or identification. They are not fine at all.

We sit by Tam's bedside. The doctors come and go, the police. All touting their nightmare theories. The room spins and churns. But Tam lies still, and I can only focus on them. We are so small in the hospital, we mere mortals. Tam is so like themself, our child. With their mother by their side, holding their hand and talking all the while, encouraging them to stay with us. Perhaps even to talk back.

I look at them, Tam, long and hard, and see in them all the certainty and vitality of youth.

You will get through this, I think. You have come this far.

Their lips are red, swollen from the impact of a stranger's fist, their shoe. Their head is bandaged. Their broken wrist is cast and bound. They are hanging on.

We stay with them, and welcome their visitors. Tam has made an impression on their London friends, housemates and colleagues, who come bearing gifts and tears. Varsha is kind to us. She suggests we get some proper sleep; we can stay in Tam's room at her parents' house. We thank her, but choose to sleep right where we are, keeping our eyes half-open.

Harry and Lauren drive over every evening. They stay half an hour, then head straight back to Alderdown. The work will not wait. But Harry has everything under control, and Lauren brings good news.

We've got a wedding booked in next spring, she grins. And maybe one in the summer.

Kerching! says Harry, his eyes twinkling.

We congratulate Lauren, all of us. Finally, some hope.

She tells us that my mother was asking after Tam. I speak to her on the phone, and sometimes she remembers me.

We talk of everything and nothing. We drink endless cups of tea, and I am sleepy and emotional.

One day, Friedrich comes. I tell him I read Stefan's journal.

So then, I say, you're my half-nephew?

Yes. And Harry and Tam are my cousins.

I soak up his company. We are related by blood, and he ties me to a part of myself I never understood. A whole world of answers to questions I never knew to ask.

Tam went drinking that night, after they left Luke's. They went by themself and bought three beers at a gay pub north of the river, called the Sass. The CCTV shows them talking to someone at the bar, maybe exchanging numbers. Tam leaves by themself, and starts walking in the direction of the tube station. They leave the main road, take a back alley behind a street of empty office buildings. At this point, a couple of unidentified men and one woman start to follow them. They cross the road, enter the shadows, and close in.

The police are confident in their investigation, even though there were no witnesses. The thugs took Tam's wallet and phone, so maybe this was a particularly vicious mugging, motivated by money. We also discuss the possibility that it was targeted, if opportunistic. Tam was wearing a women's coat and high-heeled shoes, mascara and lipstick. They must have seen these details, the attackers, when they knocked my child to the ground, when they surrounded them – three against one – and kicked them and kicked them, while Tam rolled into a tight ball, trying in vain to cover their head.

Sandra and I talk to the police about all this with a frank, unfiltered fury. We cannot pull any punches, even about our own role in our child's life. Nothing matters now but Tam.

On the fifth day, the swelling in their skull has completely subsided, and the doctors are hopeful that they can end the coma, which they induced for Tam's own protection.

They come back to life over the course of a day, under the close supervision of their doctors. They struggle into consciousness, groaning, pushing us away. The hospital room smells of chemicals and stale food, and they are disorientated and afraid.

Turn the alarm off, they say, but there are no alarms, only machines, beeping.

Can you squeeze my hand, Tam? Can you hear my voice? Can you talk to me?

Tam can do all of these things, but not without effort. Sandra and I sit either side, holding drinks and putting the straws to their lips.

When they are talking, they ask about their grandmother and the farm.

Harry bounds in and hugs Tam so forcefully that they wince in pain, and Lauren pulls him back as he gasps his apologies.

We don't talk about the attack.

At last, Tam is on the mend, chatting animatedly with their parade of visitors. So many new names to remember, Simon and Vicky and Fraser. Afterwards, Sandra and I take them down to the café, where they ask for a hot chocolate. Sandra and I get coffee, then we all sit down around a table at the edge of the seating area, as the hospital heaves around us. It is almost time to go, but Tam looks sad.

I don't understand why you're here, they say, after everything I did.

Please, says Sandra. Let's not talk about that.

It all just got out of control. You made dinner with some butter, even though... And I just... It was that night I went to my room and sent Luke a message. I told him the story, that you thought it was all a big joke, and I wanted you to...

I shouldn't have done that, I say.

It's OK.

No, it's not.

Tam looks away as I try to remember. Maybe I did think it was all a joke. Or maybe I thought I could stop my child from taking the road less travelled. Its dark, uncertain bends. Perhaps I wanted to shame them out of danger, only I pushed them right into it. Right into my own shame.

Look, I'm sorry, I say, straining for words. Really.

Tam lets out a long breath. They pick at the bandages around their head.

I never thought Luke would even see my message, let alone reply. When he did, I felt... I don't know...

Less alone, says Sandra.

At one point, I thought we were maybe falling in love. That's stupid. But I was never really part of it, of LivestockAid. After I came out to you and left home, I went to Luke, and when I told him I was done – I wasn't going to keep helping him – he went cold.

Arsehole, I say.

No. Tam shakes their head. He's not a bad guy. He just believes in something.

Then maybe he cares more about animals than he cares about people.

Tam nods. To him, people *are* animals, so animals are people.

But that doesn't follow, Sandra scoffs.

The logic doesn't matter, I guess, if you really think you're saving the world.

Saving the world? I say, and I'm still baffled. No matter who he hurts.

They shrug. Maybe that's what it takes.

The last day, Tam and I go for a walk together outside. Sandra has popped to the shops to get us some snacks. Harry and Lauren are on their way in the Land Rover. They're going to pick us up, then drive Tam back to Varsha's house before taking Sandra and me back to Alderdown.

It's the end of September and it's been raining again, incessantly. The weather makes my bones hurt. But I am now adept at balancing my weight between my good leg and my stick. Tam isn't used to seeing me like this.

You all right, Dad?

I'm fine. I'll have it replaced in the new year. It's not too long to wait.

We walk in silence for a bit. I need to start talking. There's so much I wanted to say, but it's never felt like the right time.

Tam...

Yeah?

I'm behind you, OK? I support you.

Yeah...

But I'm scared – I will my voice under control – I'm so scared that something like this will happen again. Something worse. When you're different, people notice you. It puts a target on your back.

I know. I know that.

I don't want you to get hurt.

Tam looks at me and smiles. Sometimes I'm scared too, but then I remember what the real danger is. This is me. This is who I am, and I am not going to hide, not even after this. No matter what happens, I will be myself, because these last months have been the best months of my life. Honestly. Even though this thing

– this fucking awful thing – has happened. I am free, and they can't take that away from me. I went out as myself, built a life as myself, went to work as myself. People saw me as *me*, and that was it. Dad, I can just be. It's hard to explain.

I open and close my mouth. I want to say I am proud, but words fail me. We stop by a wall, lean on it. Look out over a park and the swarming of traffic.

Dad? What is it?

The thing is, Tam, Alderdown has never really felt like mine. It was your grandfather's, your uncle Mike's. But not mine.

Tam is quiet, standing beside me.

You know how your brother took to the farm? I was never like that. I was much more like you, Tam. No, I'm trying to explain… Harry is like Mike. This is what he wants to do. And I know Pa would have liked him. I always wished that was me.

I know. I'm sorry, Dad.

Please, I say, swallowing. There's no need to be sorry. I know I've been a difficult man to live with. Your poor mum. I've been so angry, to be honest. Tied to Alderdown, and everything that came with it.

Then why didn't you leave? says Tam. You and Mum could have moved.

I suppose I thought if I stayed, I would find my way. One day. And Pa would notice, and he would… But obviously the years went by, and then he died, and then Uncle Mike died, and suddenly it was all my responsibility. And I'm not sure I've been up to the challenge, Tam.

They nod, digging their fingernails into the top of the wall. I want to touch them, to rest my hand on their shoulder. I want to hear that it's OK. But they are quiet, looking out over the roads and roofs and treetops.

Can you forgive me? I whisper.

Then Tam turns to look at me, and they are crying. Please, stop… I'm happy, OK? I'm actually happy.

312

We walk back to the hospital room, where Sandra is waiting for us. Tam says they want to go home, not to Varsha's big house, but to Alderdown. They want to come with us for a few days, as themself. Of course, we say, of course you can.

Here, says Sandra, pointing to the little table under the window. Someone has left you flowers.

Tam picks up the bunch. They're rainbow roses, artificially tinted. Swirling like cupcakes with wondrous colour.

There's a note, says Tam, peeling open the envelope.

They read it, then put it aside. When they go to the bathroom, Sandra and I take a quick look.

I'm so sorry, Tam, it says. *This was never meant to become so complicated. Get well.*

Luke, says Sandra, and we stand side by side, and breathe a sigh of relief together. That's it. The waiving of a vendetta. The last of our sleepless nights and endless questions. Luke and LivestockAid have put this whole affair to bed. Tam is back in the fold. Tam can be happy.

Tam

WE ARE DRIVING THROUGH THE countryside. It is dusk, and the starlings are out in force. A vast murmuration swirls in the sky, bulges like a great heart, then finally funnels down to roost. Harry and Lauren are in the front of the Land Rover. I'm sitting between Mum and Dad in the back. The sleepy comfort of their bodies reminds me of how I used to go to them after a nightmare. I am a child. I am a grown adult. I have never been so exhausted; it is the kind of tiredness that knocks you off your feet. Falling asleep in the car as a kid, Dad used to carry me in and up to bed. The engine thrums. We vibrate together in silence.

I wake up just before we get home.

Maisy, says Harry, as he turns onto our lane.

Hmm? says Mum, sitting up.

How'd she get out? says Lauren.

But then we see the others. The road is a confusion of cows. Harry slows down and opens his window as he passes Maisy.

Don't worry, girl, he coos. I'm coming for you.

We don't need to say anything. Somebody has hacked at parts of the hedgerow, cut would-be escape passages that the cows will never think to use. Harry parks at the entrance to the farmyard and hops out of the car.

Bloody hell, says Mum.

She and Lauren are quick on his heels.

Dad and I move slowly, helping each other. He is on crutches, and I am still frail, so we leave the action to the others.

The gate's off its hinges, shouts Harry.

314

Dad and I stand together in the fading light, blinking sleep out of our eyes.

Harry tells Lauren what to do, how to herd the cows, how to help him. Keeping her distance, a little wary, Mum calls the police, then hurries up the hill towards the farmhouse.

This is freedom. Some of the cows are huddled in their cliques; they like their face-to-face conversations. Some stand alone, in no hurry to go anywhere tonight. Some are off looking for their calves, hoofing around the buildings like they know things they can't possibly know. Others have decided to stay put, preferring the comfort and reassurance of captivity. Some cows have gone back to the fields, where they stand, chewing the cud, like this is just a rebellious late night on a normal day, not so special really. Some cows are leading, some are following. Some are standing stupidly in the farmyard, gazing up at the moon's first glow. Some are heading decisively towards the A-road, Harry and Lauren striding after them, trying to coax them back to safety.

Dad and I are left guarding the gate. It's cold now. I look back at my childhood home, through the growing dark. A light appears in the window.

Acknowledgements

I've always dreamed of being an author. Before I could even write, I was telling stories with pictures. My mum would staple these scribblings together into earnest little tomes, and I've been making books ever since, most of which will never see the light of day. Imagine my excitement to be penning the acknowledgements for my debut novel! There are so many people I want to thank.

First of all, I owe an enormous debt of gratitude to my brilliant agent, Julie Fergusson of The North Literary Agency. Your skilful, forensic reading makes my writing better, and I can't thank you enough for everything you've done for me. Second, a heartfelt thank you to my perceptive, empathetic editor, Jenna Gordon, and her fantastic team at VERVE Books – Sarah Stewart-Smith, Ellie Lavender, Lisa Gooding, and Demi Echezona – for taking a chance on a story that means so much to me, and for handling each stage of its publication with intelligence and care. I'm so proud to be a part of the VERVE family. Thank you also to New Writing North. A writer's life can be lonely, so I feel very lucky to have such a warm and welcoming community in the Northeast Novelists.

To tell this story with a realism I could never have achieved on my own, I read a lot of memoirs and nature writing. I want to thank the following for their excellent books: Sally Urwin, *A Farmer's Diary*; Adam Henson, *A Farmer and His Dog*; John Lewis-Stempel, *The Running Hare*; Richard Cornock, *A Year on a Dairy Farm*; John Connell, *The Cow Book*; Roger Evans, *A View from the Tractor*; Joan Bomford, *Up with the Lark: My Life on the*

Land; G Walter Wright, *From Corncrake to Combine: Memoirs of a Cheshire Farmer*; and Rosamund Young, *The Secret Life of Cows*. I used the following resources to research German prisoners of war in England in the 1940s: Christiane Wienand, *Returning Memories: Former Prisoners of War in Divided and Reunited Germany*; Pamela Howe Taylor: *Enemies Become Friends* and *The Germans We Trusted*; and Alan Patrick Malpass's doctoral thesis of September 2016, which gathers together anecdotes and contemporary media sources.

Thank you to the earliest readers of *Human, Animal*. Izzy Abbott, for all your encouragement, and for making me stronger. Brittany Ashworth, for reading, for listening, for being there. You just get it, and I am so grateful. Clare Dryhurst, for all your words of wisdom over the years. Catherine Ellis, for your smart, insightful feedback. Rhiannon Evans, for my very first readers' report, and a much-needed boost. Lauren Karrys, the finest Canadian export, and purveyor of dank memes! And, finally, Charles Fernyhough, an astute and sensitive critic. Your advice has been invaluable.

I'm incredibly grateful to my friends. You know who you are, but some specific shoutouts go to: David and Leigh Vassallo, you've been there through all the trials and tribulations (just a bit o' daft carry-on). Rose Tremlett, whip-smart and side-splittingly funny, my confidence hits the roof if ever you think I'm onto something with an idea for a story. Daisy Sainsbury, reading your work inspires me, and I could talk to you forever. Rachel Edmunds, a real-life Maggie, thank you for celebrating this book with me. And Gretta Mullany, I hope we can make something together one day; thank you for believing in me.

To my family, what would I do without you? Pam and Ian, my generous in-laws, I miss the cupboard under the stairs. Pat, David and Karen, you've always asked me about my writing, even when it's been like pulling teeth, and your enthusiasm has never waned. Thank you. To Bas, my sage and contemplative big brother, I'll never forget when I decided to quit the London rat race in pursuit of a more creative life and I was terrified I'd be making a mistake. That Christmas, you gave me one of the most thoughtful, supportive gifts I'll ever receive: Randy Pausch's *The Last Lecture*, a book about living the life you were meant to live, written with clarity by a dying man. It was exactly what I needed, and it still moves me to think about it. To Bryony, my clever, long-suffering little sister, thank you for indulging me that time when we were kids on holiday and I insisted on reading you the derivative, thousand-page-long fantasy novel I'd been writing! And to the late Mary Summerhays, my beloved grandmother: many years ago, you wrote to me, saying you hoped I'd be happy one day... I am!

To my parents, Sorrel and Jesús. I was a weird kid, my head in the clouds, hard at times to understand. But I lived to make things, little tributes to my ever-changing passions, and you actively facilitated this mania of mine. Dad, you were the technologist. You provided the ropes and wood for the treehouse. Your computer was for all of us to use. I was forever printing and must have got through gallons of ink and forests of paper. Still, we were always stocked and ready to go. And Mum, when I was growing up, you modelled creativity for creativity's sake. Your enthusiasm – for stories and art, for books and films and music – was infectious. I learnt to write through play, and I believe that's how I learnt to think, too. If ever I start to lose sight of why I write, I remember the freedom I felt as a child, sketching a hundred Pinocchios at the kitchen table, his long nose revelling in his fictions.

David, what can I say? Thank you for dreaming with me, for living my stories with me. We're hand in hand. We're homeward-bound, the factory lights on the black Tyne. It's winter in Madrid. It's Oxford under the stars. How many times have you saved my life?

Book Club Questions

1. Insua's debut explores the impacts of familial conflict – specifically, a conflict that arises when different family members hold seemingly irreconcilable views on political and social issues. Why might a novel about this type of conflict be particularly relevant to the time periods it explores (the 1940s and 2016), and at the time that you are reading it?

2. *Human, Animal* unfolds across three points of view and two time periods. What does this multigenerational narrative suggest about the way in which behavioural patterns and trauma are passed through generations? How has this impacted the Calverts' attitudes to tradition and progress?

3. From your perspective, what do Stefan's 1940s chapters add to this story? What does his experience as a prisoner of war suggest about the consequences of polarising conflict? What are the dangers in viewing a complicated conflict in black-and-white terms?

4. Tam can sympathise with the cause of the animal rights activists as well as the plight of family-run farms like their father's. To what extent do you understand and sympathise with each side of this issue? Is this ability important when attempting to find resolution and reconciliation?

5. How integral is Tam's queerness and self-actualisation to the novel? How much does Tam's queerness influence their need to break away from tradition and change the way things are done on the farm? What does Tam's experience suggest about queer life in rural settings?

6. The farm is a constant between the 1940s and the present day. Does this make it easier to sympathise with George's love of the place, and with his desire to hold on to tradition? Do you think his grief over his brother's death impacts his attitude towards the prospect of change on the farm?

7. A key moment in the Calvert family conflict is when the animal rights activists' video goes viral online. When you consider the portrayal of 'going viral' in this novel, do you think anyone involved benefitted? Did the video spread more information and awareness, as the activists intended, or did it only breed more tension and division? Could there have been a more constructive way for the Calverts and the activists to find a resolution?

8. Do you think Luke was only using Tam to benefit the activists' cause, or do you think they shared a genuine connection? Do you think Luke was truly invested in Tam's journey to self-acceptance?

9. Consider George's relationship with his father and brother, and how he characterises himself as a younger man. Do you think George sees parts of himself in Tam? Do you think this affects the way he parents Tam?

10. How does Insua's writing highlight the importance and possibility of conflict resolution, even when issues seem insurmountable? Do you think it's possible to find connection with people whose views – on issues big and small – might not match your own? And with that, how sympathetic did you find George, Tam and Stefan's perspectives?